Things are going good for Ravi. Sure, a bunch of vampires want to turn Atlanta into a bloodsucker paradise, and sure, Ravi's matchmaking aunt keeps shoving available bachelorettes at him left and right. Despite all that, Ravi's secret affair with the enigmatic time traveler Cayenne is making him happier than he's ever been in his life.

But Cayenne has secrets of their own, ones they can't hide any longer, past and future on a collision course to disaster.

When the truth comes out, Ravi and Cayenne face their greatest challenge yet: each other.

SHARDS OF TRUST

TRUST TRILOGY, BOOK TWO

FOX BECKMAN

A NineStar Press Publication
www.ninestarpress.com

Shards of Trust

First Edition, January 2024

ISBN: 978-1-64890-727-2

Also available in eBook, ISBN: 978-1-64890-726-5

CONTENT WARNING:
This book contains sexually explicit content, which may only be suitable for mature readers. Depictions of deceased parents, guns, violence.

Chapter One

"THINK YOU COULD maybe get off the counter? It's unsanitary."

Cayenne tosses up and catches an apple, not moving from their indolent sprawl across the kitchen island. "My *dear* Angharad, if you're so interested in where I lie, I could always move to *your* room."

Harry sighs and leans against the sink, arms crossed. And there it is, predictably; the look of disappointment they have grown so very accustomed to. A fun game by this point, to see how often they can summon it up.

"We need to talk about today."

"You know," Cayenne singsongs, still throwing the apple idly from hand to hand, "this authoritarian team leader routine really does *not* suit you, *ma chérie*."

"While *your* Pepé Le Pew routine suits you down to the fucking ground."

They laugh. See, this is why Harry is the only one of them who isn't completely insufferable. "Ah, an arrow to my heart, Harry. Say your piece, then, so I can be properly contrite and you can say you've given the bad, naughty chronomage a *thorough* spanking." They bat their eyelashes at her while taking a loud bite of the apple.

Harry massages the bridge of her nose. "Okay, look. Today was sloppy. It nearly went completely off the rails. Val got *hurt*. Where the fuck did you *go*?"

They shrug one shoulder.

She waits.

When nothing more is forthcoming, she sucks her teeth (*ooh, nice,* they mentally score another point) and shoves her hands in the pockets of her battered leather jacket. "Y'know, it's kinda hard to work together as a team when you're not *physically* together as a team."

"I had things to do," they tell her simply, wide-eyed and cheerful. "I have a life, unlike all of you. Trust me, if things were going to be *truly* dire, I would have sent you a text."

Harry manages to nod sarcastically, which is admittedly impressive. "Oh, trust you, yeah. Totally, for sure. You were so busy with your exciting, fancy-free life, you couldn't have told us about the giant fucking snake? Not even a hint?"

They roll their eyes. Mouth open on a clever retort, they're cut off by a new, deeper voice, one rich and bitter as overbrewed coffee.

"You're wasting your time, Harry," Ravi says, storming toward the sink. He throws in a bloodstained washcloth and scrubs a mixture of blood and flecks of serpent scales off his hands. The scales catch the light like glitter. "Constance has Val patched up," he tells Harry, ignoring Cayenne. He's *good* at that. It's extremely irritating.

"Oh, look, it's the Empty Suit! You made it out in one piece, what a shame," they say with scathing disdain.

Ravi whirls on them, face tight with anger. "A woman *died*," he spits out. "You could have prevented it. You *still* could. Why exactly do we keep you around?"

Keeping their expression indifferent, they take another crunch of the apple. "The only reason anyone keeps *you* around is in case our muscley *maman* gets a boo-boo, *ravageur*, so you must have been *very* excited to get a chance to throw your weight around a little. Did The Trust give you permission to go off their leash for a few minutes? Was there paperwork to fill out? Did the professor help you with the big words?"

All Ravi does is make a disgusted sound deep in his throat, as if talking to Cayenne is a complete and total waste of his time. Though their hackles rise, they give him nothing but a broad, blasé smile. Ravi shakes his head and leaves the kitchen. A second later the slam of the door to the backyard rings out.

"Was it something I said?" Cayenne asks Harry with a mocking hand to their cheek.

Harry frowns. "He had a hard time today."

Cayenne's only response is laughter.

"Go apologize."

Oh, that's a *very* good one. They laugh even harder, in true delight.

"I mean it, Cayenne. If you can't work together, we're going to have a real problem."

They let their laughter gradually peter out. It might be amusing to try to poke Ravi out of his aloofness, like teasing a chained-up attack dog. He'd never snapped at them yet, no matter how hard they've tried to provoke it, but who knows! Today might be their day.

"Sure, might be fun! See what a good little spicy pepper I am. So *obedient*." They throw the half-eaten apple in Harry's direction, not caring if she catches it or not, and slip out into the night air.

They make their way across the lawn with a loose-limbed stroll. Ravi stands at the edge of the lake, looking out over the dark water. He smiles warmly back at them over his shoulder. "Hey."

For a hint of a second, Cayenne is confused, until they notice the dew-wet grass beneath their feet has become dry, white sand.

"Hey, yourself," they say warily, stopping a few feet away. Ravi holds something in his hands, the ocean breeze ruffling his hair. "What do you have there?"

Ravi turns around, both hands flat, displaying a long sharp knife. It gleams, picking up sunlight.

Cayenne takes a step back.

"Easy there." Ravi smirks with a roll of his eyes and offers them the blade. "It's a gift."

"I know," Cayenne whispers. A storm builds on the horizon, golds and indigos darkening nearly black where the clouds meet the water.

"Here," he says helpfully, stepping forward and setting the hilt in their hand, not noticing the palm already dripping red with blood. They swallow thickly.

"Don't," they plead, near frantic. "Don't give me this." They want to run, to bolt, but their feet are fixed, tethered in place.

Ravi shakes his head and moves their hand so the blade's tip angles upward under his breastbone, where a single push would send it straight to his heart. In the sun his eyes are a deep, cinnamon brown.

"It's easy," he says, and smiles.

And Cayenne wakes up.

*

RAVI TAKES A tiny sip of the beer and gives Nate a so-so hand waggle before pushing the glass across the scarred table.

"Okay." Nate mimes checking a box on an invisible notepad. "Blue Moon is a maybe. That's six nos and two maybes. What if we—"

"Enough of this amateur-hour shit." Harry barges in and slams down a colorful cocktail in front of Ravi, sending it sloshing. "Here. It's delicious, it's fruity, and it's got more alcohol than three of those weak-ass beers. You're gonna love it."

Doubtful, Ravi picks it up. It has a cherry in it.

"Art thou quite sure they don't have any mead?" Constance leans over Val to peer at the chalkboard menu. "Marry, what I wouldn't giveth for a fine, cold gruit."

Val sits with muscular arms folded across her chest. The angel doesn't drink or eat, but seems to enjoy human company, as much as it can be discerned that she enjoys anything beyond battle. "What is gruit?" she asks, far too loud, but seeing as the bar is practically empty at 3:00 p.m., it hardly matters.

Lighting up, Constance sketches her ink-stained hands in the air. "Oh, 'tis lovely! It is an herbal ale, infused with the bitterness of myrtle and wormwood."

Nate turns away from Ravi to instead stare in horror at Constance, who obliviously keeps expounding on the merits of flavorsome sticks and leaves in beer.

Ravi takes a sip of the cocktail and brightens. "Hey. This is pretty good." It reminds him of the tiki drinks he'd been cajoled into trying at the beach. He suppresses a smile at the memory. "This one's the best so far." The tang of orange juice covers up the flavor of alcohol nicely, and it's not so sweet as to be unpalatable.

Harry raises a fist triumphantly. "Yes! The Tequila sunrise wins!" She sticks her tongue out at Nate. "Pay up, Doc."

Nate groans. He lightly punches Ravi's shoulder. "Aw, man, how could you do this to me? My pride was on the line, here." He slaps a five-dollar bill on the table, which Harry immediately whisks away. She pulls over one of Ravi's neglected test beers, claiming it.

Nate shakes his head at Ravi in mock disappointment. "I know you're new to the whole drinking experience, but, man, you've got the palate of a sorority chick."

"What, you aren't secure enough in your masculinity to enjoy a girl drink, Professor Corbin?" Ravi asks over the rim of the glass.

Harry guffaws, and even Val's lip twitches. Nate reels back with shocked delight. "Holy shit, are you a body snatcher?" Nate turns to Constance with the quick aside, "Body snatchers are a thing, right?" She nods emphatically. "You legally have to tell us if you're a body snatcher. The real Ravi doesn't have a sense of humor," he teases affably, dimples flashing.

"Sure, I do." Ravi takes another sip of the cocktail, expression flat. "Just no one ever sees it." Almost no one.

Harry finishes her beer and drags over a second. "Okay. With that first matter of business settled, on to new business. What the fuck are we going to do about this vampire thing?"

Everyone gets more serious, drawing themselves up straighter. It's slightly undercut by the jukebox flipping over to "What's New Pussycat?"

Ravi clears his throat. "The Trust's resources report unusual movement around the building complex. The financials tell an interesting story. Looks like several shell corporations bought each other out to purchase the main building. And all the adjacent ones too." He crosses his arms over his chest. "This level of organization indicates this isn't just some quick and dirty vamp hunting party, the kind that moves from town to town scraping up whatever victims it can find. If there is money like this involved, it means the vampire buying the property is older. Wiser. Much, much tougher."

Harry taps her nails on the table then grimaces as they come away sticky. "Buying up a city block is a good way to hide their tracks. If I was a smart, modern-day vamp, I'd have my money hidden in layers of shell corps." She wipes her fingers on her jeans. "But it's weird. Packs of vamps hanging around the area, but we aren't seeing any obvious vampire deaths lately. If they're making a whole new nest, it seems like that'd be hungry work, doesn't it? Shouldn't the morgues be turning up drained bodies?"

"The *really* odd thing is vampires all working together like this," Nate says, scratching at his blond-stubbled chin. "I, uh, used to know a vampire, back in the day. Don't ask. Anyway, aside from family nests, they don't like to work together for very long. They tend to be solitary. This is abnormal behavior."

"Oh, I'm *definitely* going to ask," Harry insists, propping her head on one hand, and smooshing up her cheek. Nate grimaces, neck going a little pink.

"These demons are lone hunters, in my experience," Constance adds, idly tracing a little rune in a puddle of condensation.

"Vampires," Ravi corrects Constance. She shoots him a glare. He holds his palms up defensively. "Sorry, it's just confusing when you call everything a demon." He doesn't *think* she can really turn people into toads, but better safe than sorry.

"Everything *is* a demon," she insists. "'Tis no different than you calling every fell creature a 'monster.'"

"Taxonomy has changed, Constance," Nate says patiently. "Correct categorization can be key in identifying a creature's behavioral patterns and weaknesses."

"Not this again," Harry groans. "The old demon debate."

Constance shrugs agreeably. "You folk and your orderly little boxes in your heads. I shall attempt to adjust."

Val unfolds her arms and leans forward, a stretched funhouse view of the bar reflecting in her sunglasses. "These vampires are preparing well, getting their property in order before moving in and beginning their hunts. This level of restraint is not usual?"

"No," Ravi says firmly. "There's something else going on. My sources say this could become a real problem."

Word from on high is that The Trust's seers are concerned, which means Ravi's field director aunt is concerned, which of course means as the most successful monster hunters in the region, Ravi's little team is about to be neck-deep in the thick of it.

Neck-deep. See, he has a sense of humor.

Harry sighs. "Yeah, okay, why not, vampire house-hunters. Totally normal." She points a finger at Nate. "If you know about vampire shit, which we are abso-fuck-ing-*lutely* going to dig into later, then can you put together a packet, or whatever? Any info you think relevant?"

"Sure." Nate shrugs his broad shoulders amicably. "I've been working on a paper about the gap between verified vampire facts and unsubstantiated lore."

"Nerd."

Constance drinks down the rest of Ravi's Blue Moon and licks away a foam mustache. "I shall begin gathering hunting supplies. Whittling stakes, getting silver dust, readying sunlight spells, that manner of thing."

"And I have a large hammer," Val says.

"Fuck yeah you do, big gal." Harry grins. She jabs a finger at Ravi, then quickly adjusts the gesture to use her whole hand. "Agent guy, you and me on stakeouts and recon. I wanna swing by the main building now to get a lay of the land." She stands up and pulls on her leather jacket. "If anyone finds anything useful, we can get a timeline together. Questions, concerns?"

"Yeah," Ravi says sheepishly, pushing away his half-empty glass. "You should drive."

Harry goggles at him. "I can't even handle how much of a lightweight you are. Like a literal baby. But yeah, cool. My car is probably a skosh less conspicuous than yours, anyway." Since Harry's car is a beat-up old Civic and Ravi's is an armored black Escalade, he can't argue.

Harry rubs her hands together briskly. "Let's get to gettin' and hunt some vampires, which is a real thing I just said with my mouth. Break!"

Chapter Two

ONE OF RAVI'S favorite things about Harry is she is in no way uncomfortable with silence. She's perfectly content to sit with him in companionable quiet, classic rock playing low on the car radio, watching the street. Ravi keeps his gaze relaxed as he observes his side of the road. He's done his fair share of long stakeouts, and constant vigilance is an unsustainable practice. Best to keep the eyes easy, focus soft.

Inevitably his mind wanders, drifting to thoughts of Cayenne. What are they doing right now? Are they even in the same *time* as him, or off enjoying their unfettered life somewhere in the past or future?

Suddenly he stiffens. "Movement," he murmurs. Harry immediately shifts, leaning over his shoulder. A plain, unmarked cargo truck pulls up to the curb outside the building's loading bay.

"Crates?" she asks.

Ravi frowns. A team of movers unloads the cargo, which comprises solely of several huge wooden crates, lowering each one carefully down the metal ramp on wheeled pallets. Judging by the effort the movers put in, the crates are exceptionally heavy.

Ravi thinks for a minute, recalling teenage lessons. "My guess? Crates of native earth."

"What, like Dracula shit? That's real? They need it for their coffins?"

"Not usually," he allows, his frown deepening. "That's old-school. Vamps nowadays don't need native earth or even coffins, just a dark place to hole up during the day. Only old vampires would want their native earth." He scratches his jaw, fingernails dragging against the grain of facial hair. "General rule of thumb is the older the vamp, the tougher. I don't love the implication."

Harry sucks her teeth. "Seems like a lot of dirt. That's like two dozen crates. And hold on." She grabs binoculars out of the glove compartment. Ravi tries helpfully to pull in his legs, his feet knocking around empty fast-food containers.

She peers through the binocs. "Yeah, that's what I thought. One of them has shipping stickers all in Russian, but another looks like Korean, I'd guess. And the one on the end is in English. So…these are being shipped from lots and lots of *different* places."

Tiny hairs stand up on the back of Ravi's neck. "*Really* not loving the implication."

They share a grim look.

"Whoa, who are those creepy-looking fuckers?" Harry hands Ravi the binocs and digs out her phone. "You see 'em?"

Emerging from the truck to lurk in the shadows, three unusual men watch the movers intently, occasionally directing them through the delivery doors. The men don't look to be of the same nationalities, but all three are dressed in expensive outfits of varying fashions. Each has a different stylish affectation; one with waist-length hair, one using an old-fashioned walking stick, and the other large dangling earrings in both ears.

"Yeah, I see them."

Harry lines up a few shots, pinching the screen to zoom in. She grunts in frustration. "That'll teach me to leave my good camera in the trunk. Awfully fancy threads. Why are a bunch of guys in Armani suits watching dirt get loaded into a vamp-owned building?"

Ravi can't help turning to her, incredulous. "That's a Savile Row suit, Harry." Also, a Tom Ford sharkskin, and the other only a higher-end Ralph Lauren. But the Brixton navy Savile Row is the most obvious, surely.

Harry rolls her eyes so hugely she runs the risk they'll fall straight out of her head. "Oh, I'm *so* sorry. You can tell from here?"

He blinks at her in disbelief. "Yeah."

She mutters under her breath something about rich kids and trust funds. "I got some decent face shots. Hopefully, I can run them through the recognition software and get some hits. Wanna place bets?"

"My guess would be thralls. Daytime servants."

"Ah," Harry says, tapping on her phone. "Renfields, right?"

"I think so." Ravi ruefully shakes his head. "I'm not the guy to ask. I took out some vamps in London, but I was just on the trigger." He keeps watch on the action, such as it is, since the movers are finishing up. They load up their equipment, slide up the ramp, and the three men disappear into the building. "Dr. Corbin would know."

Harry gives him one of her trademark wry smiles. "That's a zillion times more bloodsucker experience than I've had. Hey, speaking of, what do you think the story is with Nate? How's he know a vampire?"

Her smile is contagious, and Ravi offers one in trade. "You have to ask?"

With a dry chuckle, Harry checks her phone's

progress. "Our Doc, the big flirt." She scans the street for anything else, but the action is over. Things are again quiet, no suspicious activity to speak of. "Hey, I called in Bobby Hernandez to help out with the footwork. Originally to help with Constance's old big-bad demon problem, but if this vamp thing goes as shitty as The Trust thinks it will, it can't hurt to have more eyes on the case, right?"

Ravi slumps down a fraction in the passenger seat before he can clamp a lid on his reaction. He blames the Tequila sunrise. "Robert is coming to Atlanta?"

"What's that look for? You seemed to get along well during the whole"—Harry waves her hand expressively, annoyance obvious at the absurdity of her sentence—"that time we were shrunk down by the warlock with the magic dollhouse. That thing. He's a good PI, with a lot more experience under his belt than me. I thought you two were buddy-buddy?"

Ravi gives her nothing but a blank stare.

"Didn't you go to Boston to trade war stories or whatever?"

Ravi inclines his head a degree, adjusting his cufflinks. "I did go to Boston."

Trading war stories isn't how Ravi would phrase it. Getting shot down was more like it; after nursing a single drink for the better part of an evening and sidling in a careful advance that could, if need be, be mistaken for something innocent, in case the subtle tells in Robert's handshake after the dollhouse job had just been wishful thinking. Getting shrunk down and trapped with a handful of other unlucky victims was enough to rattle anyone, but for a guy with zero experience in the supernatural, Robert had handled himself well, adapting to a bizarre situation with a frank, businesslike competence that Ravi approved of.

That same plain-spoken style had been less welcome when Robert had met Ravi's discreet offer head-on with, "Look, Ravi, my closeted days are long behind me. You might be a tough guy with this weird magic stuff, but if you can't hold my hand in public, we're just not gonna work."

"Nice for you to have that luxury," Ravi had

snapped, too waspishly, before leaving. "Not all of us get so lucky."

And now Robert's coming for a visit. Which is… fine. Ravi is a professional. Robert is a decent guy. It's going to be fine.

It's not helpful to think about fiery red hair right now.

Harry's attention fortunately gets absorbed by a *ding* on her phone. "Ah, fuck. Yeah, there's a hit." She sighs deeply and turns the phone around. All three pictures turned up possible identities. "My contacts think this guy, the Russell Brand-looking asshole, is the main go-to Renfield for a major alpha vamp. This guy with the earrings is a known thrall for a *different* alpha, over in Taiwan."

"What the fuck," Ravi breathes, his blood turning to ice. "Alphas working together?" This isn't just unusual; it's unheard of. Alphas are vampire progenitors, ancient beings who've created entire bloodlines, sometimes even whole dynasties spanning generations. One alone would be enough to mobilize several branches of

The Trust to join forces against them. Three of them co-operating?

"Not sure who the third guy works for, but since our luck is just that spectacular, I'm gonna take a wild stab and say a third alpha." The set of Harry's jaw is grim. "So, this is really bad, right? I know I'm not an expert at this monster shit like you and Constance, but this doesn't sound good."

"It's not," Ravi says hollowly, not bothering to protest he's hardly any sort of expert either. He just shoots things. "Yeah. This might be big. The only upside to alphas being involved is if you do manage to kill one, every vamp they've sired goes down too. That's why it's so rare to see them. They tend to be heavily protected." He thinks for a minute, rubbing his forehead. "Right now, all we know for sure is that the *thralls* are working together. That's unusual, but not as much cause for alarm. If we knew what their motives were here…"

"Yeah," Harry agrees. "I'm going to text the rest to ramp up the research. Maybe Constance can consult her cauldron or scry or whatever the fuck she does." Her thumbs fly as she starts typing messages.

"Or the Doc can call his vampire ex."

Harry grins. "Heh. Nate was right about that. You've gotten funnier lately."

Ravi looks away, pushing up his sunglasses. He's saved from having to respond by the sudden rush of air swirling in the car's interior, lifting bits of paper trash as Valiance teleports into the backseat.

"Hello," she says with all the dignity of a queen in her regalia of athleisure and mirrored sunglasses. She flicks a crumpled Waffle House receipt from her lap.

"Fuck!" Ravi yelps in surprise, uncurling his fingers from the 9mm holstered under his jacket. "Little warning next time?"

Harry doesn't look up from her phone. "Sorry, yeah, I texted her to come. I gotta head straight to the magic shop. Constance is giving a wizardry lesson to Lucy, and I'm checking in with the kid's parents afterward. Okay if Val takes you back to your not-at-all-overcompensating car?"

"Sure," he says, with a slight roll of his eyes. "I'll

see if there's any more intel on my end." He hesitates briefly before adding, "Harry, if this *does* involve alpha vampires, it's going to move into a major operation. We may need more Trust agents on it. Other teams."

Harry wrinkles her nose. "We don't know anything for sure yet. Let's confirm before we get too psyched out about it." She eyes him, perhaps with a touch of wariness. "Do you have to report your suspicions? I don't want anyone bigfooting us on this unless we *know* we're going to need the extra help."

It is *not* standard operating procedure to withhold info, to say the least. But he'd been given leave to liaise with McAllister's team in any way he felt appropriate, and he chooses to interpret that as having discretion over what information was and was not pertinent to pass up the chain of command. He'd already fudged a great deal of the Chicago report to cover Cayenne's tracks. This is nothing in comparison.

"No," he answers after a moment. "I don't have to report my suspicions. I'll stick to the facts we know."

Harry exhales in relief and smiles. "Cool. Okay. I'll

text if we find anything else."

"Likewise." He glances back at Val and takes a deep breath. He hates teleporting. "Ready."

Val places her hands on his shoulders and the car winks out from under him. He reels, the sensation like falling in a dream right before you startle awake, then he's standing in the parking lot of the bar, his car a mere foot away. He shakes his head; teleportation always makes his brain feel staticky, but at least it doesn't cause dizziness the way time travel does.

Sometimes Ravi suspects his life might be bizarre.

"Thanks, Val."

Val releases him. "You are welcome. It was good you came for a social gathering."

It's unusual enough for Val to offer idle commentary that it gives Ravi pause. "It was also a mission brief."

"Yes. But there was a time when you would have only joined for that." Val pats him once on the shoulder, his knees nearly buckling under the weight. Then she steps back and teleports away.

*

RAVI GEARS HIMSELF up before making a hands-free call to his direct superior. To his relief, his aunt Padme sounds distracted and is satisfied with a brief check-in over the phone as he drives instead of insisting on an in-person meeting. She provides no new intel other than The Trust seers are in some disagreement, frustration evident in the steel behind her smoky voice. Ravi keeps his responses short and to the point, careful not to draw her ire.

Back at his apartment, he eats a quick meal of lefto-ver dal cheela with scrambled egg whites and grabs his fencing equipment. Sitting in Harry's cramped Civic for the last few hours has left him a little anxious, his mus-cles aching to move. Fortunately, he's on time to make the afternoon bouts at the ACN Fencing Club.

Before leaving, he checks all three of his phones. Nothing new. He lingers by the door over the candy-red phone for a moment and swipes into the picture album, where a single photo presides over the gallery.

He hasn't seen Cayenne in person since their

exuberant, champagne-fueled goodbye on the flight back from the Seychelles a little over two weeks ago. They've texted some, off and on, Ravi forcibly keeping himself from checking in too often. True to form, some of Cayenne's texts had been on the thirstier side, though all pictures necessarily faceless, which was fun up until a point.

Cayenne had responded to Ravi's shyness by texting.

> *Your modesty is UNFAIRLY CUTE. I'm honestly disgusted with myself. (winky kissy face emoji) If you change your mind, darling, my eyes are HUNGRY to feast upon you. Je veux voir ta bite, mon tigre! (kiss, kiss, chili pepper, tongue, eggplant, water splash emojis)*

Once Ravi looked up the unfamiliar French, he had to sit down for a while until he stopped blushing.

But nothing in person. As much as he wants to, he's hesitant to suggest another meeting, especially now in the middle of a potentially huge case, but also for other reasons. He still can't afford to be careless, that hasn't changed.

Cayenne hasn't proposed a visit either, leaving Ravi unsure of the rules here. He has no road map for this. Is there some unspoken etiquette on how long to wait before seeing a hookup after an extended romantic vacation occasionally interspersed with monster attacks and time travel? Does Cayenne even *want* to see him again beyond the occasional flirtatious text, or is their debt repaid and interest fulfilled?

Aside from a few contentious months with Luke in London, Ravi's sexual experience is down to short-term arrangements and one-night stands. Nothing that would count as a *relationship*, and that doesn't exactly feel like the right word to use now. But Ravi can't deny he feels…drawn. A pull he can't fight and doesn't even want to.

He has always liked the Western idiom "moth to a flame," but now it feels all too close to the truth, makes him think of smoke and blackened wings.

He shakes his head and stuffs the phone into his pocket. He's got work ahead of him and has to keep his head clear. Ravi grabs his keys and heads out.

Chapter Three

AKIKO IS FAST as ever, her footwork impeccable, and Ravi is hard-pressed to use the advantage of his superior reach against her speed. Rivals for years, they've learned each other's tricks and feints. Along with Serge, a lanky Russian, Ravi and Akiko constantly jostle for the top three spots in the club rankings.

Dodging her advance, Ravi lands a strike below Akiko's third rib. Her lamé jacket registers the hit, the indicator light on her end of the salle flashing once. "Nice," she pants, her stance relaxing, signaling a rest.

Ravi steps back as they take a short breather. Pairs of fencers on either side continue sparring among the clash of ringing iron and squeaking shoes. He takes off his mask to catch a gulp of cool air. The cumbersome things work to keep fencers' eyes from getting poked out, but they're *hot*. The club probably spends more money on air-conditioning than any other building in Atlanta.

In his quick, automatic scan of the club, other fencers glide back and forth in an athletic rhythm, the dance of advance and retreat. Ravi notes that Serge is favoring his left foot; he's the opponent to beat after a victory against Akiko, which is almost a certainty at this point. Ravi's got enough of a lead on her to call a win within a few more passes as long as he stays focused.

As he pushes back sweat-damp hair before donning the mask again, Ravi's eye catches on a shock of fox-red locks.

A full-wall exhibition window at the club's entrance separates the floor from the spectators, an area that usually has its fair share of friends and family sitting in to watch the fencers, and today is no different. What *is* different is one of those people is Cayenne.

Ravi freezes, gaze catching on them as if by hooks. Cayenne saunters through the entry room and drops into a casual sprawl on the bench nearest the glass window. Not making a big entrance, not drawing attention to themself, but for Ravi they may as well have marched in playing the trombone.

They are dressed simply in a stylish black-and-white striped boatneck tee, sunset-colored shorts that hug their toned thighs, and sockless low-rise sneakers. Oversized Audrey Hepburn sunglasses are pushed up over their hair like a fashionable crown.

"Okay," Akiko says after she finishes gulping down water. She puts her mask back on. "Ready?"

Ravi fumbles with his mask, risking a sidelong glance at Cayenne. For just an instant, Cayenne looks directly at him, lips visibly fighting a smile, before sliding their gaze away as if they were two strangers.

Ravi hastens to pull the mask down over his head, so he can grin in secret behind the tight mesh. "Ready," he tells Akiko, falling easily into a poised stance even as his heart skips madly in his chest. He wants nothing more than to show off: he's going to destroy her.

So when she easily parries his lunge and strikes a hit within the first three advances, he's somewhat put out. Against all training, he darts a glance to Cayenne, and in that instant of distraction Akiko is on him, jabbing several beats against the length of his épée until he has to attempt a risky riposte in a bid for distance.

It doesn't land. The second her épée touches his lamé, the light flashes behind him. *Keep your shit together, kid.*

Frustrated, Ravi growls under his breath, trying to regain some ground with a flying lunge, but after Akiko snaps off another two hits without him landing even one, his lead vanishes, and their bout is called.

Akiko pulls off her mask to reveal a triumphant smile. Ravi makes a face before removing his own and shaking her hand.

"Distracted," she says shortly, and he shrugs a shoulder in response. The past few years he's been sparring with Akiko at the ACN, they've only spoken to each other maybe two dozen times, and only in these short one- or two-word exchanges. Before signing on with Harry's group, Ravi would have considered it his most fulfilling relationship.

"Nice remise," he tells her, then heads for the equipment cubbies tucked alongside the window wall.

Ravi's throat feels thick as he approaches. He keeps his eyes dead ahead, off the window, keenly aware how bedraggled he must look with his hair soaked through with sweat. He unfastens the gorget to let the white jacket fall open to the collarbone and allow in some much-needed air. After several greedy swallows from his water bottle, Ravi settles back casually against the exhibition window with phone in hand. He leans with one foot kicked up flat on the glass and looks down at his device, just a fencer on a break.

His peripheral vision catches a hint of Cayenne's graceful movements. A second later his phone lights up with a text. He keeps his expression level, though every inch of his body feels electric, knowing they are just on the other side of this glass, nearly close enough to touch.

- Cayenne -

Bonjour, my SEXY samosa! I was in town and just couldn't RESIST seeing you.

There's a short pause before the next.

- Cayenne -

is this ok? me here?

Ravi's chest goes tight. He can easily imagine Cayenne's voice, soft and hesitant in a rare moment of uncertainty.

- Ravi -

Yeah, it's ok.

Only I'm going to move down in the rankings because you are very distracting. ;)

- Cayenne -

Am I, now.

Can I see you later? After you're done here?

No overt flirtation, no emojis, no extra affectations. Ravi tips his head slightly to the side. Out of the corner of his vision, he can just make out Cayenne looking intently at their phone, biting down on their full lower lip, eyes smoldering with verdant heat. Ravi takes a deep breath, and regretfully types.

- Ravi -

I can't. I have to check out some vampires. They're making a new nest in the city.

Long pause. Ravi's eyes strain. Cayenne is still for another moment, then their thumbs swipe rapidly.

- Cayenne -

Quelle HORREUR! Where at?

Ravi narrows his eyes in suspicion and sends a quick answer before Cayenne can get any ideas.

- Ravi -

You can't come with me.

- Cayenne -

Of course not, silly. Just idle curiosity! :P

He wouldn't put it past Cayenne to try to meet him there, but they were always vocal in their refusal to engage in what they call "heroics," so maybe he was safe after all. Still wary, Ravi nevertheless texts back.

- Ravi -

By Edgewood. Off Reynolds Square.

Could be dangerous. Don't.

-Cayenne-

So SUSPICIOUS, darling! Well, when you DO find yourself free, I'm going to be at a very nice hotel with a BIG, COMFORTABLE bed for the next day or two. I'll leave a keycard at the desk for you.

Cayenne sends the hotel address with a string of pepper emojis.

- Ravi -

I really want to.

He only hesitates a second before sending the rest.

- Ravi -

It's good to see you.

- Cayenne -

Of course it is, darling, c'est moi. ;)

You look absolutely EDIBLE right now. I'm tempted to press up against the glass and give YOU a show right back.

Ravi has to suck his lips between his teeth to keep from smiling.

- Ravi -

I'll text you tomorrow. I don't know my timeline yet.

Cayenne sends a bunch of Xs and Os. At the edge of his peripheral vision, they stretch to their feet and put away their phone. Ravi pushes himself off the wall and fastens up his gorget before heading back out to the sparring floor. When he next turns to the window, Cayenne has gone.

*

FRESH OUT OF the club showers, the first thing Ravi does is check his phones. A message from Harry only reads, *Call me*. Glancing around the empty locker room, Ravi dials and puts in an earbud before stepping into the pieces of his suit. "Harry."

"*Rav*, just the guy I wanted to hear! So, Nate found something." The razor-edged tone of her voice is decidedly disconcerting.

"Go ahead," he says, buttoning up his shirt and pulling on the jacket.

"Sooooo," she starts, which is never good, "Looks like there was a recent theft at an antiquities museum in Hong Kong. It was on loan from another museum. A new acquisition. Nate says they just dug it up from some old ruins a few months ago. It's an orb about the size of, let me see here"—there's the sound of paper riffling, and he can almost hear the quotation marks as she continues—"a bear's fist. It is obsidian black, wreathed with a swirling design of deep red as if it were, and I quote, crowned in blood."

"Okay?" he prods, waiting for the point.

Harry adopts a decent impression of Constance's chipper tone. "Its name is *Taquana apa Getlak Ari*. Which, according to our good professor, translates as—wait for it—the Sunwalker Stone."

Ah, fuck. Ravi bangs his forehead once against the locker door and rests it there with a groan. "Let me guess. It summons rainbows."

"Oooh, so close! Actually, it makes vampires permanently able to come out in the daytime! Isn't that *wiiiiild*?" Harry's sarcasm is reaching hitherto unknown heights. It almost helps to keep the utter dread from overtaking him.

"That would be a pretty compelling reason for a bunch of alpha vamps around the world to unite and form an alliance."

A catastrophe of historic proportions.

"And how cool they're having that little conference in our city, huh? Shows what a great job the Georgia tourism board is doing. Come for the peaches, stay because you got drained by a vampire." The clink of ice in a glass precedes the sound of Harry swallowing. "There's some good news too."

"An earthquake is going to level the city."

Harry chuckles darkly. "See, this is why you and me get along so well. We're both eternal optimists. No, the good news is we've got some time. Constance did some magical digging and found the stone can only be activated during a new moon, which isn't for another nine days."

Ravi rakes a hand through his hair, mentally racing through everything that'll need to be done. "Okay. That gives us a window. I was going to swing by the complex tonight, to scope out any new cars or anything. Get some plates to run. Check on movement."

"By yourself?"

"Just recon, Harry, I wasn't planning on leaving the vehicle."

Harry blows a raspberry. "I can't deny we could use the intel. Okay, after you do a look-see, find out what you can, then come on back to the magic shop. We're going to start getting a plan of attack together well into the night. Decide how much Trust involvement we're going to want to call in."

Ravi winces. "Yeah. This isn't going to be something your team is going to get lead on, Harry. When this gets called in, there will have to be multiple strike teams. Major ops. I can probably get us positioned where the action is, but this is going to go up the chain." Way up.

Harry grumbles inaudibly, likely holding the phone to her chest. When he can understand her again, she sounds weary. "Yeah, I thought as much. Okay. As long as Atlanta doesn't become the epicenter for a new vampire utopia, I guess I can work under close supervision. I mean if it was just Buckhead, they could have it, but Midtown? No way. You be *careful*, agent guy. I swear to God, if you get jumped and turned into a vamp, I am going to give you *such* a smack."

"Yes, ma'am," he says with a dry laugh. "No getting jumped. No bites."

"Later, square," she breezes and hangs up.

Ravi takes a few moments to gather himself,

putting his hair into place, arranging his pocket square, smoothing his lapels. When he's done, he feels marginally readier to face the job ahead of him. He sighs, securing his Glock in its shoulder holster. So much for seeing Cayenne tonight.

Duty calls.

Chapter Four

RAVI CREEPS HIS Escalade into an inconspicuous spot along a side street. Sliding the surveillance case up from under the passenger seat, he keeps his attention methodically scanning around the complex. No hint of movement, not even roaming pedestrians, but there are a *lot* more cars than there were earlier. The small parking lot has been packed to bursting with high-end cars. An inspection through tech binoculars reveals every single one has its windows tinted near-black.

Looking pretty damn likely there's a bunch of

vampires inside. Leatherette creaks as Ravi's knuckles go white on the steering wheel. He takes a centering breath and starts a careful sweep through the scope. All cars still, engines cold, nobody in sight.

Ravi drums his fingers on the wheel. Why haven't sentries been posted? If there are vamps inside, perhaps even an alpha, this place should be crawling with sentries, guards, and lesser thralls. Old vampires don't get that way without some healthy paranoia.

If something feels off, Ravi's old tactics tutor would have said, *always trust your gut*.

He drives a loop around the building, eyes peeled for any hint of a tail following him as he does. No sentries, no lurking thralls. The whole block is clear. He chews his lip, considering the benefit of reporting this back to Harry. He decides to wait, finding another likely surveillance spot with good sightlines.

This time the binoculars find an open side door, partially hidden behind a dumpster. He shifts in his seat, trying to peer inside. A long, pale shape extends halfway through the door, still and unmoving on the ground.

It's an arm.

Ravi slips out of the car and silently eases the door shut behind him. Sticking close to the wall, he slinks forward, draws his gun, and holds it low but ready at his side. He keeps constant stock of his surroundings, checking shadows and possible hiding places.

It's eerily, unsettlingly quiet.

This is no time to assault a vampire fortress, and Ravi doesn't intend to try. He just needs to get to whoever is down in the doorway and drag them out to safety. He creeps up onto the cement stairs leading to the doorway, every sense sharpened, primed for anything. Back to the wall, he breaches the entry in a swift, efficient sweep, careful not to lead with his gun. It only took one ghoul snatching his weapon from around a blind corner for him to never do that again. A stupid mistake, and pure luck he survived to absorb the lesson.

The hallway behind the open door is devoid of hostiles. Looks like a service stairwell. The person on the ground lays facedown, unmoving. No sign of breath.

Ravi crouches, angling away so as not to be grabbed in case the body is playing possum. He places two fingers on the wrist. No pulse. Do vampires have a pulse? Fuck, he doesn't know. He eases back and turns the body over with his foot, gun at the ready.

The corpse stares up blankly. Definitely dead. And familiar. One of the trio of thralls he and Harry had spotted earlier, the one with the ostentatious earrings. No signs of violence. From what Ravi can remember from his old Monster 101 lessons, thralls are just human enough to withstand the sun but are still subject to many of the same weaknesses as full-blooded vampires. But this thrall doesn't seem injured, he's just…dead.

A strobing light at the far end of the stairwell catches Ravi's eye. Emergency lights. He listens intently, head cocked, but the building is quiet save for the strange sound of irregular, cave-like drips.

Something weird is going on. He should call for backup. Wedging his back against a safe corner, Ravi takes out his personal phone to text Val, since she can arrive quickest. The moment he does, his other pocket buzzes, and he almost jumps out of his skin.

Cayenne's phone. Ravi warily pulls it out.

- Cayenne -

Hello, handsome! Just a REMINDER that there's a room key with YOUR name on it (not literally of course) at my hotel IF you aren't busy. ;) ;) ;)

Ravi stares at the screen long enough to realize with a start he hasn't been paying attention to his surroundings. He swings up his Glock, heart pounding. There's still nothing, the stairwell clear. No sound aside from the intermittent dripping.

Did…did Cayenne do something here? Why did he give them the location?

Ravi ventures from the stairwell into the strobing light. The hallway is empty but completely soaked. Water drips lazily from the sprinkler system, and it doesn't take a detective to figure out that there's been a fire somewhere in the building.

Methodically he searches, room by room.

After clearing the first floor, Ravi finds two more

bodies. The thrall with the fancy cane and the one with the long hair. By the looks of it, they died after barely making it up the stairs from the lower level. Like the first thrall, both are definitively dead, but unlike the first one, these two are soaking wet. Their skin looks burned, but more like acid burns than fire. If Ravi hadn't already touched them to check their pulses, he might be worried, but he'd be willing to bet the liquid is just plain water.

Everything is still graveyard quiet. *This is stupid.* He steps around the bodies and silently heads downstairs. *Too risky.* But his gut tells him the building is empty. It's telling him…

This was Cayenne.

He's not ready to tackle the implication head-on quite yet, so Ravi keeps his mind on the job at hand. Just in case, he dodges drips from the sprinkler system as he goes. Better safe than dead.

There's about half a dozen more bodies, all thralls judging by their shared fashion sense, each having met a similar fate as those on the stairs. Ravi also unearths a small, half-hidden maintenance room with a melted, burn-blackened plastic trash can in the middle of the room. A slurry of watery char covers the floor, scattered with scraps of burned paper.

The hallway leads to a set of double doors that have been completely scrawled over with paint. Once Ravi gets closer, he sees it's a tangle of religious warding symbols, like an ambitious attempt to recreate the "Co-exist" bumper sticker. A clever way to make doors un-touchable for a multicultural party of vamps.

He listens at the door before cracking it open just a sliver, intending a quick, cautious peek.

Instead, he stares.

Ravi swings the double doors wide, absently noting the inside of the doors have been similarly vampire-proofed, and walks headlong into the room. A dark stone altar presides over the space, the empty concave hollow in the center just the right size for, perhaps, an orb the size of a bear's fist. An inch-thick layer of gray mud coats the floor, wet ash squelching unsettlingly under Ravi's shoes.

The room is littered with skeletons.

Numbly Ravi picks his way through the bones as if walking through some macabre nightmare. The first skeleton he bends down to inspect has the fangs in the right place; definitely vampiric. They usually turn to dust if killed by the conventional methods of sun, stake, or beheading. But all these vampires had their flesh melted away.

Ravi stands at the heart of a room filled with the dead, holding his 9mm uselessly limp by his side, counts bodies, and stops around thirty.

*

HE KNOCKS, BRISK and efficient. In the space of a breath, the door flies open. Cayenne stands there as naked as a jaybird, grinning ear to ear.

"*Darling*! You made it!"

Ravi quickly shuts the door behind him and puts his back to it. The sight of Cayenne bold as brass, hair tousled, miles of skin on display, and cock already rampant, is nearly enough to distract him. Nearly.

"Cay, did you go to Reynolds Square?"

Cayenne pouts, setting a hand to their hip right where they have a little crease of lithe muscle Ravi likes to run his tongue across. "*Allez chéri*, can't we talk about that *after* you give it to me so good I can't walk? It's been *weeks*. I was hoping you'd *pounce*, like a hungry beast."

"I…I'd like to talk about it now." Ravi stares at Cayenne. Their green eyes show only mild exasperation.

Cayenne sighs then waves a hand. "Oh, very well. I should have known you'd be like this. Sometimes you are so *single-minded*, my dear. It's incredibly attractive." They saunter up to him and trail a hand from abdomen to collar. "Yes, I took care of your little vampire problem, no worries, my pet. It just took a little *preparation*." They waggle their eyebrows lasciviously and move in for a kiss.

Ravi sinks into it for a couple of breaths, the taste of their lips like a familiar song he knows all the words to, before he shakes out of it. He takes their shoulders in his hands. "That was *incredibly* dangerous."

Cayenne only laughs. "Honestly, darling, you are

making a big deal of nothing. Just a few bloodsuckers. It didn't even take that many tries, just a little research and forethought. And a lighter."

"Over *thirty* of them. That's…that's *insane*. There were alpha vampires in there, Cay."

"Were there? I don't know what that is. Is it important?" Cayenne presses their hips to Ravi's thigh and grinds slow against him. "Ooh, wait, are you *impressed*?" They grin wolfishly, seemingly very taken with the idea. "Do I get a gold star for my acts of *daring*?" They start unbuttoning his suit jacket with clever fingers. Ravi's knees go a little weak, and he rallies with effort.

"There…there was an artifact."

"Oh, *oui!*" Cayenne steps away to the nearby dresser, where they rummage around in a drawer before pulling out an obsidian orb, shot through with swirls of deep red. "I thought you might want it." They hand it to Ravi with a winsome smile.

"That's… Thanks." He holds the Sunwalker Stone in both hands, blinking. He feels…what is the word for what he feels? Awed? Intimidated? A kind of fierce, warrior pride? "This was…this was going to be the start of a big op. A major case."

Cayenne's face twists in distaste. "Yes, yes, darling, I'm sure it was going to be *very* thrilling, full of exciting shootouts and near-misses, maybe even explosions, *comme c'est excitant.* But after the whole debacle at the beach with the nix, I have to say *fuck that.*" They press up against him to nose along the underside of his jaw, breathing him in. "I want you all to myself, Ravi. Now there are no interruptions to get in the way of our upcoming cabin getaway! Which, by the way, I have already made the arrangements for."

"How did you do it?" Ravi breathes, overwhelmed with conflicting emotions.

"Hmm? Oh, I just booked it online."

Ravi lets out a startled bark of laughter. "No! The… *For fuck's sake,* Cay."

"Long story short," Cayenne sighs, plucking the orb from Ravi's hands to set it down on the entry table, "I filled up the building's water tanks with holy water, and then I started a fire." They take Ravi's hand. "Do *not* ask how I got that much holy water, darling, *so* boring. But *worth* it, because look! Here you are."

They kiss the back of his hand, lips tenderly brushing his knuckles, like the first time they met. That warm spring evening, safe and shielded between a wall and a hedge. A chivalrous kiss to the hand, like Ravi was someone who deserved to be courted.

This mad, reckless, *dangerous* chronomage. Cayenne, his beautiful, laughing monsoon.

"You did that…just to see me tonight?" Ravi swallows against a knot of emotion rising in his throat, far too tangled and complex to unravel.

Cayenne looks up through their lashes with a smile all sensuality and promise. They guide his hand down from their lips to wrap his fingers tight around their jutting cock, arching into his touch with a glad hiss.

Ravi licks his lips. Lust digs into him, clawing deep.

"For the chance to spend my evening having you fuck the brains straight out of my skull, beautiful boy?" They let out a low laugh. "Killing some dumb vampires is just the cost of doing *you*. Don't make such a big deal about it."

They drag him down for a kiss, wrapping one bare leg around his hip so enthusiastically he has to grab on to keep from toppling over, their thigh warm and smooth under his calloused palm. Cayenne sucks a biting assault along his neck, and instinctively Ravi tips his head back, giving them his throat.

Then he fists both hands into the conflagration of their hair, gasping through one scorching kiss and into the next. He strains against the placket of his trousers, needing to be inside them like he needs air in his lungs.

"Now," Cayenne murmurs against his lips, "let's say we skip back a few minutes, and you can try your entrance again, hmm? I did so have my heart set on the pouncing."

Ravi nods breathlessly.

"Good boy. Take two!" Cayenne sets a hand to their tattoo, and with a slight jolt, Ravi is back at the hotel door, his fist raised to knock. He blinks away the momentary dizziness and throws open the door.

Cayenne stands there bared as before, this time chin

lifted in a silent challenge.

Ravi barrels into the room, barely kicking the door shut behind him before lifting Cayenne off the ground into his arms. They laugh with delight as he carries them straight to the bed.

They both tumble to the duvet, kisses so fevered and hurried their teeth clash. Cayenne fills Ravi's lungs like a heady incense, that spiced cologne he's thought of all too often since the Seychelles. He's drunk on it, on teeth tugging on his lip, on demanding hands yanking at his hair, an unrelenting siege on his senses.

He tries to squirm out of his jacket, but Cayenne grabs his lapels and tugs them back into place. Then they reach down with deft hands, unzip his trousers, and pull him out. They produce a condom from seemingly nowhere and slide it on with an appreciative murmur. Ravi groans against their throat, sinking his teeth in on instinct, their pulse hot against his tongue.

Cayenne wriggles their hips against Ravi, and at the easy, slick press... Ravi hisses an indrawn breath of shock. They're already ready for him. Had they been...?

"See?" Cayenne laughs, their fingernails digging into the fabric at Ravi's hips, guiding him in greedily. "Preparation, *mon tigre*."

Fuck, but Ravi's never felt this kind of desperation before.

The glide in is so yieldingly smooth that Ravi's hips meet Cayenne's in seconds. He's buried hilt-deep in glorious heat. Cayenne moans, their spine bending into a perfect curve. Hopefully the hotel has very thick walls.

Cayenne keeps up a steady stream of delirious chatter, voice hitching at every roll of Ravi's hips. "Fuck, *fuck*, yes, oh that's perfect, my sweet. *Merde*, yes, *just* like that. *Ça fait du bien n'arrête pas*, don't stop."

The hotel could collapse around them and even that wouldn't be enough incentive for Ravi to stop. He can't even stop watching Cayenne's face, how beautifully they throw their head back, their mouth red from his kisses.

"*Aap vaakai behad khoobsurat hain.*" It escapes without his bidding, a low hiss of Hindi.

Cayenne gasps, head snapping up to look straight

at him. They bite their lip until it goes white, then grasp at his jacket to draw him closer.

Ravi growls and kneels back, dragging Cayenne's hips up onto his lap. Long thighs wrap around him, Cayenne's head and shoulders alone still in contact with the bed, hair fanning out in a bright spray on the sheets.

Khoobsurat. Gorgeous. Ravi runs a single finger up the length of their flushed and gleaming cock, his mouth watering.

Cayenne swears filthily in pure French, grinding down onto him.

Shaking hair off his sweat-damp forehead, he takes a second to stretch out his neck, rolls his shoulders, then, still fucking up into Cayenne, Ravi curls low enough to sink his mouth down around them.

Cayenne *shouts*, burying one hand into Ravi's hair and the other twisting his collar. Their hips jerk forward and back, as if unable to decide which of the twin sensations they want to chase more, Ravi's mouth or his cock. "*Mon Dieu,*" they manage in a desperate whine. "That's not playing fair." Moments later they spill down the vise of his throat, shuddering, legs dropping bone-lessly from Ravi's waist.

Every inch of Ravi is thrumming, on fire, *alive*, and he drives deep, the taste of Cayenne on his tongue as he tumbles over the brink.

How has he gone two weeks without this? Unthink-able.

Ravi pulls off gasping, short of oxygen, and care-fully extricates himself from Cayenne's lax, panting sprawl. After tossing the condom to the wastebin he collapses against the headboard, Cayenne's head pillowed on his chest, their hand idly tracing his shirt buttons.

"Well." Voice hoarse, Cayenne clears their throat and tries again. "Seemed like you missed me."

Ravi laughs as he pets their sweat-damp hair. "Did it?"

Cayenne presses their face into his chest so hard he can feel the satisfied curve of their smile. "Excellent pouncing. Just what I needed."

"Good." Sometimes he hates that part of himself, the craving to be wanted, the longing to be good… But right now, it doesn't bother him as it normally would, and in its absence he feels light and unfettered. Unburdened.

Ravi wraps his arms around Cayenne and closes his eyes. Several blissful moments pass as they quietly catch their breath. "How have you been?" he finally asks. "Things okay with you?"

Cayenne's shoulders rise and fall in a nonchalant shrug. "Oh, I keep myself busy, *mon beau*. Lately I've been working on plans for a little project." They wriggle closer, nosing at his earlobe. "You?"

Ravi hums noncommittally. He's got a date with a senator's daughter coming up very soon, the flag his aunt put on his calendar looming ever closer and closer.

He finally toes off his shoes. As they thud one by one onto the floor, he's hit with an old, errant pang of guilt; neglecting to take them off at the door would have earned him a smack upside the head as a boy. He shrugs out of both his jacket and gun holster to hang them on the bedpost, hoping the jacket won't be irrevocably wrinkled.

"What was that you said before, darling? When you were absolutely taking me *apart*, you said something?" Cayenne's inflection slides up higher than normal at the end of the question, and Ravi cracks one eye open to catch a glimpse of their coy, expectant smile before it shifts into mild curiosity.

The way they had looked when those words had tumbled off Ravi's tongue—*you are so incredibly gorgeous...* Maybe they just liked the sound of the Hindi, but...

"I said your hair is the color of carrots," Ravi says sweetly.

They immediately rear back and slap his chest, mouth open with outrage. "You did not!"

With an indignant huff, Ravi flips them, easily pinning Cayenne beneath him. "You little sneak! You could speak Hindi this whole time, and you didn't say?" Despite his embarrassment, he laughs. He shouldn't be so surprised.

Cayenne darts up to plant a cheeky kiss to the tip of his nose. "What, and risk *not* hearing you say those *lovely* things anymore? I may be many things, my beautiful boy, but a fool is not one of them."

Ravi had let slip far worse after their first time together, weeks ago, words spilling out as if from an overflowing cup, just barely disguising them at the last second in a language he assumed Cayenne wouldn't know. *The best I've ever had.* His face flushes hot.

Cayenne squirms their wrists free from his grasp to tuck them behind their head. "If you're a time traveler on the go, my steamy cup of chai, you need to blend in anywhere and any*when* you go. There's a better chance of that if you speak the most popular world languages, wouldn't you agree?"

Relinquishing the high ground, Ravi swallows his chagrin and settles in at Cayenne's side, trailing wandering fingers along their ribs. "Makes sense. How many do you speak?"

"Seven."

He angles an eyebrow. "Fluently?"

"Mm-hm. Fluently enough."

"That's…impressive," Ravi breathes into the curve

of their ear, and they shiver. *This brilliant thing.* Breezing through life with such outward carelessness it was easy to assume that was the whole truth. Like they weren't constantly calculating the spinning of the Earth and the measure of time, the balancing of timelines and para-doxes, a web of possibilities only Cayenne could see.

Ravi is hit with that awe again, and close behind it, a small shadow of a doubt; *I'm just a guy with a gun.*

Cayenne brushes a fingertip over the bow of Ravi's mouth, outlining his lips. "And what about you, my sweet polyglot? I want to hear more about *your* very tal-ented tongue." They bat their lashes with false inno-cence.

Ravi rolls his eyes. Not even a double entendre: a single, at best.

"Tamil, of course, but my family is originally from the north, so we mostly speak Hindi or just English." In truth, his "native tongue" is something of a mixed bag of Hinglish, Tamil, Marathi, Malayalam, and Punjabi, which he doesn't feel to be relevant. "Can't count Urdu, it's basically spoken the same as Hindi. A little Farsi and

Persian, enough to ask directions. I had conversational tutoring in the Romance languages. Tourist French, Portuguese, Spanish, that kind of thing."

"*¿Donde está la biblioteca?*" Cayenne teases as they trace the arch of Ravi's brow.

Ravi chuckles, leaning into the touch. "Exactly. I've got a little more Italian than the rest. There's a major Trust family there. We had to visit a lot." His ears heat up as he admits, "My Italian vocabulary is especially good with…fabrics and patterns. Tailoring stuff."

Cayenne grins. "Of course it is!" They laugh, not unkindly, as if Ravi's admission were a true delight.

He clears his throat and continues. "Picked up a few words of Hebrew while I was in Israel too. Though obviously my linguistics lessons were mainly focused on American English. The plan was always to base operations here in Georgia eventually, so they wanted me to fit the part. Blend in. *Lots* of training in non-regional North American diction."

For a split-second, Ravi has the vivid memory of being grilled on pronunciation while running the obstacle course, climbing the rope net while conjugating verbs, firing arrows while declining nouns.

Cayenne rumples his hair, seeming to enjoy the disordered fall of it over his eyes. "Why Georgia, darling? I have always wondered. Don't get me wrong, it's got its charms, but is hardly a major center of global power like I'd expect The Trust to seek out," they say, a little icily.

"We have a secret hub under the Coca-Cola museum."

Cayenne gapes at him for a second before they splutter into peals of laughter and slap his shoulder. "You… Oh, you *ass*, you actually had me there."

Ravi smiles, enormously pleased with himself.

"And the real reason, *mon comique*?"

Still grinning, Ravi shrugs. "Not sure. That's above my pay grade."

"*Do* they pay you?" Cayenne asks archly. "I just assumed they supplied you with gift cards to bespoke Italian tailors and called it even."

Ravi laughs, and Cayenne watches him with their

bottom lip caught between their teeth, like they could drink in the sight of him laughing all day. "C'mon, it's my one vanity, fuck off."

"*Mon tigre,* you can't *possibly* think I'm complaining. Keeping you dressed in all your finery while you're fucking me has been a *particular* fantasy of mine for some time."

"Oh," Ravi says with a blush. "Well, I'm glad we could fulfill that one for you, then." He shifts, zipping his trousers back up.

Cayenne slants an expressive eyebrow. "Sweetheart, there's no reason we can't go back to the moment you opened the door. We can do *exactly* what we did all over again—I knew you were *deliciously* flexible, but *mon Dieu,* we should put you in a *circus*—or we can mix things up however you like." They pry his collar out of the way to run their tongue along his clavicle, goosebumps following in its wake.

"I…I would like to. But if we start, I'm not going to stop. And I have to meet up with the team tonight." Ravi exhales regretfully and appeals to Cayenne with a crooked smile. "Let me leave while I still have a shred of my willpower left."

Cayenne makes a small sound of protest as they nibble at the divot of his throat, but he's a little surprised when they don't press for more. Maybe even disappointed, which is ridiculous, and he's annoyed with himself.

"As you wish, my dear. Soon we shall be seeing much more of each other in the mountains, *oui*?"

"Yeah." Ravi kisses the crown of Cayenne's hair. "When?"

"Next weekend? I will get you the address in a few days."

"Sure, that works. Looking forward to it." To put it mildly. Before the Seychelles, he'd never been away so long from his duties, never spent so much time with someone else. If Cayenne still wants to give him the chance for more, Ravi's eager to accept.

Cayenne's loose-limbed drape over him slowly constricts, until they are clinging tight enough to shorten his breath. "Me too." They clear their throat and pull away, propping their head upon folded arms. "I have made *certain* you will not have any schedule conflicts." They waggle their brows, beaming.

And like waking up from a dream, Ravi remembers Cayenne took out a fleet of monsters by themself a few hours previous. He sits up and scrubs his hands over his face.

"Can I tell the team about this?" He can't think of how else to explain it.

"*Ooh,*" they croon, "please do, and take a video of everyone's *faces* when you tell them how I grabbed your hair and—"

"The *vampires*, Cay, fuck! Not"—he gesticulates wildly at the bed, at Cayenne—"not *this*, you know that's not what I—"

"Yes, yes, *mon chéri*, I know." An impish wink. "You may tell them whatever you please. Tell them *you* did it."

"Yeah, that's not going to be believable."

"Oh, sweetheart. You underestimate yourself."

"I really don't."

Suddenly Cayenne perks up as if struck by a new idea. "Do you think they'll be pleased? Not that I care one way or the other, of course."

Will the team be impressed that a dark cabal of alpha vampires, the lines they have sired, and all their thralls have been exterminated in a single evening, along with their plans to hunt countless innocents in broad daylight?

"Yeah. I think they will be."

Cayenne taps a finger to their angular chin. "Hmm. All right, darling. Tell them if you wish. Maybe they'll like it better than that lovely picnic *nobody* even ate." They pout and sit up to kiss him. "Be careful out there, dearest."

"You too," Ravi murmurs, cupping their head in his hands and falling into a long, lingering kiss. When he manages to tug himself out of it, he playfully nips at their full lower lip. Cayenne yelps and tries to pinch him, but Ravi, grinning, is already off the bed and out of reach.

*

CONSTANCE'S MAGIC SHOP is closed at this time of night, but the back entrance has an electronic lock with a keypad, installed at Harry's insistence. Ravi punches in the code and lets himself in.

He heads toward the back rooms, which serve as a mash-up between library, greenhouse, laboratory, and currently war-room. Immediately, Griswold bounds up to the door, like the good little guard cat he is.

"Griswold." Ravi nods politely at the cat and keeps his distance. Too close and he'll start sneezing.

"Witch-hunter!" Griswold greets him with a strident bellow. "Thou art hale this fine eve! Much work is to be done, many foes to be thwarted." Striped tail lashing, Griswold trots ahead, weaving through bookcases loaded with esoteric items, crystals, and potted plants. "Follow, and I shall tell mine mistress the brave Turk has arrived!"

Ravi closes his eyes, gathering his patience. "Not Turkish, Griswold."

"Ah, of course, aye, thou hast said, mine sincere

apologies. Aha! I remem'br'st now. Thou hail from the Orient!"

Ravi opens his mouth, then carefully closes it. "Yes," he says eventually, "but do not call anyone Oriental unless you're talking to a rug. I'm Indian. Asian is okay, but that's…a whole thing, sometimes." He is not explaining the complexities of racial identity to an eight-hundred-year-old cat. He has his limits.

Griswold flattens fuzzy ears. "As you say, Witch-hunter."

"I am also not a witch-hunter, but let's leave it there."

Griswold clicks his small tongue, swishing his tail in annoyance. "So many new things to learn! Human-folk appear so similar betides, 'tis quite vexing. Fortunate indeed mine mistress be so exceedingly clever and wise and fair! She doth grasp nuance of this new world more readily than this humble feline."

"Yeah, once Harry had the talk with her about Moors, sure." He pushes aside the moon phase tapestry concealing the door to the back room and opens it.

"Mistress!" Griswold leaps into the room like an antelope. "The brave Indian has arrived!"

Well, he hates *that*. "I've changed my mind. Stick with Witch-hunter." He walks in with a small nod of greeting. The four others look up.

"There he is," Nate says with a bright grin. "Not a vampire, right? Harry said you might be a vampire now." He jerks a thumb over his shoulder at Harry as she pours a cup of very black, very thick steaming coffee from an electric brewer she must have brought over earlier. If left to her own devices, Constance only makes teas out of nettles and mushrooms, or brambles of bizarre things Ravi can't begin to identify.

Harry grants him a fraternal upward jerk of her chin.

Constance sniffs. "He cannot have been turned demon. None could step over my threshold without incurring considerable harm." Purring, Griswold twines around her feet, and she shifts her clunky boots until he has enough room to settle himself into a loaf between them.

Val impassively rolls out a series of papers on the central worktable. "I have procured blueprints for the appropriate buildings."

"She *bamf*ed into the city records and stole them," Nate explains. Ravi isn't familiar with the verb, but he can follow context clues.

"I will return them when we are finished," Val declares. "Borrowing is not theft."

Harry turns a tired gaze on Ravi as she opens a sugar packet with her teeth and spills it into her mug. "Find anything?"

He clears his throat. "Yes."

Constance pipes up from her inspection of the blueprints. "Jubilation, we hath scarce wisdom to go forth on thus far."

"Whatcha got us, Secret Agent Man?" Nate leans over Harry's shoulder, ostensibly to get a better view of the papers, but as his chin is nearly resting on her shoulder, Harry casually digs her elbow backward into his ribs without a blink.

Nate backs off with an "oof" and a "can't blame me

for trying" smile, rubbing his sternum. The professor flirts openly and easily with just about everyone save Val, as far as Ravi can tell, but seems to take special pleasure in flirting with (or annoying) Harry. For her part, Harry appears to not return the attention but isn't opposed to receiving it.

After their first test-run mission with Nate, Ravi offered to take him to the gun range. The guy had only a *hockey stick* for monster hunts, for fuck's sake. Without pause Nate had asked if Ravi was taking him on a date, and Ravi backed off so quickly it was likely his shoes left rubber. The last thing he needed was to get careless in such clear view of The Trust's scrutiny, and getting involved with a male member of the monster-hunting team Ravi was supposed to be liaising with was careless in the extreme. Bad enough Aunt Padme had used her intel, faulty though it was, to conclude her nephew was carrying on an affair with the angel.

Val, for her part, is utterly indifferent to human mating or romances. A safe bet for a cover, though Ravi wishes he could have asked her permission first. But that would have opened the door to yet more uncomfortable questions he was not prepared to answer, even to these people. He dislikes lying to them.

Dishonesty is a hateful practice that Ravi is very, very good at.

He's not sure if Nate had flirted with what he thought was a straight guy for fun, or perhaps to test Ravi's level of bigotry, or if he truly saw something there Ravi had always been so careful to conceal. Either way, Nate had instantly adapted to Ravi's chilly reaction and eased up. When they did go to the gun range, as colleagues only, Nate brought with him a kind of easy-going hetero energy that set Ravi much at ease. The professor flirts, but never where it's unwelcome. A good guy. Harry could do worse, if she changes her mind.

Wrenching his attention back to the matter at hand, Ravi says flatly, "The vampires are dead."

He's met with four varying reactions of disbelief and puzzlement.

"Say again?" Harry takes a gulp of her coffee that no doubt burns her throat.

Ravi shifts his balance, just a hair, and Harry's eyes narrow slightly. She *is* a detective, he reminds himself, halting his nervous movement. "The vampires are all dead. Alphas, thralls, all of them."

A brief moment of silence.

Harry sets down her coffee and crosses her arms. "Ravi. You didn't take down a bunch of ancient powerful vampires all by yourself since we last talked, did you? 'Cause, no offense meant here, tough guy, but I'm a teensy bit skeptical. You're great and all, but. Y'know. Mortal."

Ravi is hyper-aware of his rumpled suit, the dried ash on his shoes, even the smell of Cayenne's cologne surely still clinging to him.

"No offense taken. I didn't do it." He caused it indirectly though, which is a troubling thought. "I stopped by to do recon. Something was off. I saw a body. I went in, and all the vampires were dead. Just skeletons. Massive amounts of holy water. The ones who weren't killed by that died when their sires did. None escaped." He keeps his expression blank, just reporting the facts.

"Did…did The Trust move in without us? Damn it, I got this whole dossier on vamps together for nothing?" Nate slaps a manila folder on the table with a sigh.

"How can you be certain they are all dead?" Val demands flatly.

"Aye, if one of them slipped free, then mayhaps—"

"Cayenne did it," Ravi says with a calm he doesn't feel, bracing for anything. He doesn't expect the amount of befuddled confusion his revelation causes.

Harry squints. "The time-traveling twink from Chicago?"

Nate stares into the middle distance. "Wow, that would make a great title for a porno."

"Wait, wait." Harry holds her hands out as if to stop the world in its tracks. "We're talking about the chili pepper we met last month? The one who paid us to kill that chenoo? The redheaded walking HR complaint? That Cayenne?"

"Yes."

More blank stares.

Harry flaps her hands wordlessly before asking, *"Why?"*

Constance holds up a questioning finger. "I would'st like to ask *how* this was accomplished."

"How did you learn of the chronomancer's involvement?" Val frowns.

Ravi barely twitches. "They texted me." Truth.

"Oooookay," Harry says while rubbing her temples. "So, it's just over? This whole thing? Poof, like that, a major mission is resolved? The city is saved?"

She looks frazzled, and Ravi offers her a sympathetic twitch of his lips, almost a smile. "Seems that way. Cayenne was very clear the issue will not resurface. I assume due to—"

"To time travel *bullshit*."

"Yeah. Time travel bullshit."

"But this is a good thing, yes?" Constance ventures with cheer. "This threat is no more. Surely this is cause for celebration?" A small pinch appears above the bridge of her nose, and Ravi doesn't care for the speculative look she turns on him. She warned him off

Cayenne nearly a month ago. "Doth the rogue want something in return?"

Val crosses her arms. "Why have they done us this service? I do not believe it was out of a sense of altruism."

"Where's the Sunwalker Stone?" Nate's eyes go wide. "It's incredibly valuable on the occult black market. They probably wanted it, right?"

Ravi holds up his hands. "Wait, wait, no. The stone is locked in the hidden compartment in my car. Cayenne delivered it to me." Also true. "The Trust will keep it from getting into vampire hands ever again."

Harry looks dubious but unwilling to argue. Her fingernails tap an uneven beat on the table. "Val, can you confirm this? Maybe ask your bosses upstairs?" She tilts her gaze heavenwards.

"Yes." With no further discussion, Val winks out of existence in a rustle of feathers.

Harry leans her elbows on the blueprints. "Still didn't say *why*."

Ravi sighs, letting honest frustration bleed through

his wall. "They mentioned something about it being more well-received than the picnic. I think they want to make a good impression." All truth. These are true things he is telling his teammates.

Harry's lips twist into a grimace. "Ah. Before 'zhat fiasco at zhe airport in August,' right? That's coming up soon." She puts on an exaggerated French accent, a verbal caricature.

Ravi swallows. He doesn't like to think about August. It feels like a rapidly approaching deadline. "Yeah."

"Dire August must be indeed, if this doth count as fair recompense," Constance muses, still eyeing Ravi sidelong.

"But on the other hand," Nate says, "no impending doom! That's a win!"

Val reappears, the blueprints nearly going flying at the rapid displacement of air. Her sunglasses are gone, her eyes are blue-white fire. "It is confirmed. The vampires are all dead. The danger is gone."

"Ffffuuuck," Nate breathes, looking uneasy. "That's

theoretically a lot of vampires dead *globally* if their alphas have fallen. I gotta make a call." He slips around Val and out of the back room.

Harry looks around at the rest of them, one by one, expression unreadable. "Well!" She slaps her palms together. "I guess that's that! Fuck me for doing all this prep work, right?" She turns to Ravi, opens her mouth, then seems to think better of it, addressing the group once again. "Who knows why crazy chronomages do anything, right? Maybe this is our new thing. We start a case and some overpowered time wizard fuckboi just takes care of it! Hey, who's complaining." Her eyes suddenly pierce into Ravi, and he almost takes a step back. "They didn't ask for any favors, right? Payment?"

He shakes his head.

Constance breathes a sigh of relief, twisting a braid between her fingers. "If we hath benefitted along with so many innocents, while we hath not been cauled into an accord with yon jackanape in the offing, then hardpressed am I to be fashed."

"Fashed?" Ravi asks. That had been one of

Constance's harder-to-follow sentences.

Harry mutters, "Seconded." Ravi's glad it's not just his vocabulary at fault.

"Oh." Constance thinks for a moment. "I am not bothered."

Nate comes back into the room and gives Harry a subtle thumbs-up. His vampire buddy must not have been related to the alphas.

Harry rolls the blueprints back up. "Okay, well, I'm with Constance on this one, I guess. Yay, team. This is just one hell of a gift horse. We had a stroke of unbelievable luck, and I for one am going to celebrate. Drinks?"

"I'll deliver the stone," Ravi says, already taking a step toward the exit. "If it's as valuable as Dr. Corbin says, securing it can't wait."

Nate mutters something, likely another appeal to just call him Nate.

Harry shrugs. "Why the fuck not. I guess let us know if anything else comes up."

Ravi nods and turns.

"Hey, Rav?"

He looks back.

"Going into that building without backup." She shakes her head, and Ravi feels suitably scolded. "Remember what I said before. Be *careful*." By the meaningful weight of her gaze, he knows she's not just talking about the vampires.

*

SETTING UP DEAD-drops is a straightforward affair, a task Ravi's done countless times. Trust agents often turn in supernatural artifacts to be secured and researched by the upper management. Ravi keys in the correct code on his Trust phone, waits for the drop location, and drives the half-hour out to meet it, all the while careful to check his mirrors for tails.

After he secures the Sunwalker Stone in the covert spell-locked container, he inputs the code for "high-value artifact" to ensure a quick pick-up by intel agents accompanied by an armed escort. Ravi settles in to keep an eye on the dead-drop until then, using the downtime to dial up his handler.

She answers immediately, thunderstorm voice even more scathing than usual. "I pray to Ganesh you have good news, agent."

Ravi swallows reflexively. To invoke the Remover of Obstacles, his aunt must be considerably upset. "Yes, ma'am." His spine goes ramrod straight.

"Is that so?" She sounds doubtful. "Please do regale me. The network is squabbling amongst itself like children."

"The vampire threat has been eliminated." He'd given considerable thought to suitably phrasing his report. Short, to the point, and doesn't hint the team had discovered how dangerous the situation was likely to become and invite unwelcome questions.

A brief pause, and Ravi can well imagine his aunt's perfect brows rising nearly to her hairline. "That was fast." Her sniff indicates a begrudging approval.

His spirits lift a fraction. "Yes, ma'am. A magical artifact has been retrieved. It's already in the handoff. Waiting on intel now."

"Well. That *is* good news. Very efficiently done.

McAllister's team have been proving themselves quite capable, as of late." She pauses, and it's not a pause he's allowed to interrupt. He waits.

"The seers have been increasingly unreliable. Perhaps some reevaluations need to be made." The faint clink of a spoon on porcelain as she no doubt stirs honey into her tea. "Ravi. I know I am often hard on you. This is because I expect much; you are an Abhiramnew."

He's heard that countless times before. He's an Abhiramnew and expected to act like one. "Yes, ma'am."

"I am not finished." Her rebuke is astonishingly gentle. "For those of us in the old families, the responsibilities are many. And we are the oldest family, the first. It is both our burden and our privilege to see The Trust led according to the mandates. You know this. Someday, once you fulfill the requirements, you'll be privy to these inner workings."

Nothing he doesn't already know. He waits until he is sure his response is expected. "Yes, ma'am."

She sniffs, and this sniff is the rare kind that indicates she's about to reveal a truth she is hard-pressed to admit. Intrigued, Ravi leans forward in his seat. "I expect that day to arrive soon. There are many things I would like you to be in the loop on."

He blinks as she clears her throat.

"Excellent work, agent."

If he were a dog his tail would be wagging. He clamps down on the pleasure this rare praise causes before he can become too disgusted with himself.

*

ONCE THE HANDOFF is made and the relic secure, Ravi goes home. Collapsing to the couch, he's hit with a wave of exhaustion. Long day. After a few minutes of staring at nothing, he digs out his red phone and sends a quick text to Cayenne. His eyes catch on the violet lipstick mark on the framed Seychelles poster as he does, a soft smile stealing across his face.

- Ravi -

They were more confused than impressed.

He waits for an answer for a while before giving up

and taking a long shower, letting the nearly too-hot water wash the tension of the day out of his muscles. He steps out in a cloud of steam, white towel slung around his hips. Working a few drops of sandalwood oil into his hair and beard, he stops abruptly when he catches the flash of the phone's lock screen on the counter. He hastily towels off his hands and checks the message.

- Cayenne -

I'll take what I can get, darling. (shrug emoji, kiss) I'm SADLY occupied the next few days, but I'll be seeing you very very SOON. Missing you already!

Many Xs and Os interspersed with chili peppers follow. Ravi bites down on a smile.

- Ravi -

You too.

Chapter Five

TODAY, RAVI CHOOSES his armor carefully. Not one of the slimmer cut Italian customs, nor the London style three-pieces, but an Indo-Western asymmetrical fusion in sedate colors and muted patterns. The last time he'd worn it was for a funeral.

He spends a long time in front of the mirror trying to decide if the overall effect will read as staid and traditional, or too "exotic." Hard to say. He'll have to hope for the best.

Ravi arrives at the restaurant ten minutes late, as

planned, and tries to summon up some of Cayenne's carefree *joie de vivre*, hoping an echo of their nonchalance will bolster him through this dinner. He'd been far less nervous walking into a vampire den.

"My, my, Ravi Abhiramnew! Why, aren't you a sight for sore eyes, sugar!" Jessika Eaton stands up and closes in for a hug. Ravi endures it and slides into his chair as soon as she releases her grip.

"Jessika." He gives her a curt nod.

She glances at her own unchivalrously neglected chair but lowers herself into it with a thousand-watt smile. Jessika possesses long, artfully curled blonde hair and the face of someone born to generations of selective breeding. Though the American families of The Trust didn't have the head start the older branches did, they've caught up quickly. She's stunning in a form-fitting silver gown with a plunging neckline and a single, elegant chain necklace dangling exceedingly low.

Ravi remembers her well from his youth. Both Jessika and Isabella Cattano, the heir to the Italian family, were always in constant competition for his attention whenever he was forced to attend Trust functions. At least Jessika had never gone to the extreme lengths to hook Ravi into an engagement Isabella had; Jessika has often pressed her suit, but since everyone assumed the Eatons were the natural match due to the Abhiramnews' relocation to Georgia, Jessika hasn't been pursuing him as aggressively as he'd feared. She once told him she admired how dedicated he was to his "career," as she put it. As if monster-hunting was like accountancy.

"Ravi, hon, you look as nervous as a nine-tailed cat in a rocking chair factory! Surely not because you're here with little old me, is it?" She leans forward as she speaks, pressing her arms together beneath her chest. Despite her southern belle affectation, he isn't going to be lulled into thinking she's not every bit as whip smart as ever.

But that's why he's come with a plan.

"Why would I be nervous? Nah, just need a drink." He turns away to wave down a passing waiter. "Yeah, I'll have a gin and vodka martini, *light* vermouth, grapefruit twist instead of lemon. Make sure the glass is chilled." Very nearly a James Bond cocktail. *He'd* be rolling his eyes at himself if he were in Jessika's place. "The lady will have a vodka tonic. Diet. And hurry up." He waves the waiter away, then turns back to Jessika with the air of having done her a favor. "Zero calories."

It's unlikely this is enough to do it, but as Harry has said before, he's an eternal optimist. Ravi watches Jessika's expression flicker from shock to annoyance and back into her pleasant mask. "Why thank you," she gushes, "such a gentleman. It feels like forever since I've seen you. How long has it been sinc—"

"How's your father?"

Her smile turns the faintest bit frosty at the edges. "He's well. Aren't you sweet for asking." She arranges her hair becomingly over her bare shoulder, regaining some of her composure. "He's working very hard to keep the state zoning boards from—"

"Heard from Isabella lately?"

This time her smile freezes in place entirely. It takes a second for it to thaw enough for speech. "I have," she says through very nearly gritted teeth. "She's had a ski-ing accident, the poor dear. But I'm sure you remember, she was never the most graceful thing, was she?"

Ravi glances around in annoyance for the waiter. "The service here leaves something to be desired." He raps an impatient beat on the table, then takes out his phone and scrolls through it in obvious boredom.

Jessika stares at him, mouth open. He holds out hope this has been enough for her. He's so uncomforta-ble he's practically *willing* himself into another dimen-sion, but this is important. Even if he could teleport like Val, he has to see this through. His future depends on it.

The drinks arrive, and Ravi leaps on his like he tips a few back every day. It takes every ounce of his prac-ticed impassivity to hide a visceral dislike of the martini. *Hard to believe people drink them for fun.*

Jessika quickly rallies with a flirtatious smile. "You cut a very fine figure in that get-up. I'm glad I wore one of my best dresses, or you'd outshine me." She runs manicured fingers along the edges of the neckline. "Do you like it? The dress," she adds while looking up through her lashes.

He gives her a quick, dismissive glance before returning to his martini. "I think a woman's modesty is her greatest gift."

I'm unmarriable. Tell your friends.

Jessika's groomed brows climb up as she leans back in her chair. "Do you," she says flatly, finally dropping some of her artificial sweet-Georgia-peach tone.

"American women have a lot of cute ideas, but traditional values never go out of style." Ravi's tongue feels thick in his skull, heavy with lies. Hopefully she won't notice the sweat starting to bead around his temples. He should have eaten before he came, the martini hitting his stomach hard.

When the waiter returns, Ravi takes charge and orders both their meals. Jessika sits in silence as he orders himself the chicken, and a salad for her, with dressing on the side.

"What do you do to keep yourself busy these days?" he eventually asks, knowing full well she owns and maintains her own digital media publishing company. She's very popular on social media, not that Ravi keeps up with any of it, and has turned herself into a successful entrepreneurial icon. He's always found it admirable. Lots of Trust kids are content to coast on their money and privilege, if they don't go into field or intelligence work, but not Jessika.

She warms instantly at the change of topic. "Oh, I'm sure I've told you! I've still got my little business venture—"

"Still?" He clicks his tongue. "I'm sure you'll be thrilled to give that all up."

"I… Why would I give it up?" The waiter comes back with the salad, and Jessika accepts it with only a slight twist of her lip.

"Surely any husband you manage to land won't approve." He takes a perfunctory bite of chicken. It's difficult to swallow, just like his words. "I'm surprised you enjoy it. Don't you find working with all that technology a little complicated?"

It helps to imagine how much Cayenne would be laughing right now if they were here. He wishes fiercely they were. He could use the moral support. The bite of chicken roils in his stomach.

Jessika finally cracks, drawing herself up stiff. "Ravi, you have never talked to me like this before, and I don't much—"

"Calm down," he says in alarm, looking around the restaurant as if embarrassed to be seen with her. "You're getting emotional for no reason."

Oh yeah, that does it.

An arctic chill descends over Jessika.

"Emotional. Well. We wouldn't want that, would we?" She smiles, or at the very least bares artificially white teeth. She picks up her fork and spears some spinach. "*Emotional,*" she continues, voice dripping contempt, "suppose that's not your strong suit anyway, is it, sugar? You think we don't talk, us ladies? Distant, unreachable Raja Ravi Abhiramnew, *soooo* handsome, so reserved and mysterious. What a challenge, we always thought. Such a disappointment there's nothing worthwhile under there, after all. Any girl dumb enough to give *you* the time of day would be better off trying to screw a cardboard cutout." She delicately eats a bite of salad.

This is the first time in Ravi's life he's truly liked Jessika Eaton. In a decade or so she might be able to give Aunt Padme a run for her money.

He smirks with faint amusement, as if Jessika had performed a circus trick.

"I *defended* you, you know." She tosses her hair over her shoulder. "He's committed to his work, he's a hero, got better things on his mind than settling down. Trying to fill those big shoes left to him.

"Maybe I was wrong. You really *are* just a smug, stuck-up *douchebag* who thinks you're better than the rest of us just because your family gets some superpowers once per generation, and your mother was *actually* somebody important. Unlike *you*." She takes a substantial drink of her zero-calorie vodka tonic. "I thought we could do some real good together, you and me. Finally drag The Trust kicking and screaming into the twenty-first century, unless—"

Ravi kicks back in his chair. "Fuck, you sure like to

talk." He grabs the waiter's eye and lazily raises a hand to request the check. Then he sets his chin on his hand in a bored, insouciant lean while tapping on his phone.

Jessika's eyes narrow into slits. "You should count your lucky stars you've got the fate of the world dangling between your legs, else I'd plant one of my Blahniks there hard enough to stick. I always wondered if there was a reason you never got your mother's powers, or her sword." She fluidly rises to her feet, smoothing that fantastic dress over her hips. "Now I know." She doesn't even bother looking back as she leaves.

Once she's gone, Ravi lets his shoulders drop with a sigh of relief. He leaves a stack of cash on the table and walks to the men's room.

Ravi splashes water on his face with shaky hands. He stands head bowed over the sink for a long, long while, breathing out and in until his nausea subsides. He's done it, he realizes with something that could almost pass for triumph. He's bought himself more time. Hopefully, he won't get raked over the coals too badly for this.

*

"I AM EXTREMELY disappointed." Ravi winces, pulling the phone away from his ear an inch, as if that would protect him from his aunt's ire. "Jessika Eaton has retracted her interest."

He had planned something to say here, castigating Jessika's character perhaps, her unsuitability as a bride; but now, in the moment, he can't bring himself to go through with it. Instead, he braces himself for the incoming wrath.

"The girl didn't say much, other than she doesn't think the two of you will make a good match. I would say you should have tried harder to win her over, but anyone who would throw away the chance to marry into the Abhiramnew line is clearly too foolish to be entrusted with our noble lineage."

Ravi blinks. This is beyond unexpected. His aunt takes Jessika's disinterest as a personal affront.

"The Eatons were never my ideal choice, anyway. Obviously, I would have preferred a nice Indian girl, though nobody is allowed to say that kind of thing anymore." She sniffs expressively. "True, the Eatons hold some significant political clout, but they are one of the newer families." Padme says *newer* as if it is some personal failing. The Eatons can trace their roots back to *The Mayflower*, which by her scale is hardly any time at all. "They don't fully understand what is at stake. The legacy we are trying to build. We hold the fate of the world in our very blood, and any silly girl who would balk at that is not worth our time."

Ravi's mouth moves soundlessly. He's so taken aback he doesn't know what to say. "Yes, ma'am," he defaults. Always a safe bet.

Aunt Padme sighs, and to his great shock, the sound holds a touch of sympathy. "Don't be discouraged, Ravi. There are always more daughters."

*

RAVI RIDES HIS good mood through the next morning's boxing practice and well into the afternoon. No current missions, no looming doom, no forced dates with eligible bachelorettes. Instead, he has the weekend to look forward to. The address Cayenne sent leads to a cabin nestled deep in the forest, secluded by a long drive into the Appalachians.

Another gift of respite, another oasis carved out of time. Good thing there aren't any current monster hunts brewing, because Ravi would have a difficult time keeping his mind on task. All he can think about is the comfort of Cayenne's easy laugh, their clever, wandering hands.

He's never felt this way about anyone before. And he *knows* it's not wise. Cayenne is still so much of an unknown quantity, a book with its pages torn out. They could casually end a supernatural city-wide threat with all the nonchalance of sweeping away an anthill. It is one thing to suspect it abstractly, as he had when they first met in Chicago, but it was a far different thing to see it first-hand. It had been so unnervingly *easy* for them.

Ravi takes all his misgivings and keeps them sectioned off in a corner of his mind labeled, *August: to be Thought about Later.* He had bought himself some more time with his ploy to repel Jessika, but it won't last forever. He needs to snatch whatever happiness he can before the hourglass runs out.

His personal phone vibrates on the coffee table. Messages from both Harry and Nate. He'd sent a short text to Harry informing her he was going to be unavailable for the weekend except in case of emergency, but he hadn't sent anything to Nate.

He swipes into Harry's message first.

- Harry -

All right, I'll bite. Been bugging me. Why'd they text you? First time round the Pepper was my client. Paid stupid money too. Did they say why they didn't text me about the vamp sitch?

- Ravi -

No.

- Harry -

Just no huh

- Ravi -

I assume because I was on the scene already.

- Harry -

Must be

Have a good weekend

She leaves it there. Harry is good at boundaries, another reason he likes and respects her. Nate, however…

Harry once called Nate a human capybara, those cute animals that seem chill and amiable with every living being to cross their path, no distinction made between predator or prey; just good vibes regardless of species. The comparison suits Nate down to the ground. The professor's brand of openness is nothing like Ravi's used to and makes him feel like he's always trying to catch up, trying to guess how a normal person might respond. He opens Nate's message having no idea what to expect.

- Nate -

Hey Secret Agent Man! You seemed super weird the other day.

Oh, by the way, Constance says hi. She's letting me

ask nosy questions about medieval folklore. Surpris-

ingly filthy!

- Ravi -

Hi, Constance.

- Nate -

She actually said a bunch of ancient nonsense, but I

translated her Olde English for you. Just another an-

thropological service I provide. :)

Anyways, you seemed rattled the other day. Well no,

that's not true, you seemed like a brick wall. I thought

we'd been making progress getting some cracks in

that thing. Just checking in.

That is…very kind. The sincerity of it compels Ravi
to answer with some of his own.

- Ravi -

I guess I was. Kind of crazy seeing that many skele-

tons.

I've seen some stuff in my time, but it was unex-

pected.

- Nate -

"Your time" lol

Like you're this grizzled old beat cop

Ravi's lips twitch in amusement.

- Ravi -

Feel like it sometimes.

- Nate -

Psshh, you whippersnappers. Try defending a thesis some time, that'll really grow some hair on your chest.

For real though, sounds like it was super unsettling. Sorry you had to do it alone. If you wanna talk, I'm good for it.

He can't decide how to answer for the longest time.

- Ravi -

Thanks, Nate. I'm fine.

- Ravi -

I had a martini.

- Nate -

Oh ho! Do we get to add one more approved drink to the list?

- Ravi -

No. Hated it.

- Nate -

Tsk tsk, what kind of self-respecting secret agent are you?

He considers sending *who said I was self-respecting?* but Nate might not read it as a joke.

- Ravi -

The kind who might requisition you something better than a hockey stick.

If he feels like it.

- Nate -

Ah, there he is. Knew you were in there. ;-) Why would I need to upgrade when there's a badass like you on the front line?

- Nate -

And Val. You two got the heavy hitting covered. Though I wouldn't say no to a pen that shoots knock-out darts, if you have one of those laying around your Q-branch.

- Ravi -

Good night, Doc.

- Nate -

It's like 9:30, dude, you're so lame.

- Ravi -

Us grizzled old beat cops need our beauty sleep.

The typing prompt animates for far longer than Nate's brief answer warrants.

- Nate -

HA! Ok ok, good night.

Ravi plugs in all his phones and settles in with a favorite video game. With feet kicked up on the coffee table and a coconut water by his arm, he gets busy fighting monsters and saving the world.

Chapter Six

THE TREES ARE thick and fulsome with their summer greenery, the winding asphalt river of the mountain road flanked by exquisite views of glimmering lakes and clear sky. Ravi drives with the windows down and the wind in his hair, the late morning sun bouncing off his aviators and scattering along the dash in little pinpricks of light.

One decided point in North America's favor is how much space has been set aside for the pleasure of driving. India wasn't built for cars, and the English think over an hour spent in one is an eternity. But here, when done right, long drives are a meditative experience, listening to music and watching the land unfold ahead forever. Peaceful.

Ravi harbors the hope he'll someday get to go on one of those fabled American road trips. Not just racing somewhere to kill ghouls in a graveyard or get pelted with books in a haunted library in some other city but meandering around at his own pace seeing some scenery. The job requires a lot of travel, but rarely affords the opportunity to enjoy it. Maybe someday.

The cabin isn't what he expected, as it appears from behind a veil of forest; a cozy, wood cabin affair with a tall A-frame roof, the north side clad with windows stretching from foundation to roof, catching every scrap of the mountain view.

Ravi steps out of his car, unkinking his back. The cabin appears empty, with no other cars out front. No lights, windows shuttered. He gathers up the take-and-bake he brought as a surprise, slings his duffel over his shoulder, and approaches the cabin.

The path leading to the cedar stairs has been intersected with a red chalked circle, surrounded by sigils and a few pocket watches. It lines a space just big enough for one person to stand in. A heart, a chili pepper, and an arrow pointing inward decorate the bottom step of the stairs. Scrawled underneath, as if added in hasty afterthought, is a shape vaguely recognizable as a snowflake.

With an amused snort, Ravi digs a sweater out of his bag and pulls it on. Then he takes a deep breath and steps into winter.

Snow falls in thick fluffy clumps, the cabin now lit up and glowing in the early evening, smoke rising invitingly from the chimney. Ravi blinks off the momentary vertigo, a puff of his breath hanging in the air. He likes winter in small doses, so he takes a moment to scoop up a handful of snow and enjoy the novelty of cold. Then, with a shiver and a smile, Ravi walks up and knocks on the door.

"Entre, étranger!"

He doesn't know what he expected to find once he

opened the door, but it certainly wasn't this: a huge faux-fur rug liberally scattered with rose petals stretched between an overstuffed couch and a stone fireplace roaring with a freshly laid fire. Nearby is a silver ice bucket with a bottle of champagne. And lying languidly on their side in the middle of the snow-white rug, inadequately covered by only a red silk robe, is Cayenne.

Ravi stares while Cayenne grins up at him. "What…what is this?"

"It's a romantic gesture, darling!" Cayenne waves a hand in invitation to drink in the scene, and it is *quite* a scene. "And here's me, in only this thin little robe." Their smile turns sultry and they tug their lower lip between thumb and forefinger while their other hand drifts down to their bared chest where the robe gaps wide.

"It looks like a slow jazz album cover in here."

Cayenne grabs a piece of ice from the champagne bucket and lobs it at Ravi, eyes sparkling. "*J'y crois pas!* I went through all this trouble, and you have the *audacity—"*

Ravi ducks the ice, laughing. "I didn't say I didn't like it. The robe, especially."

Cayenne bites their lip and lets fabric drop from one shoulder. "Why don't you help me take it off, then, *mon tigre*?"

Ravi shrugs, drops his bags, and says, "Okay." He vaults over the back of the couch to press Cayenne down into the fur. Their delighted laughter melts into a desperate kiss. Desire rushes in, a river overflowing its banks, sweeping Ravi along with it.

He unties the silken belt and slides his hand underneath to meet the taut planes of their stomach. Cayenne shivers, then surges forward to bear Ravi down to his back with their nails at his scalp and their tongue hot in his mouth. He goes willingly, stripping layers of shirts over his head in one smooth movement while Cayenne unzips his jeans.

Cayenne meets Ravi's gaze before yanking down his waistband. They grin, then pull out every aching inch of him to lick a slow, wet stripe from root to crown.

Ravi's head falls back against soft fur and his eyes flutter shut. It's intensely good, nearly overwhelming. But not watching Cayenne skillfully suck him strikes him as very stupid indeed, so he props up on his elbows to enjoy the view.

The firelight is *very* kind to them both. The flickering light paints Ravi a warm golden brown and outlines Cayenne's lithe physique. Their hair picks up an ember-red glow which Ravi sinks his hands into, not guiding, but letting Cayenne do as they please—and what they please seems to be swallowing down Ravi's entire body cock-first.

"Fuck, I missed you," he whispers, syllables escaping without conscious thought, muscles twitching with the effort of keeping his hips still.

Cayenne pulls off with a gasp, lips swollen. They look up with uncharacteristic solemnity and rasp something in French so thick it would be hard for Ravi to follow even if they *weren't* also stroking his cock with deft, clever hands.

"Didn't catch that," he gasps, thrusting up for more.

"I want," they say while running their lips up and down the length of him, the tease setting his teeth on edge, "to have you every way I can. How's that sound, dearest?" Their tongue darts, lapping a bead of moisture from his tip.

Ravi's eyes roll back. "Sounds good to me."

Cayenne chuckles warmly before swallowing him down. It only takes a few more blissful moments before Ravi comes hard, barely biting back a loud moan.

He catches enough of his ragged breath to unclaw his grip on the fur rug, keen to return the favor. He sits up, but Cayenne shoves him back down with surprising strength and clambers over him, flashing a gamin grin. Their robe falls away in a red waterfall of silk.

"Shall we shift back for another go, *mon trésor*? The jump from the circle might intensify the side effects, but you just let me know when enough is enough, *oui*?"

A little lust-drunk, it takes a moment for the question to click with Ravi, but once it does, he smiles. "Yeah, let's go again."

Cayenne kisses him, and with a slight jerk in his

gut, they spin time back a handful of minutes.

This go-around Cayenne flips a corner of the rug to snatch up a condom, and when they sink down on him, they fling their head back with a greedy cry, hands braced on his chest. They follow the loud, unselfconscious sound with a stream of mingled languages. "*Merde*, yes, you beautiful thing, oh fuck, *oui*, I've been absolutely *desperate* for you, *juste ici, juste ici*—"

The heedless spill of Cayenne's tongue sends Ravi wild. Folding upright and mouthing along their throat, he strokes them through a shuddering orgasm. They paint his stomach messily. Ravi shivers at the intimacy of it, at the pleasure of being marked, drinking in every praiseful gasp Cayenne gives him.

Some of their usual grace has fallen away when they kiss him, teeth sharp at his lips. "Ravi," they breathe into him, an odd weight behind their voice.

A prickle goes up Ravi's neck. "Cayenne," he returns, turning it into a questioning tease at the last second, as if his tone could banish the strange gravity of their mood.

Cayenne blinks back an unfamiliar, grim expression until it gives way to their classic seductive smirk. "Another round? Wanna ride this ride, handsome?"

Ravi laughs as he nibbles the edge of their ear. "*Haan, ek round or,*" he murmurs—*one more round*—and Cayenne purrs a little laugh as they spool time back again.

This time, as dizziness sets in more strongly, Cayenne squirms back onto the rug and drags Ravi on top so his scarred thighs bracket slender hips. Hair spilling wildly into his eyes, Ravi bends down and whispers into the kiss, "Last one. Getting a little dizzy."

Cayenne manages a laugh through bruise-bitten lips, gripping the furrows of Ravi's hips as if they'll never let go. "Well then, *mon chéri*, we'll just have to make this one count extra, won't we?"

*

LATER RAVI HEATS up the Sichuan, which exhausts his aptitude in the kitchen, and they share a meal on the couch in T-shirts and pajama pants. Their legs tangle together under a knitted blanket. Ravi watches Cayenne eat their mapo doufu, the back of his foot roving alongside their thigh in a light caress.

"Like it?" he asks over the movie playing in the background.

Cayenne makes an affirmative noise as they chew, dipping their chopsticks into the container for another bite. Ravi props his head on his fist, obscuring a smile. It's a weird predilection, he knows, watching them enjoy capsaicin levels the average Caucasian can't handle, but it delights him, nevertheless.

"So, darling," Cayenne asks, stroking Ravi's ankle. "How's tricks, as they say? Things quiet on the home front?"

Ravi shrugs a shoulder. "Yup. The schedule has recently been made pretty damn clear."

Cayenne winks. "You're welcome."

A gunfight on the screen briefly distracts them. Ravi rolls his eyes. "In the future, shotguns can fire twelve shells without reloading, huh?" His favorite thing about action movies is critiquing the fight scenes.

"Well, either this film is a *brilliantly* accurate portrayal of the future's policing of time crimes—and spoiler alert, my sweet, it's *not*—or they thought everyone would be too distracted by a shirtless Jean-Claude Van Damme to count how many bullets have been fired." Cayenne sets their takeout container on the floor and languidly stretches out, settling their long legs in Ravi's lap.

"Good way to get hit. Not counting shots."

"The time travel is hardly accurate either, but I'm not complaining. *Except* the part about the same matter not being able to occupy the same place. They accidentally stumbled onto a temporal truth, there. Fortunately, your group's little foray with that whatever-it-was ice monster didn't take overlong, or else you'd have started feeling the effects from there being two of you at the same time. One in Chicago and one in Atlanta. It's terribly unpleasant, though *far* worse for me, darling. I can't even bear being on the other side of the planet from myself for more than a moment."

They top up their champagne and wave the bottle

at Ravi, wordlessly offering a refill. Ravi passes the flute over. He needs to remember to add champagne to Nate's running list of alcoholic drinks Ravi doesn't actively dislike. Growing up, he was surrounded by the stuff at Trust functions and balls but never allowed to try a sip. His body was to be kept "pure." When he finally had his first taste at the age of twenty, it was a disappointing experience. The forbidden allure of it led him to believe it would be some delicious treat, but instead it was just vaguely inoffensive bubbles. The bottle Cayenne brought is nice, though. Or maybe he's started acquiring a taste for it.

"I think you mentioned that the first time we met. About not being in two places at once."

Cayenne glances at him sharply for a split second, then relaxes. "Ah, in Chicago? *Oui*, I believe I did. Sadly true," they say, eyes darting away for a moment. Ravi watches with a shadow of concern. They've been acting out of sorts since he'd arrived.

He tries a joke to lighten the mood. "That's probably a good thing. If there were two of you, I think things could get pretty explosive." He sets down his glass and sweeps his thumbs over the arches of their feet, then pulls them up higher in his lap to apply a slow, sensuous massage. He wonders if they understand the cultural significance of the gesture, the intimacy it implies. If they do, they give no sign.

Cayenne groans, head falling back onto the armrest. "Ooh, you lovely thing, *c'est bon.*" They enjoy it in silence for a half minute, then their face flickers, going distant. "You don't know how right you are, pet. Explosive may be an appropriate word for me."

"I just meant metaphorically. You know, my head would explode." Ravi scrunches his nose as he smiles, trying to cheer them out of their ill mood. Cayenne gives him a fond smile, but it falters at the corners. "You okay, Cay?"

Cayenne digs the heels of their hands into their eyes. "Why are you so unnervingly *perceptive*? Can't you just be dumb and pretty?" They drop their hands and stick their tongue out at him, removing the sting from their words.

They clamber into Ravi's lap like an oversized cat, all elbows and angles, and squirm under the blanket until they sprawl across him with their tousled head on his chest. "This movie, *c'est ridicule.* Let's keep moving down the watchlist, yes? We still have not seen the last of that trilogy, this *Back to the Future.* One must hope the third is better than the second."

Ravi murmurs agreement, letting Cayenne change the subject as they please. He'd let them do anything they want; if they don't want to talk, he isn't going to make them.

He wraps his arms around them, reveling in skin on skin. Aside from the odd handshake, Ravi doesn't think he's touched anyone outside of combat situations for the past year, before meeting Cayenne. Now he craves it, hungers for the casual intimacy of touch; the way their chest rises and falls with his as they breathe in near unison; being present, being someone different, someone who could have this. The outside world feels miles and miles away. Maybe years away too; he didn't even ask if this winter was in the same year they had left. He can't bring himself to care.

He watches the movie lazily, never paying it more mind than the redhead in his arms. Currently Doc Brown and Clara are sharing a view of the stars, heads close together over a telescope as they talk rapturously about Jules Verne. Cayenne shifts, burrowing closer. They set one slim hand on Ravi's arm and idly trace small circles. Ravi shuts his eyes and basks in the sensation, drifting.

After some time—Ravi has no idea how much or little—Cayenne takes a deep, deep breath and says, "Do you ever think… Wouldn't it be nice if we could do that?"

Ravi opens his eyes. On the screen, Doc Brown and what must be his new family are on a flying train. He's dozed through a few plot points, it seems. "Do what?"

Cayenne sets a sharp elbow on Ravi's sternum and props their head on their fist, attention firmly fixed solely on the movie. "If we could do *that*. Go wherever we want."

Ravi blinks, ignoring the movie to watch Cayenne's

face instead, angular features carefully composed into nonchalance. "You have a train?"

"Ah! Would that I did, my sexy samosa." Cayenne laughs, frivolity strained and frayed at the edges.

Dread creeps over Ravi.

"It *would* be *très drôle*, wouldn't it? Flying around together on our time-traveling train? Minus the *petit enfants*, of course."

Having one boyfriend for a handful of clandestine months of midnight hookups didn't really prepare Ravi for navigating the emotional landscape of anything beyond casual sex. Despite that, Cayenne's forced indifference rings immediate alarm bells.

Luke once asked Ravi in his Jamaican-London patois, laughing as though it were a truly crazy thought, "Wouldn't it be funny if we invited Emery to join us sometime?"

Want disguised as a joke to test the waters.

Ravi swallows. He has no idea what to say, so he's perfectly surprised at what comes out of his mouth. "You don't want kids?"

Finally, Cayenne looks at him. "Be serious," they say reproachfully, brows drawing together at a sharp red-gold slant.

"Uh, who are you? I thought you were never serious."

Cayenne noisily exhales, looking back at the television as credits roll. "I wouldn't bring children into this world, even if they weren't all messy, smelly, noisy things that demand constant attention and refuse to listen to reason." They lick their lips. "It is not possible for us, anyway, *non*?"

This is… That's…

Ravi's brain shorts out. The question had been a casual hypothetical, the way people often asked each other, *hey, do you want kids someday*? An abstract thing. Not…not framed as *them* having kids. He literally would be less shocked if Cayenne unzipped their skin and revealed themself to be a green alien.

Ravi doesn't have a navigation chart for this. He's adrift and grasping for anything to stay afloat.

So, he matches Cayenne's serious tone and says,

"It's not *likely*, no, but that shouldn't stop us from try-ing."

And when Cayenne laughs, shaking their head with true mirth, Ravi relaxes. He hadn't even been aware of how tense his shoulders had gotten during this conversation until he rolls them back into the cushions. He runs the pad of his thumb over Cayenne's tempt-ingly plump lower lip. Cayenne captures it in the heat of their mouth. Ravi's breath hitches, and he moves in to replace his thumb with his tongue.

The instant before their lips touch Cayenne asks, "You do want them, then? Children?"

Ravi's jaw tightens, his head falling back to the arm-rest. He chooses his words carefully. "Not if they're go-ing to be raised like I was."

The green of Cayenne's eyes shines brightly, too lu-minous, like dewed grass. "What if…what if you left?"

Ravi groans, putting his hands over his eyes. "Cay…why are you… Are you trying to start a fight?" Cayenne pushes up off the couch and Ravi follows them, sitting up and letting his hands drop loose between his knees. "Can't we just…enjoy our time together? We don't have to—"

Cayenne paces across the white fur. "What if you *left*," they ask, their accent as thick as he's ever heard it. "You could leave it all behind you."

"Cayenne—"

"Pick a decade!" Their voice rises, their hands tracing expressive shapes through the air. "As long as I am not there already, we can go anywhere, you and I. We can—" They yank at their hair. A shadow of *something* creeps into the set of their mouth before they smooth it away. "We can skip the next few months, *oui*? Just jump ahead a little; 2050 is very nice, no one cares who fucks who anymore, we can be—"

"*Cayenne.*" Ravi's heartbeat trips wild and uneven at his throat and wrists, trying to pound a way through his skin. "Stop. That's…that's great to hear about the future, but it's not just about…*that*. You *know* it's not just that, don't you?"

They had to know. From the very beginning, they knew so much about him, even the secrets. His skills, his preferences. His mother. Everything important.

"Whatever it is about, you can leave it behind."

A sharp sound makes its way up from Ravi's chest. It's not even close to a laugh. "I can't do that."

"Yes, you can! I do it all the time! We can go right now! You and I, we can do *anything* you want—"

"It doesn't *matter* what I want!" Ravi pushes himself unsteadily to his feet, heels sinking into the white rug.

Cayenne grasps him by the shoulders and shakes. "What you want is *all* that matters, *homme fou*! Nothing else in the whole world does."

"Look, it's…it's the dharma of sugar to be sweet, and the dharma of a blade to be sharp."

"*Quoi*— What the *fuck* are you talking about?"

"I'm saying that my path is… I can't change it, Cayenne. I wouldn't want to even if I could."

"It's not your job to save the world." Ravi can't help it—he flinches. An old wound tears open. If Cayenne notices, they ignore it. "Even if it was, who the fuck cares? There are *so many things* I want to show you, darling, if you'd only *let* me."

He smirks mirthlessly. "If only we could all have magic powers that let us ignore any consequences. If we could all run away from our problems."

Cayenne isn't insulted in the least, nodding agreement at the harsh words. "*Je pourrais te donner ça.*" They shake their head in frustration. "I could give that to you, Ravi!"

"Stop, Cayenne… I *can't.*"

"They don't value you, *mon tigre,* my beautiful boy. They don't *deserve* you. They treat you like an *attack dog,* risking your life for *nothing.* And if you're truly lucky, you'll live *just* long enough for them to finally pair you off with some social climbing bitch and use you like a farm animal!"

"Stop," whispers Ravi.

"And you are so, *so* broken you *thank* them for it! You think you deserve nothing in the face of 'the greater good!'"

"That doesn't matter."

Cayenne splutters a vicious, humorless laugh.

"What does then? *What does?*"

"My responsibilities matter."

Cayenne laughs, loud and mocking. "Oh, *fuck* your responsibilities."

"I don't expect you to understand. Because you're…you're *selfish*, Cayenne."

Cayenne doesn't even blink, just shakes Ravi's shoulders again. "*Oui!* I *am* selfish. And I want *you*, I care about *you, you* matter to me!"

Ravi pushes Cayenne off him. "But I *don't* matter!"

Cayenne nearly pulls out their hair by the coppery roots. "*Aaarrgh!* You're *impossible*. This fucking *martyr* routine, I can't—"

"Nineteen seventy-seven," Ravi says evenly, crossing his arms over his chest.

"What? You…want to go to 1977?"

"No!" He takes a deep, centering breath, wrangling his volume under control. "It's the year the Chosen Ravesh, my *grandfather*, defeated a giant white worm before it finished digging the tunnels that would have collapsed three cities. He went down fighting, like most of us do. Hundreds of thousands of people were saved.

"Nineteen sixty. The Chosen Ayudhina dies preventing the sinking of an entire island. In 1953, it was hundreds of *kaftars*. Werehyenas. Nineteen thirty-four, a Germanic demon cult. Nineteen twelve, a sentient plague. Eighteen seventy-two. Eighteen seventy. Eighteen sixty-eight, it goes on like that for a bit; lots of us were chewed through on that one."

If pressed, Ravi could recite every single one of his ancestors to have fallen by name, by year, by what evil brought them down—a list going back and back to when India was still trading silks and spices for Roman gold.

"I didn't have what anyone would call traditional schooling, but *this* I know backwards and forwards. My line goes back more than a thousand years, Cayenne. It's skipped generations a few times before, I'm not the first, but you know how many Chosen *haven't* been Abhiramnews?"

He holds up his fingers. "*Three*. Once in World War 1. Once in 1556. And the first way back in 554, at the collapse of the Gupta Empire. All the way back to the third century, Cayenne, it's been *my* family's responsibility. The first of us to be Chosen was Abhira Dakshayani, in 262. She was twelve."

He rakes shaking hands through his hair. "It's been eight years since my mother died. Eight. A gap like this has *never* happened before, in over a thousand years. Not once. It's only a matter of time before another crisis arises. We *need* the Chosen again. And I know I wasn't… It's not me. You're right, it's not my job to save the world. But I am the scion of my line, I can do *something*. If that's to be a…a farm animal, as you say, then I'll do it."

Cayenne abruptly turns away from him, covering their face with both hands. They heave in several long, ragged breaths, shoulders trembling. When they turn around, a bleak, haunted expression gets quickly overtaken by grim determination.

"Can't you just give them a *jar*?" Cayenne mimes an emphatic vulgar gesture. "I volunteer to help any way I can. How many pints do they need?"

The jagged edge of Ravi's laugh hurts his ears. "Can't be serious for five minutes."

"Who's not serious? If they just want you to knock up their broodmares, surely they can make do with a few donations?"

"Tell you what, I'll ask," Ravi jokes, gallows-humor. "It's sure to go over well." His shoulders round in a defeated slump. "To answer your question, yeah. I do want children. I like kids. I want…" He bites it back, because it doesn't matter what he wants, no matter how badly he wants it. "But how can I have any, knowing what it'll mean for them? They won't have a normal life. They're going to…have a life like mine." He can't look at Cayenne, doesn't know where to put his gaze, so ends up sightlessly staring at the flames licking over charred logs in the fireplace.

"I can't do that to them, to my own blood. I can't just leave them alone like I was, to be trained by strangers to kill monsters while I fuck off to some other decade with you. I *can't*. I have to *be there*. To make sure they know that…that someone's in their corner. No matter if they're Chosen or not."

He covers his face, desperation clawing at him and dragging him down until he's drowning in dark waters with no hint of the surface above. "It's…it's fucking *impossible*, Cay. No matter what I do, it's unforgivable. If I have them, I'm dooming them to a short life of violence. If I refuse outright and walk away, then the world loses the Chosen, maybe forever, and the next apocalypse goes unchecked. There's nothing I… *I can't do anything right.*"

Cayenne's face crumples. They pull him into their arms, shushing softly. Tears have long been trained out of Ravi, but he shakes as Cayenne holds him, face buried in their fragrant hair.

"I wouldn't mind, you know. Being your little secret on the side, if that would make you happy. Then you'd get everything you want. It's just… It's so *medieval*, darling. It's the twenty-first century." They comb his hair back with a light, soothing touch.

Ravi gathers himself with an ease born of long years

of practice. "I can't do that to you, Cay. I...I have only scraps to give you. Don't ask me for more. It's not fair." He takes their face between his hands so he can look at them, eyes tenderly sketching every perfect line.

"*Merde*, I want you to keep looking at me like that forever," they whisper. "If I could stop time altogether I would." Cayenne's eyes squeeze shut, and Ravi wipes away their tears, thumbs brushing the proud arch of their cheekbones. He kisses each one, then presses another, long and sweet, between their eyes.

"It's okay. We still have time. This is good, right? Getting away for a while, going on vacations?" Ravi tips their head back to kiss them properly. "It's going to be okay."

Cayenne pushes him away with a strangled gasp and claps their hands over their ears.

"*Stop!* This is…this is *fucking unbearable!* I can't hear it." They lose some of their usual poise, posture angular and sharp while their fists clench and release in a restless pulse. "You selfless *idiot*, you're trying to comfort *me*? Like *I'm* the one who needs saving? If you think I'm going to let you be kept on a *leash* your whole life, Ravi, you're *insane.*"

"Cayenne, there's nothi—"

A sudden grin, wild and savage. "I am a *fucking* chronomage, my beautiful boy, and it's not all parlor tricks and multiple orgasms."

Cayenne crushes them together, biting and clawing and tearing at his clothes, spiraling into each other the way ships go down in a squall, and Ravi plunges into the depths willingly, holding on to Cayenne for air.

Chapter Seven

THE NEXT TWO days are thankfully peaceful, passing by without further argument. By unspoken agreement, they avoid contentious topics and emotional outbursts, trading them instead for lazy mornings in bed and cozy nights by the fire.

Ravi wakes up warm and relaxed, the bedroom overly hot from the still-burning fireplace. He kicks off the comforter with a languorous stretch down to his toes.

An appreciative murmur. "Oh, now *that's* the best

sight I've ever woken up to, *à coup sûr.*" Cayenne watches him, lip caught between their teeth. Just to amuse them he flexes a little, and sure enough their face eases into a wide smile. "Have you tried fighting one of those nasty monsters like this, my sweet? Surely the sight would stop a *few* beasts in their tracks." They run a finger through the line of dark hair trailing down his stomach. "Didn't the Greeks fight in the nude?"

Laughing, Ravi rolls on his side and kisses Cayenne's chin. "I think just for the Olympics."

"Such a shame. Another fine idea *ruined* by reality." They lean back, assessing Ravi with open approval. "You look *very* relaxed. It's a nice look on you, darling, truly."

"I feel relaxed. No monster hunts on the horizon, no mysteries to unravel. It's a nice break."

Cayenne's smile goes brittle for a sliver of a second. "No monsters here, my sweet." They sink into a slow, exploring kiss.

When they pull apart for breath, Ravi teases, "I'm just glad we haven't run into a marauding yeti up here in the mountains."

Despite years of honing his situational awareness, he's taken by complete surprise when Cayenne smacks him across the face with a pillow.

"Why would you say that! Now you've doomed us. I was *going* to teach you to go snowshoeing today, but now *for sure* there will be a yeti attack."

"That's the thing with the tennis racquets on your feet?"

Cayenne chuckles. "*Oui,* my dearest, that's the one. You want to bundle up and tromp through the snow for a bit?"

"Sure," he agrees, "teach me."

*

RAVI HAS ALWAYS liked the look of snow, and up in the mountains it falls pure and clean into a white blanket marred only by their tracks. He quickly learns the necessary loping stride to navigate with snowshoes as Cayenne guides him up a trail to see the view. The mountains are barely visible, shaded blue by snow and distance. All the little noises of nature are so muffled that the slight rise of their voices could be the only sounds in the whole world.

It's beautiful, but *cold*, and when Cayenne mentions he's getting a little blue around the lips, they head back to warm up inside.

In the kitchen, Ravi wraps his sweater around him while Cayenne makes cocoa. "*Bon appétit*, my dear. I have put in a *very* special ingredient." They wink as they slide his mug over and crowd into the breakfast nook bench beside him.

"Is it drugs?"

Cayenne bursts into a loud laugh. "*Non*, silly. Why would…" They devolve into giggles.

Ravi smiles lopsidedly. "You did say a 'very special ingredient.' Awfully suspicious, if you ask me."

Cayenne snorts and pushes the mug up to Ravi's lips. Chocolatey sweetness soon gives way to a fiery burn. "Oh! It's spicy."

"The very special ingredient is *quite* fabulous, sure to turn any old boring thing into something *extra-*

ordinary, darling."

Ravi takes another sip, rolling the cocoa over his tongue. "You put cayenne in it."

"I did, *mon cher.* Do you like it?"

"You put *cayenne* in it. That is…so *fucking* cute." He leans in and kisses them on the cheek. To his delight they blush, complexion going as pink as the inside of a seashell. He leans his head on his fist and drinks in the sight of them, the burn of the cocoa spreading warm and radiant through his chest.

"I've been thinking. About the other day. Something you said."

Cayenne's head tilts.

Ravi's heart climbs up into his throat, and he has to cough to get it back down in its proper place. "About going away. Why don't we go somewhere in October?"

Cayenne's expressions go through a swift, strange metamorphosis, from curiosity to guilt to hope, before settling into a tightly controlled wariness. "October?"

"Yeah." He gives them a gentle nudge with his shoulder. "You want to go somewhere with me? For a couple of weeks. I know that's a few months away, and I know August is"—he rotates his wrist, searching for the right words—"is going to be some big deal and all, but after. Where do you want to go? My treat this time."

The bottom half of Cayenne's face is hidden by their mug of cocoa. "Why October?"

One side of Ravi's mouth curls up. It is not a smile. "Durga Puja," he says with false apathy. "Big days-long Hindu holiday, and a major Trust event."

When he was a child, his mother would come home for Durga Puja and take him to temples on pilgrimage, just the two of them. She'd bring flowers to offer at the altar—lotuses, hibiscus, marigolds. Sometimes she would weave a few into Ravi's hair.

"I've managed to avoid it for the last eight years by finding pressing matters that demand my immediate attention." He fiddles with the handle of his mug. "I was hoping you'd be my 'pressing matter' this year."

Cayenne's throat moves. "You won't want to go anywhere with me after August," they say matter-of-factly, jaw tightening.

Ravi bites his lip, looking up through the fall of his hair. "You've implied as much. But… We fight, we make up, we fight, we make up…" He smiles over his cocoa. "We've gotten *very* good at that. Especially the making up. So, in August, we'll probably fight, and…"

He looks away, ears burning like coals. It's quite an admission, a promise of faith. But as ever, his barriers don't work around Cayenne. They pull apart all of his defenses as easily as unraveling a sweater, thread by thread, until Ravi's fool heart is bared naked, soft and vulnerable and hopeful.

Cayenne takes a deep breath and stares out of the window at the gently falling snow. When they turn back, there's a determined set to their chin. "I want to teach you something."

"Oh? I'm…game."

"For once, dearest, I am not being salacious. I want to teach you to say something in a language you do not speak."

Though perplexed, Cayenne's beseeching gaze means Ravi can only give one answer. "Sure, I'll try."

The handful of words are in a soft-sounding language with rounded vowels and sloping consonants. Cayenne listens to him repeat it four times before they are satisfied.

"What does it mean?" The syntax is unfamiliar, even to Ravi's ear.

They flip a lock of hair away from his eyes, fingers tracing his brow. "Just trust me, sweetheart." They crawl into his lap and press a dozen scattered kisses to his face. "You'll know when to say it to me."

*

RAVI LOSES TRACK of days after a handful of spins back in time. Four or five? More? He's not sure, and honestly isn't too concerned about finding out. The problems of the real world belong to somebody else right now.

The cabin boasts a fully furnished attic library, the room coming to a sharp triangular point at the peak of the A-frame, one side all window. Low bookshelves line the sloped walls with a random assortment of crime thrillers and dog-eared romances, none dated later than the '80s. Muted daylight spills in while snow falls thick past the glass.

The morning had been spent thoroughly enjoying each other in a slow, spectacular session that left Ravi loose-limbed and lazy. He lounges on a nest of pillows, book in hand.

Ravi isn't a big reader. He has a hard time sitting still for more than a chapter or so before the need to get up and do something useful becomes too strong to ignore. But he found a pretty engaging espionage mystery on the nearest shelf and was halfway through the villain's first appearance while he waited for Cayenne to return with a fresh bottle of Tempranillo.

Cayenne comes back without any wine, their shoulders held stiff as they stop at the edge of Ravi's spread of blankets, fingers clenching at their sides. They lift their head, lips set in a resolute line, and approach him.

Ravi quirks a brow. "What's up? Yetis finally show?"

Cayenne doesn't smile. They pour themself into his

lap, straddling him. Ravi lets his book drop to the floor with a surprised grunt. A bit more sudden than their usual advances, but Ravi is more than onboard. Hard to imagine he'll ever get enough, ever be sated. He traces his hands up over the lithe curve of their spine and urges them down for a kiss.

"Wait, wait," Cayenne whispers, lips pressed to his temple.

Ravi stops. "Hm?"

"Can we just stay like this for a minute, my pet? Only for a minute."

Ravi stills his wandering hands and gets himself under control. "Sure." If they just want a hug, he's all for it. He rests his head on their shoulder and savors the moment, breathing in their familiar scent. It goes on for a long time—minutes, going on five, until finally he shifts. "Cay…"

"Just one more second," Cayenne rasps. They suck in air as if preparing to jump off a cliff. Finally, they untangle from Ravi's lap and sit cross-legged in front of him. Their hands convulse, twisting fistfuls of blankets.

"I have something to tell you."

The flow of Ravi's pulse turns cool, dread skittering icily up his spine. He takes a deep breath of his own, steadying himself. "August," he guesses, not really a question.

"I'll…I'll try. But first, there is something else, *mon coeur.*"

A mad, sudden beat trips in Ravi's chest. The endearment is a new one: *my heart.*

Cayenne exhales shakily, tugging at their hair. "*Mon Dieu, je suis un idiot.* I shouldn't have taken you here. It's only going to make things harder, once you see what I did. I shouldn't have done *any* of this; not that first dinner, not the Seychelles, none of it. If I had any sense in my fool skull, I would have already sent my mind all the way back to that park in Chicago, gone as far back as I can possibly stretch, and not gotten involved. That's what a hero would have done. What *you* would have done." Cayenne looks straight at him, eyes red and lips pale. "But I, my darling Ravi, am not a hero. I am a monster."

"You aren't a monster, Cayenne."

Cayenne hugs their arms around their body, shaking their head. "You don't *know*."

"Then tell me!" Ravi gesticulates forcefully, at his limit for being kept in the dark. He's sick of having this fucking time travel *bullshit* lurking in the corners of his vision, haunting their every second together. "Just *tell me*, Cayenne."

Cayenne drags a hand over their face. "You know we knew each other. From the future. My past."

"Yeah, I know. You work with the team." A horrible suspicion creeps over him. "Were we…enemies?"

They wince, arms tight around their middle. Their eyes slide away. "*Non*, it is not… It is not like that, in the future."

"Lovers?" That would add an extra layer of complication, but not one he thinks warrants this level of agitation.

"*No*," they scoff, almost a laugh, "not lovers, not even friends. We…we *hated* each other." They take another deep breath, and Ravi realizes it's one of *his* breaths, his ingrained sniper exercises Cayenne must have picked up. It doesn't look like it's helping.

Cayenne looks up as if seeking answers in the exposed attic beams. "This was supposed to be *fun*. This was supposed to be… I don't know anymore. Paying a debt. Charity. Or—"—their voice goes raw—"a *joke*, to be honest. But you… I can't… I didn't *know*. It's not my fault that I didn't—" They hide their face in their hands before dropping them back down, visibly quivering.

"Boring, emotionless Ravi Abhiramnew; professional errand boy, an empty suit, my *ravageur*, who wouldn't even sneeze unless The Trust gave him leave to do so, who never had anything as interesting as an original thought." Cayenne shakes their head with a humorless scratch of a laugh. "It was clear you *desperately* needed to get laid, so I thought I would…do you a favor. Because *c'est moi*. Granting you the *pleasure* of my time. Harmless fun, to make up a little for my transgressions against you. And then we would go our separate ways, and I would be well and gone before that grim day in August arrives. Gone before you find out. That is how it was supposed to go.

"Then, that dinner, in Chicago… I had never seen you *blush* before. Or laugh. Or make a joke. But there you were, sitting across from me, funny, and sweet, and…fragile. One peek behind the brick wall and I wanted more. You…intrigued me. This beautiful, breakable boy.

"You were just an asshole in an expensive suit, and I *never* saw past that. Why couldn't you have been a cold, arrogant prick like I was expecting to find? Why did you…" They cover their mouth with a trembling hand, then force it back down again, dragging in a shuddering breath.

"When I texted you I liked you, it wasn't even true at the time. It was just what got the best results. I tried a lot of other ploys, first, before you said yes. I figured out what it would take, what you needed to hear. It took me *so many* tries to crack through that wall of yours; to know what to say, how to look at you, how—" They choke on a scathing laugh. "How *French* to be."

Cayenne puts both hands to their ribs, gasping like

they can't get enough air. When they finally continue, their voice drops low, harsh and accusing. "It's your fault. Why did you…why did you have to be like this? Why did you have to be so, so…so *fucking* wonderful, so— Why did you have to…to *see* me so well as you do? Why couldn't you have just been a thug in a suit? I was never supposed to *care* this much, Ravi. *C'est pas juste,* it's not fucking fair."

Ravi's anchor has been cut. He drifts without a course through choppy waters. His voice dredges up from his chest, a tangled bramble of a sound. "I bet it was funny. Making me want you. Was it?"

Cayenne flinches, curling their tattooed hand into a tight fist. They don't speak, biting their lip so hard it goes white and bloodless.

Ravi nods slowly.

"Ravi," they say in a broken-glass whisper. "I shouldn't have let it get this far. I am such a fucking idiot, a selfish disaster. *Je suis une catastrophe.* You don't know how true it was when you called me a monsoon. You were right all along. I bring destruction and ruin, like you said."

Ravi can't stand to see them like this, a crumpled wreck, no sign left of their bright, carefree confidence. Anything he might feel all seems selfish and unimportant in the face of Cayenne's anguish. "Cayenne. A monsoon, even if it's a complete disaster, even if it tears your house down to rubble, it still makes things *grow*. You've…you've done that to *me*, Cayenne. I'm a different person because of you."

Tipping their head back, Cayenne breaks into a hideous, lifeless laugh. "And how *horrible* that is! Of *all* people, I'm the only one to bring you a little joy, to offer you true freedom… M*e*! It's a sick joke." They reach out and jerk back. It's a broken, abortive move, like they can't stand to touch him.

"I can't take back what I did, *mon coeur*. What I will do. There are things I can't change, even if I—no matter *how much* I want to." Cayenne stares down at the back of their hand, at their artfully rendered tattoo. "A chronomage can't exist at the same time as their past self. If I get even close, it's…it's *agony*. The Cayenne you'll meet in August won't know you, and they won't trust you. All I can do is hope—" Their throat works around a hard swallow, and they tear their gaze away from Ravi's. "All I can do now is hope you'll still want me. After you see what I did. What I *will* do."

"*What the fuck are you going to do?*" Ravi yells, frustrated beyond measure. "*This* isn't enough? This isn't what I find out in August?"

"*Non.* This is not…this is not… *Merde.*"

"*Just fucking tell me.*"

Cayenne sucks in a shaky breath, finally meeting his eyes. "I'll…I'll try."

Their tattoo flickers. Any determination in their features has been stricken away, replaced with a rictus of grief. The tattoo flickers again.

Again. And again.

Faster and faster they send themself back, trying over and over, crumpling more and more with each flash of their tattoo. Ravi loses track of how many times they attempt it, how many bright flickers on the back of their shaking hand, while for Ravi no more time has passed than the space of a breath.

Finally, Cayenne scrambles to their feet and turns away from him. Arms limp at their sides, Cayenne throws back their head and laughs, high and hysterical.

Ravi stands up, twitching with the urge to go to them, to offer them some solace.

Cayenne turns back with a bitter smile he's never seen them wear before. "Well. Of fucking course anything I say will only make it worse." They laugh again, strange and unfamiliar, a jagged, jaded bark. "The smartest thing would be to not see each other anymore."

Heart seizing, Ravi freezes, limbs useless.

Quicker than he had ever seen them move before, Cayenne snakes forward and cups his head in their hands, holding him fast. Their eyes *burn*.

"I may be a monster, *mon chéri*, but no matter what happens, remember I am *your* monster." They pull him down until their foreheads touch and close their eyes. "I love you, Ravi."

And they kiss him, savage and feral as a storm, take a step backward, and disappear.

Chapter Eight

"HEY, SO…YOU'RE okay, right, agent guy?" Harry asks from over the top of her phone.

Ravi doesn't look at her, shielded behind his sunglasses. He keeps his attention on the band-poster-plastered door and his back to the wall, alert for anything. "Why wouldn't I be?"

"Your top two buttons are undone."

Ravi resists the urge to glance down and fix it. "It's summer," he says flatly. "It's hot." Like she's one to talk, with her long hair piled into a messy bun, wearing a shirt with bleach stains that just barely manage to look intentional.

"Okay." Harry shrugs, leaving it alone. "The place looks clear. If we're going to find this"—she sighs with deep irritation—"*haunted guitar* today, we're going to have to split up into even smaller groups. Nate and Constance are checking out all the blues bars in Ansley Park, and Val's taking Downtown." She pauses to take in her surroundings with a sardonic eye. "Isn't it weird how so many of our cases bring us to bars? Do monsters love two-for-one rail drinks or something? Good thing none of us are in recovery or anything."

Ravi waits for instructions, leg bouncing under the table. He hadn't gone to the group mission brief, just met Harry when she texted him the location, and hadn't asked to be filled in. The mission parameters were to find a haunted guitar somewhere in one of the city's dozens of blues bars. The three likely spots they've searched turned up nothing. Ravi itches to do something *useful*. "You want to split? I'll try the place on Flat Shoals Road."

"Actually," Harry says with a suspiciously bright cadence, "I'm taking East. You can hang back here for a bit."

Then Robert Hernandez walks into the bar. A vigilant eye already on the door, Ravi clocks him the instant he appears, a stocky silver fox of a man in casual attire.

Oh, what the fuck.

Harry waves Robert over, then glances askance at Ravi. He's unconsciously balled a fist on the table. Hastily he flattens it, reining in his control.

"I did mention Bobby was coming in for a consult." Yeah, that was just a few days for her, but nearly two weeks for Ravi. It had completely slipped his mind. *Sloppy.* "I told him to meet us here to check in. We're not kicking the tires on Constance's demon hunt thing until tomorrow."

Bobby gives them both a friendly wave and a smile, weaving around the tables to join theirs.

"Free advice," Harry mutters, "take off those fucking sunglasses. It's a dark bar and you look ridiculous. Only Val can pull off that look without everyone assuming she's hiding a week-long bender."

Ravi scowls and pulls them off. "Yes, ma'am." He barely manages to keep the bite out of his words.

She arches a brow and turns a welcoming smile onto the new arrival. "Hey, Bobbo! Haven't seen you in a brick. How was the flight?" The PIs shake hands as Bobby slides into the far booth.

"Gotta be honest, Harry," Bobby chuckles in his gravelly voice, "first time I've ever flown first class. I think I'm ruined for coach now." He dips his chin at Ravi, a perfectly casual greeting between friendly acquaintances. "Hey, Ravi."

A polite, stiff nod in return. "Hey."

Harry snickers. "Heh, yeah, Constance doesn't have a great concept of how much money today is worth. She sent enough, right, along with the info?"

Bobby nods emphatically. "About that. The retainer she sent me was *generous*. Extremely generous. I'm a little worried about how it's gonna show on my taxes, to be honest, but that's another thing. Can't be safe to send that much money through the mail. You got to teach her about wire transfers."

Harry grins and rolls her sleeves into haphazard cuffs over her elbows. "There's apps for that now, old-timer. Just thank your lucky stars she sent cash instead of diamonds."

"You kids lead some weird lives."

"You have no idea. Guess what we're doing? Did you guess tracking down a lead on a possible haunted guitar? Wow, you're good, man. Actually..." Harry glances at her phone. Ravi notes her lock screen is clear before she angles it away from him and stands up. "I am so sorry, Bobbo, I've got to run. But you guys should stay and catch up! I already paid for a round."

Ravi tries to catch her eye, telepathically asking her what the fuck she's doing. Unfortunately, he has not developed any magic powers overnight, and Harry ignores him.

"It's so good to see you, man." She claps Bobby on the shoulder as she passes by. "If you come by Constance's shop tomorrow around noon, we can go over the details for this demon hunt. This fucker's *shifty*."

"Sure, can do."

"Awesome. Oh yeah, Rav, if we find the right bar I'll give you a call, okay?" She flashes Ravi a double thumbs-up and whirls away.

Ravi crosses his arms in the ensuing silence. "Robert."

Bobby smiles. It's a kind smile. Warm. "Hey, *chavo*. She's sweet, huh?"

Despite himself, Ravi almost laughs. "Yeah. Real peach."

Bobby leans on his elbows with a heavy sigh as the waitress drops off a couple of beers, Harry's buckwheat favorite. Ravi snags one and takes a big swallow. He doesn't prefer the taste, but maybe it'll help him get through this. At least it'll give him something to do with his hands. He feels like he might crawl out of his skin any time he sits still long enough to think.

"She's sharp." Bobby twists off the cap and takes a long drink punctuated by a satisfied sigh. "Picks things up."

Ravi grunts. "I know you didn't tell her anything."

Robert hadn't been interested in discretion but would respect it in others. Ravi appreciated that, at least.

Bobby watches Ravi drink. Another detective. Another reason to clamp down even more carefully on his facial expressions. Bobby nods as if to himself. "Look…I know we didn't part on what you'd call great terms—"

"I made a pass. You called me a coward. I left." The words are out before Ravi can bite them back. So much for clamping down.

Robert sets aside his beer. "Kid, when Harry suggested meeting here, I was hoping to get the chance to talk with you. I'm not happy about how things shook out in Boston. But if you don't want me here, if you don't want to talk, I can go." He thumbs back over his shoulder, and Ravi knows he means it. If he wants to be alone, all he has to do is say so.

Ravi manages to keep a dead stare for another few seconds before his shoulders fall. He leans his weight forward on one elbow, scrubbing at his beard. "Sorry, I'm not…I'm not trying to be an asshole. That's just what happens when I open my mouth."

Bobby smiles. "Nah, you're doing fine."

"That's me," Ravi scoffs, balancing the words carefully on a tightrope so they don't waver and fall. "Doing fine."

Bobby's broad shoulders stretch wide as he rests his arms on the back of the booth. "I'm gonna guess this isn't just about me, right? Doesn't seem demon related, either. Nah, this feels personal. I'm gonna guess something happened recently. It's reeeeaaal subtle, but the clues are there. I am a detective, you know." He grins wryly.

Ravi stares at him, swallowing.

"You wanna talk about it?"

Ravi opens his mouth, closes it. Where to begin? What even to say?

"Well," Bobby starts, taking a swallow of beer, "I was in the closet a long time, you know. Wasted a lot of time in there."

Ravi looks away, fiercely wishing he had his sunglasses on. "That's not..." He rubs the back of his neck, grasping for words and coming up empty.

Mouth dropping open, Bobby jolts up straight in his booth. "Shit, is this about a *guy*? Did you meet someone?"

"You…*fucking detectives.*" Ravi buries his face in his hands, cursing in Tamil under his breath. After a long minute, he finally says, "Yeah, I met someone." His voice comes gruff and muffled through his fingers. He reaches for his beer with an aggrieved sigh; he's either had far too much alcohol or not nearly enough for this conversation.

"Ah, hell, *chavo*. That's nothing to be so worked up about. That's a good thing."

Ravi grimaces at the bitterness of the beer. "Just broke up with me a few days ago," he adds mildly, summing up a complex situation in a handful of words.

"Oh, damn. I'm sorry, Ravi. If you wanna talk about it, I'm a great listener."

It's…a nice offer. Next to no one even knows about Ravi's preferences, much less would be willing to hear some sob story about it. As long as Ravi doesn't also drive Robert off, it's a rare opportunity. Might be smart to get a normal person's perspective, something Ravi has even less experience with than romance.

"I'd…I'd like that. Yeah." He takes an automatic scan of their surroundings. The bar isn't busy, and they're sequestered far in the back. Canned blues music plays loud enough to foil any eavesdroppers or listening devices. Ravi isn't likely to get a better chance.

"I met someone. Little over two months ago. Sort of. Longer, really. The timeline isn't…normal. Weird supernatural shit we don't have to get into. But it was…good. Really good," he says hoarsely.

Bobby is an attentive listener. He likely has the same genial demeanor listening to clients, and no doubt it helped in gathering confessions back when he was a Boston badge. "Okay. Weird magic shit. Check. What's he like?"

"They," corrects Ravi gently.

Bobby nods with only a brief lift of his salt-and-pepper brows. "Oh, sorry, I just assumed. Very modern, huh?"

"Not really. Maybe here in the States, but we've had

a third gender in India for centuries."

Pausing with the bottle at his lips, Bobby looks genuinely surprised. "Huh. I didn't expect that, given the things I've heard."

"Well," Ravi reluctantly admits. "You're not wrong. It's not as enlightened as it sounds. Still a struggle for equal rights. Used to be better for *hijras* in…the old days. Pre-colonial. Lots of things were. It used to be different for them. And for…for people like us." He barely gets it out, throat tight, avoiding eye contact. Even now, he can't say it. Still a coward. Robert hadn't been wrong there.

Mercifully, Bobby brings the topic back on track. "So, let me guess—a real flashy, out-and-proud, larger-than-life type?"

"I… Yeah. How'd you guess?"

"Eh, just an old cop's hunch. I've been there, myself. I'm also guessing they're pretty easy on the eyes, yeah?"

A half-smile sneaks unbidden across Ravi's face. "The easiest."

"Heh. Knew it. Only thing that makes sense." The

grin he gives Ravi almost borders on flirtatious. "Don't know why *you* were chasing after a beat-up *viejo* like me anyway."

He slants Robert a skeptical look; the guy has to know he's good-looking. "Not that I wasn't interested for other reasons, but older men usually don't mind keeping a secret." He sighs. "In India, anyway."

"Yeah, I've heard some not great things. It must have been tough growing up there. I'm sorry."

Ravi truly looks at Bobby for the first time since he walked in. Friendly eyes set in a rugged, well-lived face. No one would know his orientation at a glance; a guy would have to know what signs to look for, or maybe recognize something he'd seen in himself.

Perhaps they traveled it in different decades, and in different countries, but it was the same well-worn road. They've both walked it, along with so many others. Carried the same weight.

Ravi offers the barest hint of a smile. "Thanks, Robert."

They drink beer in a silence that stretches out so

long Ravi itches to fill it. An old cop's trick, he realizes with distant amusement.

"Ten years in jail, if they catch you. If the law doesn't, the blackmailers will. And then you might prefer jail." He absently peels the label from his bottle in thin, ragged strips. "It was decriminalized back in 2009. Great, right? Not quite. That only lasted four years. And what do you think happened to everyone who came out in that time? Couldn't go back in again."

Sudden firings. Street violence. Kids kicked out of their homes. Arrests for "traffic tickets," when anyone who's been in India a hot minute could tell you traffic enforcement was a joke.

"Damn," Bobby mutters. "Your family support you, at least?"

Ravi snorts, not looking up.

"No, huh."

"No." He drops a long peel of label paper on the table.

Bobby sighs. "That's rough, kid."

All he can do is shrug and start picking at the other

side of the label. "It is what it is."

Bobby shifts forward in the booth. "So, what happened with this easy-on-the-eyes person? You said things were going real good."

Where to even start? Cayenne's monologue of revelations has been running on nonstop loop in Ravi's head. No matter how he's tried sieving through it for clues, it all makes less and less sense; a broken mosaic that must have once made up a true picture that is now only shards. Days later, Ravi still feels the lingering dizziness from the trip back through the chalk circle, nausea still rising at odd hours of the day and night. He's not sure if it's from chronal energy residue or something else entirely.

"It's…complicated." To say the fucking least. "They…told me they loved me." It spills out of his mouth without his conscious volition, a thought that's been perched in the middle of Ravi's heart for days, its sharp-taloned grip unceasing.

"Oh, wow. Okay." Bobby whistles low, brows climbing to his hairline. "Isn't that good? Bad? I can't tell, you're hard to read, kid."

"It's…unexpected."

"You love them back?"

Ravi opens and closes his mouth like a fish gasping for water. He doesn't even know how to begin to answer. His family hadn't been the loving sort. They never said it, never practiced it, never taught it. Pure practicality: Abhiramnews are short-lived, globe-trotting monster-hunters with arranged marriages, destined to fling themselves at every emerging apocalypse until death. Love was for other people, people without destinies. *Focus on your bladework, kid,* he'd heard more than once. *That'll never let you down.*

"I don't even know what love looks like," he admits.

Bobby rubs his chin with a distant look of remembrance. "You know, when I came out, I was still on the force back then. Boston PD. There were guys I knew for years, saved each other's lives, who suddenly wouldn't give me the time of day."

Ravi nods grimly, but Bobby holds up a preemptive

finger. "But the strangest thing happened. All sorts of folks on the force and otherwise, folks I didn't even know very well, came up and offered their support. Got some of my best friends that way, and some I still got to this day. Damnedest thing." He motions around to the world at large. "Just goes to show you, there's probably love all around you that you're just not seeing."

Ravi nods again more slowly, giving this some thought while he shreds the label a little more.

"So, they told you they love you and then, what? Broke up with you?"

Ravi sinks a little lower in his chair and nods again.

"Ah, damn. Hell of a thing. I'm sorry."

Ravi contemplates the woodgrain of the table.

"Hey, look, you're still young!" Bobby leans in and slaps his shoulder in an avuncular manner. "You're what, in your early thirties? Maybe thirty-five?"

"Twenty-five."

"Whoa. No shit? I mean, sorry?" Bobby palms the back of his neck with an apologetic wince. "I didn't mean *whoa*, I just meant…you look older. Act like it too."

"No, it's okay. I…grew up fast."

"No kidding. Anyway, you're *really* young. You got plenty of time to go out there and try again. Maybe this is a good thing; kind of sounds to me like you got given a big bouquet of red flags. If this person doesn't appreciate you, doesn't treat you the way you deserve, better you find out now, right?"

Ravi focuses on breathing steadily. "Right."

"That's how it goes; you fall in love, you get your heart broken, maybe even break a few hearts yourself. Which I'm sure you do anyway without even knowing it. Pretty thing like you." He throws a teasing wink. The tips of Ravi's ears warm. "*Chavo*, you got a good group of people around you. Harry and the rest, they're all real good people. If you can tell me, then you can tell them too. Take this old queen's advice and rely on your friends. Ain't good for you to keep this all bottled up."

*

HE TALKS WITH Bobby for another half hour, thankfully moving away from the painful topic of his love life.

Eventually his phone buzzes with an update from Harry:

Found it! Gather up, crew.

Plugging the address into his navigation, Ravi promises to get another beer with Robert before he leaves town. When Ravi leaves the bar, he feels…a little lighter. Just a bit.

Before he starts up the car, he drums his fingers on the wheel. He reaches for the ignition button, then pauses. Reaches for it again. Stops. Against his better judgement, he pulls out the cherry-red phone and glances at the screen.

Blank. No messages. He shoves the phone away again.

"*Muttaal,*" he mutters in sharp castigation, then starts up the engine and heads to the rendezvous.

*

JOHNNY RAY'S IS a more upscale bar than the others he and Harry had scoped out. More authentic, with con-siderably better ambiance. Ravi is a sucker for classic

Americana, and this place has it in spades; lots of country tchotchkes on the walls, autographed photos of famous musicians, and a large display of musical instruments.

Normally he'd be all for it, but he's too busy being irritated with himself. Why'd he even bring the phone? Really? Cayenne tells him they've been lying to him from the start, they're *going* to do worse to him, and he hasn't thrown the thing away? Unbelievable.

While the others investigate the wall of displayed guitars, Ravi stands vigilant off to the side, arms crossed. The others are the brains, anyway. He's just there to shoot things that get past Val.

"None of these musical instruments fit the given description," declares the angel. The bar is relatively crowded for a weekday, and the Amazon with ash-white hair is getting the lion's share of side-eye. Their whole group looks…unconventional, to put it mildly. At least Constance left her talking cat at home.

"Nothing?" Nate asks, leaning up against an artfully graffitied display piano. His broad-shouldered frame also attracts a measure of attention the professor appears oblivious to. "We're sure this is the right bar?"

"Indeed," says Constance with a pensive tap to her chin. "The item in question is assuredly present. The auguries were very clear." She steps back to fit the whole wall of guitars in her field of vision, all fifty or so.

Ravi shifts impatiently.

Harry rubs the bridge of her nose with a world-weary sigh. "So, what, you read some tea leaves and they said this was the place, right?"

"No," Constance answers primly, "thou speaketh of tasseomancy. Augury is reading the flight of birds."

No one has anything to say to that.

Harry puts her hands on her hips, facing the group like a coach giving a pep talk. "Well, if the ghost guitar is here, then we've gotta find it. Let's take it room by room. If someone can cause a distraction, I'll pick the lock to the back room."

Nate looks intrigued. "You can pick locks?"

"I was a wayward youth. So, let's—"

Without a word, Ravi spins on his heel and heads

to the bar in long, determined strides. Harry splutters behind him. He ignores her.

"Hey," he barks at the guy kneeling behind the bar. The man stops fiddling with the ice basin and stands up.

"Uh, yeah, can I help you, man?" The bartender has a bald head and an open, pleasant face.

"We're looking for a guitar." Ravi automatically scans for possible threats, checking the mirror to keep an eye on the patrons. In the reflection, his team gives each other significant looks as they follow Ravi up to the bar.

The bartender steps over with an indulgent smile. "Well, we got a whole wall of 'em over—"

"A specific guitar."

The guy's smile dissolves. His eyes flick nervously to the door at the back, and Ravi's suspicion lasers in tight.

"What's your name?"

"Uh. Ray?"

"Okay, *Ray*, you know what guitar I'm talking about, don't you?"

A hand comes down on Ravi's shoulder. He barely manages to tamp down the ingrained impulse to break the wrist before he sees Nate's reflection in the long mirror. The rest of the team flank him. Val faces out as if standing guard, muscular arms crossed. Constance whispers into Harry's ear, who just nods, providing silent support at Nate's shoulder.

The professor smiles his friendly, dimpled grin. "Heyyyy, Ravi. My guy. Coming on a little strong, don't ya think?"

Ravi shakes off his hand. "Nope. This guy knows something." He points an accusing finger at Ray. "Where's the guitar, Ray?"

Nate laughs flippantly and sidles alongside Ravi, reclining his elbows back on the bar in an everything's-fine-here lean. "He's just passionate about music," he tells the bartender with an expressive wink. To Ravi he adds, voice gentling, "And we're just here for a drink, right?"

"We're here," Ravi enunciates every syllable clearly and precisely, "to find a haunted guitar, and so far, we've just been wasting time."

Nate opens his mouth, but Ray holds up his palms and cuts in, sweat beading on his scalp, "Okay, okay, man, look. I got the guitar in the back. You can have it; I don't even care anymore. I'll go get it. I don't want any trouble, all right?"

"No trouble," Ravi agrees with a nod. "Not going to sneak out the back, are you, Ray?"

Ray gives his head a vehement shake. "No way! Seriously, I don't know who you people are and I don't care. You can have the guitar. Thought it'd be cool, but damn thing has been more trouble than it's worth. It'll be a relief to get it off my hands. I swear."

"Sounds good," Ravi says. The guy seems sincere. And if he's not, easy enough to chase him down.

Nate looks back at Harry and mouths, *what the hell?* She throws her hands up in the air. Ravi ignores them both.

Ray heads out from behind the bar and stops, still with a tightly plastered-on smile. "And uh, can I get you a drink? On the house."

"I'll pay for it. I'll have…" Ravi scans the shelves behind Ray and picks more or less at random. "That whisky." Why the fuck not. It's got a nice Art Nouveau label.

"Yeah, man, no problem. One of the good ones, you got taste." Ray pours with considerable haste. "Here you go. You and your pals can grab a table. I gotta dig the guitar outta the back. Won't be a minute."

"Sure. Thanks."

Ray crab-steps away. Ravi takes a tentative sniff of the whisky. It smells like kerosene.

"What the fuck was that?" Harry hisses.

Nate waves her back, like he needs some space to work, and watches Ravi slap down a handful of cash. "So. You've graduated to top-shelf whisky since last week?"

Taking a sip, Ravi answers, "Yup."

"Oh, cool, cool. How is it?"

"Awful." He throws back a huge swallow.

With a surprised grunt, Nate snags the tumbler out of Ravi's hand. "Dude, that's meant to be sipped."

Ravi scoffs through the burn in his throat. "I can make decisions for myself."

Before he can react, Val's adamant hands grasp him by his shoulders and pull him away from the bar. His feet barely touching the floor, she maneuvers him to the most secluded table and forcefully sets him down in a chair.

Harry is the first to pull up a chair next to him. The rest soon follow suit, all four of his teammates facing Ravi head-on. He's painfully aware he left his sunglasses in the car.

Harry gives him a piercing once-over, leaning on folded arms. "Rav, what the fuck is up with you?"

He meets her stare evenly. "I found the haunted guitar. Wasn't that the goal?"

"Forget the guitar," Nate says. "You look like shit. You're drinking *whisky*. And it seemed like you were one second away from clocking that poor guy in the face."

Ravi can't help but recoil. He wouldn't hurt an innocent person. Did he look like he was going to?

A thug in a suit, Cayenne had said.

"I'm fine," he says.

Nate rolls his eyes. "Harry is a detective and I *literally* have a PhD in observing people. You cannot bullshit us. What is going on?"

"Witch-hunter," Constance says, then in a kindlier tone, "Ravi. We hath talked freely before, thou and I, hath we not?"

He glances away, fighting the desire to fidget. Eventually he sighs and meets her encouraging gaze. "We have."

There's no telling what Val is thinking behind her sunglasses, but she says, "You do not seem well."

Ouch. If *Val* feels it's necessary to say something, he must look worse than he thought.

Harry frowns. "Did something happen with Bobby? I thought you guys would want to talk. Sorry if—"

"No," Ravi says. "We had a good talk. That was… that was fine." Robert told Ravi he should rely on these people. His friends.

Fuck, he's being an asshole again.

Just then Ray walks up with a beautiful white guitar and offers it to Ravi. "Here, just like I said. You can have it." He seems truly anxious to get rid of it.

"Ah!" Constance sticks out her arms and makes grabby hands. The confused bartender passes over the guitar. "Thank thee kindly, barkeep. We shall take it from here onwards."

Ray makes himself scarce as Constance settles the instrument in front of her and lightly runs her hands over it. The others lean in.

Saved by a haunted guitar. Ravi quietly exhales, grateful to no longer be the center of attention.

Constance produces a small vial from her satchel and places a single viscous drop of green fluid on the tip of her tongue. She blinks several times and winces at the overhead lights, dimmed though they are, then turns her attention to the guitar. Everyone watches with open curiosity.

Val leans over and tilts her glasses very slightly down, affording a small glimpse of her burning white-hot eyes. "I have seen haunted items before. If there is a soul tethered to this instrument, we shall surely see some sign of it."

Eyes brightening, Nate sits up very straight. "Some ghosts *are* trapped souls? There's a lot of theory about apparitions being echoes, or psychic flashbacks, or —"

"Doc," Harry interrupts.

Nate ducks his head with an apologetic smile. "Right, right. Later."

"Constance, can you, you know, sense anything?" Harry makes a waggly stage magician flourish.

Constance is so absorbed by the guitar it takes a moment for the question to register. "Hmm? Oh, indeed, my niece! There is no specter in this lute."

Typical. "So, it's *not* haunted," Ravi growls. He turns around to face Ray, but Harry's hand goes vise-tight on his forearm. He subsides, settling back into his seat with an irritated sigh.

Constance rubs at her eyes, her pupils enormous. "Nay, not haunted, but there is indeed a malediction. Someone has laid a curse upon the lute so it causes great fear and apprehension to whomsoever plays it."

"Aww, no ghost," Nate pouts. "But, hey, curses are easier, right?"

"Verily, my scholarly fellow. A simple spell of banishment shall suffice. I can do it now, should thee wish it?"

Harry pushes her black boots against the table, leaning her chair back on two legs. "Ugh. Okay. Great, no ghost, but I'm not thrilled someone is going around cursing stuff. Can we track it somehow, through the curse? Is that a thing you can do?"

Constance lifts her chin. "Mine niece, 'tis foolishness to assume magic can achieve any goal. There are laws and limits to mine abilities."

"So, you can't do it?"

Constance sheds her haughty expression for a toothy grin. "I *absolutely* can do it."

Nate laughs, and Harry rolls her eyes through a smirk. Constance bends down over the guitar, ink-stained hands tracing esoteric runes. The whole of her eyes, pupil and all, go white. Claiming a side effect of her breach into the future, occasionally the hedge-witch can "peer through the very veil of time itself," as she describes it.

Ravi scans around the bar for onlookers. Folks are mostly ignoring the table of weirdos holding some sort of guitar seance. Nice that some people still appreciate minding their own business.

Constance raises her head, eyes clearing to their normal hazel. "You shall be pleased to hear, my niece, the man who cursed this guitar is long since dead. The guitar has been passed around for nearly two decades, accumulating renown for its unluckiness. It has caused some harm, but mostly just dismay." She shrugs. "'Tis a mild danger."

Val grunts. "Mild danger or no, this is the object we have been contracted to find and exorcise."

"Okay, exorcise away. Or banish it, whatever." Harry lets her chair fall back to the floor with a *thunk*.

Without a moment's hesitation Constance spits on the guitar. She looks up at Harry's cough of surprise. "What? Would'st thou prefer blood?" She traces a rune in the saliva. A slight *twang* reverberates from the guitar, not so much heard as felt. Constance smiles brightly. "Done!"

Nate gives her a double thumbs-up. "Nice! Easy-peasy, another mission in the bag. Look at us. We're just crushing it lately. What should we do with the guitar, Harry?"

"I guess keep it? You want it, Doc?"

"Eh, I've already got one. Acoustic dreadnought."

"I can just picture you in college, sitting in the quad playing Dave Matthews in between rounds of hacky sack."

"I'm feeling personally attacked here, McAllister."

Great, job done. Ravi starts to stand up, but Harry forcibly drags him back. "Nuh-uh, no way, my dude, sit the fuck down and talk to us." She's unusually serious, a wrinkle of concern drawn across her forehead. "You've been off for a while. You went into the vampire situation by yourself. You've been even cagier than usual, which is saying something. You practically made that bartender piss his pants, and you're..." She pauses, regarding him with keen scrutiny. "You're jeopardizing the efficiency of the team."

Fuck. Of all the things she could say.

He plunks himself back down into the chair with a heavy sigh. That big gulp of whisky was a bad idea. He's definitely feeling it, alcohol acrid at the back of his throat.

"Okay. Okay. You want to talk. So, let's talk about it. *Once.* And then hopefully never again." He rubs the bridge of his nose, heartbeat drumming in his ears loud enough to drown out the music. Deep breath. In and out. *I got broken up with.* Easy. Just five words, and even true.

Ravi opens his mouth and what comes out instead is, "I got my heart broken a couple of days ago, all right?" And immediately he wishes he could disappear into the floor.

Except for Val, the others look as if nothing has ever surprised them so much in their entire lives. After her initial astonishment, Constance's face morphs into something unsettlingly akin to horror. Whereas Val merely inclines her head to the side as if hearing an unfamiliar note in a song.

Breaking out in a full-bodied cold sweat, Ravi has to drag both hands through his hair to keep himself upright, to not sink below the table.

"Oh. Okay. Well," Harry rallies. "Personal stuff, then. That's, uh, that's…"

Nate delivers a sympathetic pat on the back. "Sorry, my guy. I've been there. That's rough."

Harry clears her throat, shifting in her chair. "I thought maybe it was some big Trust stuff going on."

Ravi lowers his face into his hands. "They're not mutually exclusive. The Trust affects my 'personal stuff,' and my 'personal stuff' interferes with The Trust."

"Ah. Sounds complicated."

Jagged, bitter shards grow on the edges of Ravi's laughter. "Complicated, yeah."

"Anyone we know?" Nate asks. "The heartbreaker?"

Constance has not moved her knowing gaze away

from Ravi once since he made his confession. He swallows and looks away.

"Cayenne." And there it is. There's no rewinding and taking it back. No clock tattoo on Ravi's hand. What's done is done.

"*What?*" Nate's voice rises in shock. He checks around the bar before turning back with his volume more under control. "You're saying *Cayenne* broke your heart? Cayenne with the…the face and the hair. That Cayenne?"

"Ah," Harry says with a grim sort of satisfaction, staring into the middle distance. "There's that last puzzle piece."

"Oh, *Ravi*," Constance murmurs, shaking her head.

"We are speaking of the chronomancer?" Val asks. Her expression is virtually unchanged but for the slightest lines of disapproval around her mouth. "You have been engaged in an intimate relationship with the chronomancer?"

"*Fuck.*" Ravi lets his head sink to the table, swearing under his breath in muffled Hinglish. "Yes."

Nate again puts a hand to Ravi's shoulder. "Broke your heart in less than two months, huh? You fall *fast*, my guy."

Ravi's distantly grateful for the touch, the gesture of support. "It was longer than two months," he tells the inside of his elbow.

Harry snorts. "Uh-huh. I bet there are all sorts of ways being a time wizard can improve your dating life."

"Sure," Ravi says bitterly, words still tripping heedless off his tongue, "you can go back in time to date a guy you despise, know all his secrets and weaknesses, and then tell him you can't see him anymore because you're going to do something so terrible and awful in August that he's going to hate you for it."

"Okay, wow." Harry blinks and fans her hands out expressively. "That's a *lot* to process. Shit. Yeah. We are definitely going to have to circle back to that. *Hey, Ray!*" She spins around in her chair and shouts at the bartender. "Gonna need a round, here!" She turns back and places both hands flat on the table. "Now normally I would not pry, you know that, Rav. But if we're talking about the time traveler who claims to work with us all in our future, the same one who can end a city-wide vampire threat for no reason—" She pauses. "I guess not for no reason, huh? They were clearing your schedule, weren't they?"

"Yeah," Ravi manages through a dry throat.

"Yeah," Harry sighs heavily. "The same time traveler who is going to cause some kind of airport mayhem pretty soon, then I'm sorry, but it isn't just personal."

"I know. It was stupid to get involved. *I* was stupid."

Constance clucks her tongue and takes his hand in hers. To his surprise, he lets her. The whisky must be affecting him, lowering his defenses. "Indeed, it is foolishness to follow your heart, Witch-hunter; but then we are all among us on this earth made fools equally."

Ray comes by with a round of beers. Harry cracks right into hers, Constance quickly following suit.

Nate still looks a little dazed, not yet reaching for his beer. "I thought you were straight. After the gun range thing."

At least there was that small mercy. Ravi gives him a grateful nod. "Good to know. I was worried I was giving off clues."

Nate's forehead furrows in obvious confusion, then smooths. "Oh," he says softly. "No, you weren't."

Harry again clears her throat, her arms loosely crossed over her chest. "So, this is a cultural thing, right? Why this is a problem for you?"

"It's…it's *partly* that," Ravi admits.

"Well, you're here in the land of the free, etc. etc., not that we're all by any means a bastion of progressive thinking, but you're in a great city for it. Atlanta pride, baby. You can date whoever you want, at least, who the fuck cares."

Ravi wishes it were that easy. "It's more…a family thing. Or…a Trust thing."

"Which is it? A family thing or a Trust thing?"

He gnaws at the inside seam of his lips. "They are one and the same, for me." He finally picks up his beer but doesn't drink, just runs his fingers over the cool condensation.

Constance twists a thick brunette plait over her shoulder. "Pray tell, these past days where you have been unavailable. You have been with this…this *clapper-dudgeon*?"

"Okay, I immediately need to know what *that* word means," Harry breaks in.

Constance flicks her fingers dismissively, her diction briefly sliding into antiquity. "'Tis a term of reproach. Thou hast been played false by this time wizard, Ravi? Would'st thou be fain I place a hex upon them? Perhaps a geas?"

"No!" Ravi sits up in alarm. "No hexes."

Constance sits back with a cluck of her tongue. "I hast not placed a geas in *forever*," she mutters.

"Hey." Though Harry doesn't raise her voice, everyone shuts up and listens to her regardless. "Ravi." She scoots her chair to face him, uncharacteristically serious. "We're circling back now. So, Cayenne works with us in the future, and you two aren't pals there. Weren't pals? Fuck if I know how cause and effect works with this time travel bullshit."

It's a little easier for Ravi like this, facing Harry like it's a mission brief. He takes a few breaths to steady his nerves. "That's correct."

"Okay. I'm going to guess in Chicago when you hung back, something happened."

"They…asked me to dinner."

Harry bites her lip. "Sorry if this is too personal, but do you date a lot?"

Ravi shakes his head.

Harry seems to choose her words carefully. "Do you think…do you think they knew that? When they asked you out."

Ravi can't meet her eyes for a moment. "They knew a lot about me."

Her mouth screws up sideways and her nostrils flare. "Yeah, I bet they fuckin' did." She rubs her forehead for a few seconds, and looks off into the empty air, tapping her boot. "Okay. What did they want? Let's hear it."

Ravi stares in blank confusion.

"What info was Cayenne after? You don't go

through all this trouble running a honeypot for nothing."

"Perhaps to gain goodwill for their past self's actions in August," suggests Val, "whatever they may be."

"Wrong fucking way to go about achieving that, wasn't it?" Nate snaps. His characteristic ease has vanished, jaw set squarely. "Pulling this sick shit with us."

"They didn't want anything, okay?" Ravi wishes fiercely for a monster to come crashing through the walls and start attacking. Anything to take the spotlight off him. "There wasn't... I didn't give them any sensitive information. They didn't ask for any. Not about the team or any of you, or about The Trust."

About himself though? Completely different matter. He told Cayenne things about himself he'd never even said aloud before. And some truths he hadn't even known were in there, until Cayenne coaxed them out. "It was just... They said it was for *fun*. To pay a debt. That they didn't mean to let it get as far as it did."

Harry's brows climb higher and higher as Ravi talks. "And the Pepper broke up with you because you are *going* to hate them? After whatever goes down in August, what their past self does? Did. Will do. Fuck. That's what they said?"

He nods again, rubbing his temples. This might be the most difficult conversation he's ever had in his life. Almost as bad as some of his dressings-down from his aunt. He's utterly exhausted, hollowed out.

"Huh. Okay." Harry's short nails rap on the table as she gives Ravi an appraising, sideways once-over. "I get it. It's *extremely* shitty, but, like, I *get* it. Any idea what Red's gonna do in August?"

Rueful, Ravi shakes his head. "Very little details on that. I know it will be the first time Cayenne meets us. They're not going to trust us. It's likely going to be…" He closes his eyes for a second, tilting his head back. "It's probably going to be pretty bad."

"Fun," Harry mutters.

"Though I don't think anything is set in stone. From what I've gathered, time travelers can't change their *own* past after a certain point, but that's not to say their past can't be changed at all by exterior influences. Timelines *can* be changed, I know that. So…so we can fix whatever they did in the past—I mean, what they will do, in August."

"Damnation," Constance grumbles, "this modern tongue is bewildering enough without the surfeit of tense shifts."

"I'm with Constance," Nate says. "You're saying we can make sure they *don't* do what they *did* do? Ugh, that sucks. Good thing I'm not a linguistics professor, this would drive me crazy."

"Pretty sure," Ravi says, hesitantly. "I'm not sure if that will change the present-day Cayenne or not. Or if we'll keep memories of a future we change. I don't know anything useful." Some agent he turned out to be. Too busy getting led around by his dick to get any decent intel.

Harry digs a knuckle into the inside corner of her eye, as if fending off a headache. "I'll be frank, guys. I'm more concerned about August than ever, after how easily the Pepper took down those vamps. Big, bad, powerful vamps. Not to mention how easily they were able to get under the skin of an extremely guarded, naturally suspicious guy with literal secret agent training."

Ravi slips minutely down into his seat.

Harry immediately shakes her head. "No, that's not a slam on *you*, Ravi. You… They *like* you. You got under their skin too. They weren't expecting that. Or they would have done things very differently."

Ravi swallows, meeting her eyes. She hikes up one half of her mouth. It's not quite a smile, but it's comforting, nonetheless.

"Nate, can you look into legends about chronomancers? If I were a time traveler, I'd make sure nothing important ever got written down, but it can't hurt to see if there's anything we can use."

Nate nods, features still knotted with anger, and finally drags over his beer to take a long swallow.

"Constance, can you—"

"Place a hex upon the time wizard? *Aye.*"

"No. Well, maybe. Anything that can temporarily stop them from time traveling if we need to. They don't like you being near them, maybe we can use that?"

"The two of them touching *might* collapse space and time. I'm not sure if it was a joke or not," Ravi adds. He remembers Cayenne on the rented jet, apprehensively telling him about their fear of flying, of being unable to shift time around them at high speeds. Ravi's instant, unthinking promise not to tell anyone.

He had been such an easy mark.

Harry nods. "Okay, let's save that for an emergency then."

Constance hums. "I shall endeavor to find whatever I can to assist. I suspect Val shall be our best bet, as she is the fastest among us. Should this red-capped varlet try to flee, methinks they will have a hard time outrunning an angel."

Val says passionlessly, "I could simply strike them down with my maul."

Ravi freezes, blood draining from his face. "You can't."

Harry slides down in her chair with a groan. "This is going to be extremely complicated and very annoying, I can already tell. Val, we're going to try using our words first. Ravi, I know you care about them, but—"

"I know!" he says sharply. "I know we might have to get…physical."

Nate raises a hand. "Let the record show that I am not making the very obvious joke that has been perfectly set up."

Harry sighs. "Your restraint is truly admirable, Doc. Yeah, we might have to fight. But we're all going to do our best to fix this, okay?"

Ravi is surrounded by solemn, earnest nods and has…*no* idea what to do with that. He's been assigned to hunter teams before. The usual scope of offered support had never gone much beyond watching one another's backs in a fight and slapping on the occasional trauma bandage. Efficient. Professional. Nothing like this.

"Look, I know I'm not…the most forthcoming guy. But you…" Ravi shoves hair out of his eyes and struggles to marshal his thoughts. "I'm not great with words, and I'm even worse with people. But the four of you are… I've never told… This is—"

Mercifully, Harry places a gentle hand on his arm. "Hey, it's okay. You don't gotta say it. It's cool. You got our backs, we got yours." She spreads her arms wide in a gesture that encompasses the whole table. "We're a team. If you want us to kick your ex's manipulative ass, we can do that. If you want us to calmly talk your ex out of committing unknown heinous crimes, we can do that too. We just gotta get through the next couple weeks and be ready for anything."

Chapter Nine

EVERY SINGLE MEMBER of the team checks in via text or teleportation over the next week, for the single, simple reason of making sure Ravi is doing okay. It's like being in a foreign country with no idea of the language or customs; he'd been tutored in six different ways to de-escalate a werewolf threat, but never how to say *thanks for being there.*

Offended by the hotel-like sterility of Ravi's apartment, Nate brought him a cactus. "Liven the place up a little," he'd said with a clap to Ravi's back.

Constance presented Ravi with a homemade stew of some kind. An old Shaw pottage recipe, she had called it. Leery at first, Ravi was pleased to find it tasted of black pepper and honey. Vegetarian as well, so either she looked up Hindu dietary restrictions, or more likely Harry or Nate told her to play it safe.

Val quite literally *appeared* one afternoon, causing Ravi to nearly fire off a shot through his own walls after grabbing the gun taped under the kitchen counter.

She hadn't come bearing gifts, but a solemn vow: "I shall endeavor not to kill the chronomage unless their actions demand it." Very Old Testament, this angel. He told her he'd appreciate it. And to call before she came over.

Today seems to be Harry's turn. She arrives with the uncursed guitar. When Ravi protests that he doesn't know how to play, Harry scoffs in disbelief, and throws herself in a careless sprawl onto his couch, socked feet up on the coffee table. "Whaaaat, rich Asian kid like you, your parents didn't force you to play an instrument?"

He huffs a laugh. "Yeah, my encouraged talents were more…on the physical side." An amalgam of combat styles and martial disciplines, strategy and warfare, supernatural threats and how to counter them, intelligence gathering, basic spycraft, and how to not break under pressure.

Music lessons, not so much.

"No extracurriculars?"

It would take nothing short of torture to make him 'fess up his dance lessons to Harry, and he'd been taught to withstand a considerable amount. "My humanities tutor let me take extra art history courses."

"*Tutors*, Jesus tapdancing Christ," Harry laughs. "Someday we're gonna dig into your family situation, bud. Really crack into you." She mimes breaking an egg.

Ravi shifts, scratching his jaw. "I'd prefer to keep as much of the tattered remnants of my mystique intact for as long as possible, thanks."

"Fair," Harry concedes, slinging the guitar strap over her shoulder and strumming a few chords. She's pretty good. It's obvious someone had made *her* take lessons.

"You should keep it," he tells her.

"Yeah? It is a pretty sweet ax."

Laughter hits him unexpectedly. By Harry's smirk, she hit what she'd been aiming for. "*Ax.* Yeah, you definitely should keep it. You already speak the lingo."

"Guns and guitars: any good Georgia girl's best friends." She plays another couple of bars while glancing around his apartment. Her gaze falls on the poster of the Seychelles. Ravi can't help but tense up. She gives it a professional once-over, keen eyes snagging on the small, unobtrusive lipstick mark in the corner. "That where the two of you went?"

After a moment of hesitation, he nods. "First time, yeah. Second time we went to a cabin in the Appalachians."

"Nice," Harry says mildly. Her fingers are deft on the frets as she plays a soft, sliding lick that Ravi recognizes as bluegrass. "I'm guessing you don't normally get a lot of vacations."

"Some," he says, which is true enough. He's

allowed a few days off a year, and sometimes he even uses them.

"So, what's keeping you from kicking the chrono-thot to the curb?"

"What?"

Harry shifts into a bluesy chord, her voice affecting a slight country twang. "You've been done wrong, man, been done real, real wrong. Why haven't you washed your hands of Cayenne altogether?" She tips her chin pointedly to the poster, still hanging in pride of place.

His mouth twitches, and he sits down across from her on an uncomfortable ottoman. "Why don't you just say what you want to say, Harry."

She levels a reproachful frown. "I'm not here to listen to *myself* talk. I can do that at home. C'mon."

"I..." He passes a hand over his face. "They... I guess I'm having trouble because they said...they love me."

He can't stop thinking about the naked truth written on every line of Cayenne's face, pages and pages filled with *I love you, Ravi* scrawled across from margin to margin.

Harry's eyes narrow. "When? At the Seychelles?"

"No, definitely not. This was at the cabin before they left. Seconds before, actually." He clears his throat, watching as his hands twist together between his knees as if somebody else was controlling them. "A couple of days before that, they asked me to run away with them. To another time." He lifts his head and forces some cheer into his voice. "Good news, by 2050 there's no discrimination against sexual orientation."

Harry flashes an equally false smile, matching his tone. "Hey, there's a silver lining here after all."

Ravi's laugh is a barren little thing.

"Just so I'm clear," Harry says, again picking through her words with care. "Cayenne didn't bust out the L-word *before* they came clean with you. They said it afterward and then, what? Time-teleported away?"

"Yeah."

Harry blows out her breath in a heavy gust. "*Fuuuuck*, dude. You really did a number on them." She shakes her head, unslings the guitar, and sets it down beside her.

Ravi frowns. "What do you mean?"

She waves at his gaming consoles. "You play, right? Me too. You ever do that thing where you save the game, destroy the town and slaughter all the villagers, and then just reload the save like nothing happened?"

"Not…often. But I know what you mean. The stuff you do when quests get boring."

"Exactly. Cayenne's got a save and reload button tattooed right on them. I'll bet the comparison has occurred to you before. You're not dumb."

"All evidence to the contrary," he half-jokes. "Yeah, that's come up before. I told them I didn't want to be an NPC, and they promised to not rewind time without me. As far as I know, they kept that promise up until…until that last day. When they tried to tell me about August."

"Oof. That pretty much confirms it. Look, I don't mean to minimize what they did, because it is *deeply* fucked up, and Cayenne is one hundred percent a horny trash goblin you should kick to the curb. But I also think they weren't lying about being in love with you."

The unexpected strike stabs right through him, wounds him. "Why would you tell me that?"

She offers up a sad little smile. "Because I don't want you to keep beating yourself up about feeling something for them. Which you're obviously doing. Yes, they originally were in it for a little hate-fuck, or on a whim, or whatever messed-up reasoning they had, and then *lied* about it, but also… Look. If you were playing that video game, and you were a capricious god who could do whatever you wanted with no consequences, razing villages and stabbing merchants or whatever; what would it take for one of those little villagers to make you want to stop? To try to fix what you've done. To make you say you're *sorry*."

He bites his lip and looks away from her.

"Because no offense, but I don't think just some good dick would cut it, y'know?"

This manages to startle a laugh out of him. His shoulders lose a bit of their locked tension. "Maybe some *really* good dick."

Harry throws her head back and guffaws. "Ah, you're gonna be okay." She gets to her feet and straps the guitar over her back. "Nothing's on the schedule right now, monster-wise. Bobby is helping out on some basic footwork with Constance's ongoing demon hunt, but apart from that? Things are quiet. So take some time off, okay? Rest up. When August rolls around, we'll all have your back."

She doesn't wait for a response, heading for the door. When she passes by the kitchen she tosses, "Nice cactus," over her shoulder, then pulls on her boots and lets herself out.

*

IT'S LATE, THE moon a waning crescent over the kappa's lake. Ravi sits alone on the wooden bench in the backyard, wearing a rumpled suit and tired eyes.

He hasn't moved from this spot since sunset. The surrounding houses are dark and quiet, all the neighbors down for the night. With perhaps the exception of the kappa at the bottom of the lake, munching on the waterlogged cucumber Ravi had earlier thrown in.

The lake house had been a stroke of good luck for the team. After their peaceful resolution with the local kappa, they'd driven past the *For Sale* sign and Constance had remarked, "Zounds. Should mine demon nemesis e'er track me down in mine shoppe, I'd be fain to weather his siege in a redoubt such as this," and from there things had evolved to Harry handing a flabbergasted realtor the entire asking price in diamond-traded cash. A sound strategy, having a fallback location. Ravi approved. And by happy coincidence, it also meant that *he* didn't have to worry about any curious family eyes upon him here, as the purchase had been completely under The Trust's radar.

The first of August looms close, only a handful of days away, a rapidly narrowing divide between now and the inevitable future. A brief snapshot in time where Ravi can still enjoy blissful ignorance. He's alone, the curtains already drawn against prying neighborly eyes.

Take some time, Harry had said.

Cayenne took time effortlessly, as one would pluck a fig off a tree. If Ravi were a chronomancer, able to freeze sand in the hourglass, what would he do with his slivers of stolen time?

Ravi takes out the crimson phone and takes a picture of the moon as it hangs in a narrow slice over the lake. He hits send, then follows it with a short snippet of Devanagari.

The moon tries every month in vain
To paint a picture of your face;
And, having failed to catch its grace,
Destroys the work, and starts again.

With hands that shake only a little, he adds, *Can I see you? Please. We don't have to talk.*

He's not a chronomage. He's just a guy with a gun. He doesn't have the luxury of rewinding time to try again, so he needs the right combination of words to get Cayenne to show, and to get it right the first time. Manipulative, sure, but turnabout is fair play.

He waits, pulse thudding in his ears. *This is so stupid. This is such a bad idea. What the fuck am I doing here?*

It feels like hours instead of minutes before the screen finally lights up.

- Cayenne -

No talking. Lake house?

He'd judged right. No talking. A final goodbye without the burden of unwelcome questions, of being held accountable, was too tempting for Cayenne to resist. Excitement and panic surge through Ravi, and he starts pacing like a trapped animal before getting a hold of himself. *Keep your shit together, kid.*

He texts back a simple *yes*, then goes inside, leaving the back door unlocked. He drapes his suit jacket over a chair, pulls the magnetic whiteboard off the fridge, and sets it on the counter. He erases the shopping list and writes two words. Then he leans against the sink and waits, fingers drumming on the countertop.

He doesn't wait long before the phone buzzes on

the counter. No doubt Cayenne spent a lot of time getting to the right spot, hours maybe, before simply jumping themself back the moment after the texts were sent. But for Ravi, barely a minute has passed.

He stares in disbelief at the message for long, long seconds, his chest tight.

Cayenne sent a selfie.

They're at the front step with the door of the lake house barely in frame. They look… Ravi bites his lip. They look good, as always. But *tired.* Pinched and nervous. Emerald eyes slightly bloodshot, hair hastily finger-combed into a semblance of order.

Ravi swallows hard against a rising lump. Cayenne doesn't allow pictures of their face in the world, a time traveler's guard against discovery. This itself is a message, one of complete trust. A pang pierces behind his heart like the snap of a wire.

Text follows the photo.

> *Your monster is lurking outside your front door. If you still want me.*

He exhales shakily.

Back is unlocked. Kitchen.

Heart clambering into his throat, Cayenne bursts in not thirty seconds later, an overnight bag sliding off their shoulder onto the hardwood. They look almost as nervous as he feels.

Ravi takes a centering breath, the kind he learned young to line up a perfect shot.

Cayenne's steps falter, as if they're thinking about vanishing into the breeze. Quickly, Ravi holds up the prepared whiteboard. *No talking,* it says. Then he uncaps the marker with his teeth and jots down under it, *I know, this is cheating. Let me?*

Cayenne barks out something between a laugh and a sigh of relief, then nods. They take a few hesitant steps closer. The July night air isn't anywhere near cold enough for the way they're shivering like a leaf.

Ravi erases the words and scrawls new ones. He holds it up in front of his chest, intently watching Cayenne's face.

I was okay being a fling. I'm used to that. When he's sure Cayenne has read it, he turns the board around and erases it. He tries to write fast. *What I'm not used to is someone wanting more. To take me on a vacation. To make me happy. To ask what I wanted, what I needed.* He hesitates before the next part, throat sticking as he swallows. *No one has ever told me they love me before.* He holds this up, chest hitching, then he erases everything. The next scrawl is slanted, jotted hastily.

What did you think was going to happen? That I could walk away? His hands betray the smallest tremor as he holds up the board. Again, he erases and writes, this time underlining the first three words. *I'm fucking help-less here. I was trained to fight everything but that. No defense for it.*

Cayenne lets out a wounded, strangled gasp before they press a shaking hand to their mouth. Ravi pauses a long time before the next board, lower lip caught be-tween his teeth, gaze still locked on Cayenne. Their ex-pression is frozen, unreadable, and their breathing shal-low.

I know you can't make any promises, and I can't either. I don't know what's going to happen after the airport, or if I'm going to be able to forgive you. He draws in a shuddering gulp of air and writes, *But no matter what's going to happen in the future, you're here tonight. And I'm here.*

He attempts a crooked little half-smile.

Cayenne's shoulders lift as if they're gathering themself for a great leap. Their eyes flash as they storm up to him, closing the distance in long, predatory strides. "Ravi, for the love of *God* quit being so *fucking* romantic and *kiss me already!*"

Without wasting another second Ravi throws the whiteboard across the counter, lunges forward, and swings Cayenne up off their feet. They taste of rum and toothpaste and tears, and at the slightest brush of their lips Ravi feels like one of those desert flowers that bloom sudden and vibrant with the first drops of rain.

It's torture breaking apart long enough to rasp, "Stay tonight?"

"*Oui*, yes, of course you idiot, *oui!*" Cayenne kisses him hard enough to bruise. They flow into his arms while a moan claws past their throat, a desperate, wanton sound that sends Ravi's pulse rabbiting wildly.

He spins around and lifts them up onto the kitchen island, surging between their thighs to pour himself into an artless kiss. He drinks down their increasingly frantic moans as if he'd die of thirst without them.

Clever hands slide under the hem of his shirt, over Ravi's ribs, his shoulders, and up into his hair. Cayenne kisses him like he's the finest thing they'll ever taste, licking into his mouth with furious hunger, all advance and no retreat. They rake their nails down his back, and he hisses, arousal surging so fast his head swims.

Grabbing two fistfuls of disheveled copper hair, Ravi pulls them back just far enough to speak, distantly surprised by the throaty scrape of his voice when it finally surfaces.

"Can we just be together tonight? Just for... I don't—" He shakes his head, frustrated with his stumbling tongue.

Cayenne cups his cheek and nods. "No past and no future, *oui*? Just us, here right now?"

"Yes," he says with relief, "that."

"Yes," they hiss, eyes agleam with something like triumph, and yank at the buttons of his shirt, pulling his clothes into disarray, undoing his belt. All the while they continue their assault on his mouth, biting at his lips and stealing his breath. Ravi shoves their shirt up so he can get his tongue on the fine cut of their hairless chest and unzips the fly of their jeans. He reaches in and they fit like they were made for his grip, already gratifyingly hard and beading moisture.

"Ah, fuck!" The shout rings off kitchen tile as Cayenne pushes into his fist. "*Oui*, come on, hurry up, darli—" Ravi cuts them off with another devouring kiss, a fierce joy sparking at the naked *want* in their words. He wants to give them everything, anything they want.

Clothes hanging off him, Ravi spins Cayenne around and bends them over the counter. Their moan is all urgency and enthusiasm, and they kick off their jeans, hands shaking as they grip the edges of the marble. "Please, *mon tigre, baise-moi*..."

With a growl, Ravi scrambles for the condom in his

wallet and realizes, "The lube's upstairs, I didn't—"

One knee slung up on the counter, Cayenne scrambles across the cooktop, scattering spices. They snag a bottle of olive oil and slap it into Ravi's hand with a wild, desperate grin. "If it's good enough for the Romans, darling, it's good enough for us."

Ravi laughs, glad he's always preferred non-latex condoms, and it's only another few intolerable seconds of waiting before he's sliding home, Cayenne's breath hitching as they throw themself back, tight, eager heat driving onto his cock again and again.

Fuck, he's missed them, deep down to his bones. Their voice, their smile, the warmth of their breath against his shoulder as they sleep, their bodies an artless four-legged tangle. He missed moving in tandem under the multicolored lights of the club, the drumbeats throbbing up through his shoes, covered in golden glitter and laughing, freedom and happiness running in him like a river.

He uses the bunched handful of Cayenne's half-shucked shirt like a handle as he moves into the fast, forceful rhythm he knows they most favor, and the kitchen fills with the sounds of their joining bodies and rising voices. Cayenne keeps up a string of lovely multilingual encouragement until they go tense beneath him, shuddering with a soft, satisfied cry. Only then, pulsing hot, does Ravi let himself shatter.

Struggling for oxygen, he blinks back to awareness collapsed onto Cayenne's back. He pushes himself up on trembling arms. A line of freckles peeks out below Cayenne's rucked-up shirt. Ravi feels compelled to find each one with a slow, lingering kiss.

"Sorry," he murmurs, lips pressed to overwarm skin, "am I too heavy?"

Cayenne's laugh might have been scraped up from the bottom of the lake. "*Non*, my beautiful boy, *c'est tellement bon*. Mmm, stay like that for a moment. Oh, you lovely thing."

They drag in a shaky breath that lifts Ravi up a few inches with its force. He stays as requested, nose nuzzling into sweat-dark hair at the nape of their neck, and breathes deep the heady scent of sex and spice and skin.

After a long moment Cayenne shifts. "You know, I fear this counter may never be the same."

Ravi laughs, voice gone raw. "Then we'd better move to a bed, hm?" Reluctantly he pulls away from their warmth with a final press of a kiss to the top of their spine before moving to the sink to clean up.

Cayenne joins to help him skin out of his remaining clothes They're now both naked in the middle of a kitchen, which is a first for Ravi. Cayenne tilts their face up to kiss the tip of his nose. "Bed, my sweet."

Hands join, and it's uncertain who leads whom through the living room and up the stairs to the first bedroom they find. Curled together under the sheets, they get lost in kissing, barely separating but for the occasional gasp of air.

It's easy, so much easier than Ravi had thought it would be, to push aside all the reasons they shouldn't do this, to let himself fall into this perfect sliver of time without worrying about inevitable regret. Nothing has ever felt this easy.

Cayenne rolls on top, tongue licking sweet into his

mouth, their cock a hot brand at his hip. He's already responding in kind but can't tear himself away from the pleasure of their mouth, so he reaches down and takes them both in hand. Cayenne bucks into the touch with a throaty groan, briefly falling out of the kiss just long enough to wrap their clever fingers around his; twin throbs trapped in the cage of entwined fingers.

Cayenne whispers filthy endearments against Ravi's lips as hands slide, and Ravi can't help the ceaseless trip of his praising, begging, not even knowing what he's pleading for. Cayenne curses and shivers all over, spilling messily over their linked hands. Toes curling and spine arching, Ravi follows a bare instant later.

They catch their breath, Cayenne murmuring warm and intimate at Ravi's ear. "*Je savais que tu reviendrais vers moi.* You'll always come back to me, won't you, my pet?" They punctuate their words with an ellipsis of biting kisses.

Ravi arches his neck to give them the whole of his throat, not caring if they're leaving marks, letting them do as they please until he's liquid and sleepy, blissed out from the roots of his hair down to the soles of his feet.

Finally, he rolls Cayenne onto their back to rest his head on their chest. For a long while he basks in the sound of Cayenne's heartbeat, mind euphorically empty, simply drifting.

Graceful fingers trace shapes across his skin, and if they spell out words, Ravi can't make sense of them. "I do love you, you know," Cayenne says savagely, in a rush, like it's an impulse they can't control.

That's *unfair*. Stung, Ravi pushes himself upon one elbow. "Why would you say that?"

"I don't know. Because I am a foolish, idiotic monsoon and I throw myself around without any regard for the damage." Cayenne sits up and takes his face between their hands. "But I do, my darling, and I *know* it's…it's *cruel* and *vicious* to tell you this, but I don't *care*. I'm not a good person like you, Ravi. *Je suis ton monstre.* If I have to be a monster to get what I want, then I am happy to be one. And what I want is you."

For a fleeting instant Ravi wishes only to bolt, to turn around and hide, to be anywhere else but here; but then he leans hard into Cayenne's touch, wanting even more to bury himself in their arms and be held again.

"I thought we agreed no talking." His whisper drags out of him, fluttering like dry leaves.

A barren, pained chuckle. "*Oui*, you already broke that little rule. Very clever ruse, my sweet, to get me here. I thought your word was your bond with you hero types."

"Yeah, well. Looks like you're a bad influence."

Cayenne laughs, long and bitter. "The worst." They sling a thigh across Ravi and roll him back, pinning him to the bed with their hands at his wrists. He lets them. He'd let them do anything. "I know *you* are too kind-hearted to say it back, my brave, beautiful boy, that's not why I told you. I just need you to know." Their gaze lingers on his face as if memorizing every feature. "I've told other people I love them, but you're the first time it's been true. I need you to…to remember that, before we say goodbye."

Ravi wishes he was better with words. "Cay, do you think I've ever sent someone a picture of the moon because just *looking* at it made me think of them? Nothing like you has ever happened to me before."

Cayenne squeezes their eyes shut. "I truly hope nothing like me will happen to you again." A long, brittle silence. "But you're right, we shouldn't talk like this. For us, here, there's no past and no future. Only now."

Ravi shivers against their lips as if the warm summer night were the depths of winter.

"We're running out of time, *mon trésor*. Let's enjoy it."

Chapter Ten

THE SUN RISES much too quickly through the bay window. They watch it dawn together in silence, limbs entangled.

With a determined shift of their shoulders, Cayenne takes Ravi's chin between thumb and forefinger. "Here is what we are going to do, my sweet. We are going to get up, get dressed, and go to brunch."

"Brunch?"

"Yes."

"There's food here. We keep it stocked."

"Ah, darling, this is not just any brunch. We are going to have a very *gay* brunch! I know a place that does a fabulous drag bingo and serves bottomless mimosas. I, for one, intend to dress for the occasion." They toss their bed-mussed hair and grin.

Ravi blinks. "You want us to…"

Cayenne sneaks a quick kiss, stalling his protest. "And you and I, *mon beau*, we can be as obvious as we damn well please. We can even—*un tel scandale*—hold hands if you so fancy! Because I'm going to rewind the *entire* day right back to here, right now, at this very moment." Their smile is bright with promise, a sunrise of their own. "Today there are no rules, darling. Nothing will count. My gift to you."

It takes Ravi a moment to absorb the full implications; this whole last day of July enjoyed to the fullest, then rewritten. Anything goes. No consequences, no chance of being caught, of being found out. A day to be a normal person, just for one day, to live like somebody else.

Ravi has to take a deep breath, but not to quell his

nerves. Excitement wells up in him almost like adrenaline, the sheer amount of possibilities on offer making him a little lightheaded. "No rules?"

"As free as birds, my dearest. And *then* I'll reset us again, and we can spend today anyway you like, and then I'll rewind us *again*. And we..." They swallow, forehead pressed to his, red hair feathering through his coal black. "We just keep doing it as long as we can. *Oui?*"

Another sliver of time, another oasis. Living a life inside the hourglass. Leisurely, Ravi rolls onto Cayenne with a kiss he draws out long and unhurried and wonderful.

"*Haan,*" he whispers. "Yes."

*

MIMOSAS DEFINITELY MAKE the list of acceptable cocktails. Ravi's already on his second glass, crowded up in the corner booth against Cayenne's side with an arm slung over their shoulders, and nobody cares. It's amazing.

The stage show is loud and boisterous, all sorts of folks in a rainbow of configurations laughing and singing along. Cayenne offers him a morsel of fruit, and Ravi eats it straight from their fingers with a boundless thrill. The best part of the whole experience might be Cayenne's delighted smile, happiness beaming from their every pore.

"Look at you," they murmur in his ear. "You are *stunning* like this." They creep a hand across his knee.

Ravi ducks his head, flushing, and nudges their shoulder. "Come on, take it easy on me. Even though this is getting reset, I'm suppressing a lifetime of instinct, here." Cayenne squeezes his thigh once and mercifully pulls their hands above the table.

One of the announcers passes out bingo cards to those who want them, and Cayenne's hand shoots up to bring her over. She's a blue-haired East Asian queen with a sassy bob and a flapper aesthetic, just shy of hitting six feet with her heels.

"Well, hello to you, Red. You want a stack?"

Cayenne's painted-on white denim jeans have more

holes to them than fabric, and they're wearing the hell out of a crop top emblazoned with *Scream King* in pink bubblegum lettering. They twist their wrist with a little extra flair as they stretch out a hand to accept the cards, the glitter-shadow on their eyelids catching the light.

"You know we do, beautiful." All charm, Cayenne smiles, and the entertainer goes a little pinker under her blush.

Next, she gives Ravi a once-over, and he feels underdressed in his black jeans and collarless shirt. But he doesn't need the armor of his suit. Today he's just a regular guy out with his…his Cayenne.

"How about you, Broody?"

"Um, sure." She hands him cards and a dauber, then brazenly ruffles his hair before pivoting on her impressive heels to leave them to it. Ravi huffs and sweeps his hair back out of his eyes, fighting a blush. "Okay, so how do you play this game?"

Cayenne looks at him as if he's sprouted a second head. "You've never played *bingo*, sweetheart?"

"You have?"

They wink. "Of course not. It's one of the few forms of gambling that isn't worth the trouble to rig." They peer over at the stage. "Though they haven't yet announced the *prizes*, so I could be wrong. Still, *mon chéri*, it's easy enough to learn, no? I believe you mark the squares the lovely ladies call out until you win."

Yet another thing they have in common, Ravi muses; two outsiders with no idea how normal people function. With only a fleeting skip of his heart, Rave dares place his hand over Cayenne's, right there on the table.

Cayenne smiles radiantly.

They nibble at their food, drain a few more mimosas, mostly ignoring their bingo cards even as numbers are called out in favor of casual conversation. The whole time their fingers interlace in plain view of the restaurant.

Conversation meanders easily, wandering to the topic of the lake house. "Whose idea was the huge basketball hoop in the driveway?" Cayenne asks, spearing a syrup-soaked square of French toast with a fork. They offer Ravi a bite he politely declines.

"Actually," Ravi says, piling all his untouched toast onto Cayenne's plate, "it was my idea."

"I had no idea you played, darling."

"I don't. I mean, I've had a few pick-up games every so often. But that hoop has never been used."

"Never? Why did you get it then?" Cayenne pours Ravi another mimosa from the pitcher after he drains his glass. He's experiencing a pleasant tingle. Maybe from the drinks, and maybe from…well, everything.

"As I'm sure you noticed, that particular gated community doesn't quite reflect the diverse reality of the city of Atlanta."

"Oh, believe me, I noticed, my samosa."

"Ha. Yeah. The HOA has a 'no basketball hoops allowed' rule."

Cayenne rolls their eyes hugely. "How *typical*."

"Yeah. So, I felt it was my civic non-white duty to buy the absolute biggest fuck-off basketball hoop I could fit in the driveway." He grins toothily. "The HOA sends a fine each month, and they can't do a thing as long as I keep paying it."

Cayenne's eyes shine. "Well, now we *have* to play a game."

"Oh, yeah?" Ravi's grin widens. Too long without physical activity makes him antsy, and even considering their athletic coupling, he'd love the opportunity to get more exercise in.

"It's a date," Cayenne promises, voice silken.

When the latest performer finishes a song, they applaud. Next comes the prize reveal for the upcoming round of bingo, and the ladies make a big show of presenting the assortment of goods. There's a lot of *questionable* items that make Ravi cough into his mimosa while Cayenne makes bawdy remarks about each one. One of the prizes is a pair of tiger print shorts, and although the queen announces them as "running shorts," they are barely long enough to qualify.

"*Mon Dieu*," Cayenne gasps. "They are *perfect*. We *must* win." They whirl to face him, deadly serious. "Ravi, I will win those by any means necessary."

"I bet you can just buy tiger print shorts if you want

them, Cay."

Grinning mischievously, they purr, "Oh, they're not for me, darling."

Ravi gives them a blank stare. "I am not wearing those."

Cayenne crows, "But they're *tiger striped!* It's practically fate, *mon tigre!*" They press their cheek to his, extending an arm as if displaying the view on some distant horizon. "Imagine it: the two of us in nothing but the *smallest*, most *salacious* booty shorts and *nothing* else, shooting baskets in your fuck-off hoop in an *extremely* homoerotic manner, right in view of all the neighbors in that bigoted little suburb."

Ravi can't help but laugh at their genuine excitement. "Cay, that's…"

Cayenne holds Ravi's hands flat between their palms, as if in prayer. "Please, it'll be *so* much fun. You don't think it'll be a *little* bit satisfying? Really think about it. Don't automatically shut it down because of your sweet, modest nature, *mon chéri.* Remember, today is about freedom. We can do *anything.*"

Ravi runs his thumbs over the back of Cayenne's knuckles and glances around the restaurant. Other couples, men, women, a whole spectrum in between and beyond, all enjoying themselves, calling out bingo wins, and sassing with the drag queens. No one is paying them the slightest mind, and it just feels…normal. Both ordinary and extraordinary all at once.

Finally, he sighs. "Well…"

"Ravi, I will literally do *anything* to make this happen. I'll change the course of history, if I have to. Please tell me what you need to say yes."

Laughter shakes through him, and he has to cover his face for a second. "You are *so* dramatic."

An impish smile. "Does that mean you'll wear them if I win?"

Ravi adopts a stern expression and holds up three fingers. "First, you are a huge brat. Second, *I'm* going to win them." He snatches up a bingo card. "Third, no cheating. I mean it. If it is 'fate' or karma, then I will wear the stupid shorts."

Clapping their hands with glee, Cayenne nearly

squeals with delight. "Yes, *merci! Merveilleux!* No cheating, promise." They kiss him on the cheek, beaming fit to burst.

Really, it's just Ravi's luck they end up winning fair and square.

*

CAYENNE IS A decent free thrower, though they keep traveling with the ball no matter how many times Ravi calls foul. It's been a few years since he's played, though it hardly matters since Cayenne is less interested in winning than in running bodily into Ravi at every opportunity; sweaty chests colliding while fighting for control of the ball, "accidentally" grabbing his ass more than a few times.

Curtains are twitching up and down the street. As they first started their game, stripping off their shirts and stretching, the lady next door came out onto her porch, stared, went back inside, and a minute later came back out to settle into her veranda with a big bottle of chardonnay and a book she clearly had no intention of reading. Cars would slow down as they passed. One neighbor was on her fifth dog walk of the day.

Shaking off a lifetime of hiding is *hard.* Ravi isn't used to being so exposed, hates being the center of attention, but Cayenne is so obviously gleeful about the situation that he can't object. And it does admittedly feel pretty good not caring what anyone thinks. Freeing.

Though the shorts are still ridiculous, and Ravi isn't changing his mind on that.

Juking sideways, he manages to spin around Cayenne and throws a scoring jump shot.

"*Très bien,* handsome." Cayenne admires him, hand at their hip. They're almost golden in the fading sunlight, miles of skin sheened with perspiration. Their only concession to modesty is a pair of what surely are the world's tightest athletic shorts. It's incredibly distracting. "I thought you said you didn't play?"

"Not exactly the sport of my people, no. I bowl a mean game of cricket, though. And you should see me at soccer."

Cayenne walks close and casually takes the ball

from Ravi to dribble a crossover. "Mmm, I really should."

Ravi makes a half-hearted attempt at stealing the ball back, but Cayenne dodges, holding him at bay with an armbar. In a real game, the ref would have blown the whistle on the way Cayenne slid their palm savoring-slow up over Ravi's slick stomach. A flagrant foul of excessive contact.

On her nearby porch, the next-door neighbor pours another glass of wine. Cayenne runs up to the hoop and tips the ball in.

Landing back on his heels after an attempted block, Ravi says, "When we were really young and our parents would meet up for Trust business, the kids would sometimes get together and play soccer for hours. The Italians *killed* at it. The rest of us had no choice but to catch up. Competitive bunch, unsurprisingly." He catches a throw and dribbles in place, scanning Cayenne's balance for any indication of their next move. "I'd come back inside covered in grass stains."

Strangely, Cayenne looks at him with something a

lot like apprehension. They hesitate before asking, "And then what?"

Ravi cants his head, confused. "Then nothing. That's the whole story."

Their shoulders relax. "*Je suis désolé*, darling, I was expecting… No matter. It *is* nice to hear you have the odd happy memory in that head of yours."

Ravi snorts, throwing the ball at Cayenne. "I *do* have some of those, you know. A handful."

Cayenne tucks the ball under their arm and steps close enough for Ravi to catch the scent of sunshine on their skin. "You deserve nothing but happiness," they say, completely serious. "If I could give you that, I would." A shadow of guilt lurks behind their eyes, which is just not going to work for Ravi at all.

He moves closer, so they're only inches apart. "You're doing it right now." He pulls Cayenne into him and they kiss, exposed in the driveway in the late afternoon sun, as the next-door neighbor drops her wineglass.

*

EVENING CICADA SONG nearly drowns out the abundance of frogs holding their chorus in the mirror-smooth lake. Trees trace the water's edge, oaks dripping with Spanish moss and willows with long leaves trailing down like curtains. It's a sizable lake, especially for one in the heart of a suburb, dotted with small verdant islands. A beautiful home for the kappa, though presumably the creature only lurks at the muddy bottom unless some other monster encroaching on its territory draws its ire to the surface.

It's just gone dark, and Ravi stretches out on a picnic blanket, watching the moon rise. The balmy night paired with the glow of the city on the horizon reminds Ravi a little of being back on his family estate, of climbing up to the roof of the haveli to see the bright, distant lights of Chennai out past tea fields and evergreen forest.

Cayenne saunters out from the kitchen while balancing a bottle of wine under an arm, two glasses in one hand, and a premade picnic platter in the other. They are also, to Ravi's astonishment, completely naked.

"Only the finest of grocery store cuisine," Cayenne breezes, hips swaying as they stroll out into the evening air. "Hmm, what am I missing? I swear, I've forgotten *something*. Maybe the corkscrew?" They shift their balance from one hip to the other, looking down at their bare flesh with feigned puzzlement. "Ah, no, this wine has a screw top. What ever could it be?"

Ravi's shock is quickly followed by delight. Cayenne looks otherworldly under the cresting moonlight, like something wrought out of porcelain and dreams. "You are just… You're *shameless*, you know that?"

Kneeling on the blanket, they set down the makeshift picnic and give Ravi a playful peck on the cheek. "I know, *c'est moi*! It is one of my *best* qualities. But do you know what *you* are, sweetheart?"

With a soft roll of his eyes, Ravi smiles. "About to hear a very risqué proposition?"

Cayenne scrunches up their nose. "Wrong! The correct answer is *overdressed*." They shift close enough to start undoing Ravi's shirt buttons. "Before I met you, darling, I admit I never knew the more prettily wrapped the package, the more *satisfying* it was to open it."

"Cay…" Ravi looks around, half-expecting to spy some slavering beast lurking somewhere out on the shore—or worse, faces in the windows of nearby houses. "Anyone could see us." But he doesn't reach down and stop their nimble fingers.

"So? Today does not count, *mon coeur*. And the only monster lurking besides yours truly is the kappa. The little beast is *far* too busy living its best life at the bottom of the lake to bother *us*. At most, we merely risk giving your *dreadfully* boring neighbors a display of two of the most *magnificent* specimens they have ever seen. They should be thanking us, to tell the truth."

Ravi bites down on a smirk as Cayenne urges the shirt off his shoulders, fabric pooling around his elbows. With an approving hum, Cayenne runs a fingertip down his bared chest and dips it under the top of his joggers.

Ravi's breath catches in his chest, but he helpfully lifts his hips and lets Cayenne tug off his pants. He's still wearing the dumb black-and-orange shorts underneath, far better suited as they are to be underwear than athletic apparel.

Cayenne pauses for a moment of open admiration, then snatches up one of Ravi's legs and kisses the back of it, right over a set of raised scars spanning the swell of his calf. They punctuate each press of their lips with a loud, silly smacking sound.

They are so…*ridiculous* and *irreverent* and *beautiful*, and Ravi has never had this much fun with anybody his entire life. Grinning, he tilts his head to one side. "Were you planning on us eating any of this food, or is the plan to get me naked and have your way with me on the grass?" Ravi wouldn't be opposed, the way he's feeling: light and untroubled, his heart full to bursting.

Cayenne gives him a gamin grin. With startling speed, they grab the ludicrous shorts and yank them down and off in one smooth movement. They lean back on their haunches to get a good look at him.

"You are a sight," they whisper, then clear their throat. "Regretfully, I think food first. We must replenish ourselves after that workout, yes? This is just *freedom.*" They spread their arms up in a lazy feline stretch, clearly enjoying Ravi's eager eyes on their body as they do so. "I thought you might appreciate it. Also, *I* most certainly enjoy the view. Don't you, my dearest?"

Ravi takes one more cursory glance around the lakeshore, but between the arrangement with the kappa, his ingrained vigilance, and Cayenne's innate powers, the chance of anything catching them unawares is very low. He breathes out slowly, wrestling with training and habit and self-consciousness. But then his searching gaze lands on Cayenne, apprehension fading as he drinks the sight of them in, so ethereally handsome and effortlessly at ease.

Ravi runs his thumb over Cayenne's clock tattoo before giving their hand a squeeze. "It's a hell of a view. Yeah. Let's eat."

The picnic unfolds pleasantly, the July night feeling even warmer after they enjoy a few glasses of wine— one-and-a-half for Ravi to Cayenne's three. Eventually, they're both pleasantly buzzed, lazily cuddling on the blanket, Cayenne the little spoon in Ravi's arms. They watch the stars together, listening to the drone of insects and the calls of whip-poor-wills.

"This has been a really nice day, Cay," he murmurs into their hair. "Thank you. Today was…" He huffs, not quite a laugh. "It was very different."

"Good different?"

He presses a kiss behind their ear. "Good different."

It takes a long time for Cayenne to speak, and when they do, the words are slow, halting. "I…I wish we had more time together. I don't know how many times I can safely spin you back. I've never taken a passenger with me quite the way I have with you." They're still in his arms, not even breathing for another prolonged pause. "I want to live this day over with you as *many* times as we can, my sweet, but…I don't want to hurt you. Again." Their throat clicks as they swallow.

Ravi doesn't want to think about this day ending. He doesn't want to think about how Cayenne has hurt him, how they still will after this endless day ends.

So he sets a hand to Cayenne's jaw and turns them

around into a fierce, demanding kiss. They gasp in surprise, stiff posture melting as Ravi delves deeply into their mouth, sucking on their tongue and nipping at their lips.

Ravi breaks the kiss, and his voice has gone low and husky. "We'd better make the most of the time we have." He reaches down and they gasp, quickly responding to his sure touch.

Groaning, Cayenne shivers head to toe. "*Parfait.*" They twist back with a ravenous kiss, thrusting into his palm even as they squirm back against his lap. Their wild enthusiasm makes Ravi's stomach flip over and his throat go dry, the way it always does, their naked *want* for him far more intoxicating than wine.

"*Oui*, Ravi, *baise-moi.* Take me, you beautiful—" they begin a stream of breathless, aroused babble until he kisses them again. Even then, they moan a muffled plea into his mouth.

"Fuck," he mutters, grinding his cock against the firm, round swell of their ass. Cayenne grabs his forearms with bruising force, fingernails digging. Their wild, rising voice hits Ravi hard, like every one of their eager cries sounds an echo in his loins. He has to take some deep breaths to settle down, already knowing he's going to be hard-pressed to last.

"*Now,*" Cayenne demands, shoving a mysteriously procured bottle of lube into his hand. "*Tu dois me baiser tout de suite,* Ravi, please, don't make me wait for it—"

He grinds his teeth in frustration. "Cay, we don't have any cond—"

The sound Cayenne makes is nearly a scream of aggravation. "This whole day is a do-over, yes? Nothing counts, *tu homme exaspérant!*"

"Bad habit," he hisses the token protest into their ear but doesn't argue, too far gone to be careful. Without wasting another second, he pushes their top thigh aside and smoothly works into them.

"Bad habit is my middle naaaame—ah, fuck, *yes!*"

Ravi gasps, almost losing it immediately at the greedy way their body swallows him in, at the silken, velvet grasp. Perfection, incredible, stars bursting behind his eyes. Ravi has to bite down on his tongue to hold out.

He wants to give as much of himself as Cayenne wants to take, wants to pour himself empty and never come up for air, wants to feel their heartbeat rattling swift into his chest. He wants them wrecked with passion, begging and writhing and so ruined with pleasure they forget every last lingering hint of past or future, *now* the only time that matters.

He laps a hungry stripe from the nape of their neck to their earlobe, reveling in the salt of their skin. "This good?" It doesn't come easily, words scraping rough out of his throat; Ravi's accustomed to keeping quiet, to holding his breath against his ecstasy and worrying about thin walls.

Cayenne bucks against him so vigorously he's almost thrown back. "*Yes!*" Their shout is loud enough to be heard over the cicadas, and Ravi glances up at the neighbor's houses before remembering their opinions don't fucking matter.

He deliberately slows the rhythm of his hips, drawing out the smooth glide. He's never done this without a barrier before and the friction is almost too much, overwhelming. He's only clinging to his control by sheer force of will. "Yeah? This what you wanted? Fuck, Cay, you feel *so*..." His next thrust is so demanding that Cayenne braces an arm on the ground to stay put, clawing past the picnic blanket and into the grass.

Their shout is *definitely* going to bring out the neighbors. The last thing Ravi wants right now is an interruption, so he slides his hand over Cayenne's mouth. They suck his fingers into the heat of their mouth with a hungry, muffled hum, and that's... He wanted to pull Cayenne to their climax before he went tumbling off the edge himself, he's always been good at that, keeping himself under control but...

The last vestiges of Ravi's control erode. Cayenne is an assault on his senses, stripping every ounce of his discipline and lifting his yearning beyond measure. He could no sooner hold back than he could will his own galloping heart to stop beating.

Ravi smothers a helpless growl against a freckled shoulder as he strokes into Cayenne's shuddering heat with everything he has. He comes with a bitten, breathless cry, spilling and shattering into the bliss of their willing body.

As if this was all they had been waiting for, Cayenne follows him to their peak, vise-tight around him as they scream their pleasure into Ravi's palm. Then all their muscles go loose and lax, a rag doll in his arms.

It takes a moment to catch some air in his lungs. "*Fuck,*" he rasps.

Cayenne moans agreement against his skin, and he belatedly frees their mouth. Syllables spill soft and slurred, as if drunk, a babbled stream of consciousness. "*Oui,* so good. Oh, Ravi, *je t'aime tellement—*"

They freeze, boneless pleasure evaporating as they realize what they've said.

Ravi knows enough French for *that*.

But nothing today counts, not even "*je t'aime.*" So, Ravi nuzzles a kiss into Cayenne's hair, giving them the comfort of his body until they relax once again. A breeze kicks up cool against sweat-slick skin, bringing the distant smell of woodsmoke from some summer bonfire.

Later, Cayenne stirs in his embrace, reaching back to card through his hair. "As truly sorry as I am to move from this spot, we should get some sleep. Just a few hours, my sweet. After we catch a little catnap, I'll take us back."

Ravi leans into the caress, skin prickling with pleasure. Strange how being touched even after sex was what really made Ravi's heart skip, his throat tight. Such a simple thing to make him feel so helpless, like he'd do anything for more, no matter how unwise.

"Back to this morning already?"

Cayenne sighs. "If we stretch it out overnight, it'll be more of a strain to repeat today. The temporal expenditure…" They wave a hand vaguely in the air, grasping for untranslatable concepts. "A handful of small jumps rewinding minutes can have the same effect as one big jump undoing a few days, but this…this is somewhere in-between, and it is…" They blow an annoyed gust up into the untidy riot of copper hair falling across their eyes. "This is unknown territory for me. You must let me know the *instant* you feel anything unusual, *mon coeur.* Promise?"

Ravi sits up and plants a kiss on the wing of their shoulder blade. "I'm sure it'll be fine." He scatters small nibbles to make them laugh and squirm, and they fortunately don't notice he neglects to make any kind of promise at all.

Chapter Eleven

THE DAY DAWNS for the fifth time. Suitably impressed with the omelets Cayenne whips up (barely burned at all), they enjoy a quiet breakfast over a thoroughly cleaned counter. Ravi's contribution is to make coffee, black for him, and practically white with cream and sugar for Cayenne.

The chronomage taps restless fingers against the counter.

"Something up?"

Cayenne purses their lips tightly before moving

into a bright, careless smile. They stand up and lean over the back of the chair. "Our *delightful* little sporty scrum the other day got me thinking, my dear."

"About?"

"You've never seen me fight."

Ravi blinks, looking up from his coffee.

"I was drugged to the gills with that *connard* nix. As such, you've never gotten a chance to see me in action. Not *that* kind of action, anyway." A lascivious grin.

He had noticed Cayenne moving into some unfamiliar fighting stance back at the fight on the dock, but Ravi had been able to take down the nix with iron before more violence had become necessary. He'd wondered about it, once or twice, about the secrets under Cayenne's surface.

"We should spar! It'll be fun." Cayenne smiles as Ravi perks up in his seat. "I *thought* you might enjoy that, *mon beau.*"

"You're sure?"

"Very sure."

He won't insult them by questioning their prowess.

Surely easy enough for a time traveler to pick up a few combat tricks here and there. If Cayenne wants to play, Ravi is more than game. He stands up and stretches his arms back over his shoulders, loosening up in anticipation.

"Where, the backyard?"

"As you like, my dear," and they lead the way onto the grass.

*

RAVI'S FEET AUTOMATICALLY slide into position; he raises his arms with hands loosely curled. Cayenne lowers into a swaying stance Ravi's never seen before. It looks graceful, snakelike. He'd be very interested to see more of it.

Cayenne sticks their tongue out at him.

Ravi lunges with an open-handed strike at their face. He lets the blow swing too far wide, testing them out.

They easily step around it. "Oh, you *almost* mussed my hair," they say with a toss of their head. "You mustn't be afraid to *bruise* me a little, sweet thing." A sudden burst of movement—Cayenne feints at Ravi's ribs and jabs up at the last second, extraordinarily quick. The heel of their hand narrowly clips the edge of Ravi's jaw as he manages a dodge. Any closer, and it would have rung his bell pretty good.

Huh. Sneaky.

Watch the feet, but never trust them, his instructor had often insisted. *The attack starts in the eyes.* Up on the balls of his bare feet, Ravi moves in a slow circle around Cayenne. They follow his movements with a verdant predatory gaze, smiling with a harmlessness he in no way trusts.

"I knew the moment I saw you that you'd fight dirty," he says, then drops to the grass to sweep their legs out from under them. Cayenne barely jumps out of the way, laughing as Ravi hops back up onto his feet into a guarded stance.

"Me, fight dirty? What do you call *that*?" As they speak, Ravi throws a couple of cheap shots that Cayenne ducks without any trouble. They laugh. "Don't they teach you hero types honorable combat?"

They tense the set of their shoulders, telegraphing an incipient attack. Arms up, shielding his face, Ravi says, "Sure, until they found out I wasn't going to get Chosen superpowers. Then I had to learn more survivable skills."

Cayenne's eyes drop. They spin into reach with a strike at Ravi's solar plexus, snaking under his raised arms. A good hit, solidly struck. If Ravi hadn't been shifting his heel back, he would have had the wind knocked out of him.

"Nice," he says admiringly.

"I always go for vulnerable spots," Cayenne tells him, suddenly serious. "If you leave me any opening, I'll take it." They aim a swift kick at his throat. Ravi ducks under it, and that's when he realizes this isn't just for fun.

It's a lesson. A weapon to use against them. A gift.

"You know," Cayenne continues casually, moving like liquid around him. "You've got an advantage. I haven't been practicing much lately, since...well."

Another high kick Ravi deflects with a forearm. He attempts an ankle grab to pull them off balance, but with a graceful little wriggle they pull their leg right out of his grasp.

"What is that style? I haven't seen it before."

A small, bashful smile. "Capoeira, darling. With some jiu-jitsu, and just a *soupçon* of your own brand of violence."

"It suits you," he says approvingly. Martial arts that favor grappling over striking would work best for Cayenne's frame. "And you haven't been practicing?"

"Well," they begin airily, but he picks up on a slight trill of nervousness and shifts his focus to their face, reading the veiled play of emotions. "I haven't always looked like this. I'm built a bit differently, now. You know, after Lucy worked her particular brand of magic." They laugh, a delicate sound, eyes darting away. "*Scrawny* could be an applicable description."

Ravi absorbs this and nods, jumping back to avoid a swing. "Krav Maga is a smart style to learn if you're going to be up against larger, stronger opponents.

That's why I learned it, to combat monsters bigger than myself. My Krav instructor was only five three in boots, and she could regularly kick my ass across the yard."

He turns to accept a blow on the meaty part of his shoulder, which brings Cayenne close enough for him to slip over their guard, twist his arm around their wrist, and bend it backward. They grunt and squirm out of his grip with a sharp kick to his shin. He ignores the sting, breath thickening with exertion. Sparring with Cayenne is much more strenuous and interesting than he had assumed. He's having *fun*.

"I wasn't as…controlled at seventeen as I am now. Took me almost a year to get anywhere close to holding my own with her."

"You know, darling, some would say a single year is a remarkably short time to get near a professional level."

He barks a laugh. Cayenne turns his kick aside and leaves their flank open for a quick knuckle jab. They take the hit and stick their tongue out at him again.

"Well, it helped that I had a thorough foundation in

kalaripayattu, thang ta, and *shastra-vidya* already. And it's not like I had anything else to do except learn. Every day in Israel was…wake up, train until I pass out, then do it again the next day."

Cayenne pouts sympathetically, then lashes out with a series of rabbit punches and advancing high kicks Ravi is hard-pressed to stay out of range of. "No monster hunts for young baby Ravi? No special missions?"

He doesn't say anything for a few exchanges, sidestepping a few open-handed swings. "No, no missions." He shifts far back, buying some space to regain oxygen. "They didn't know what to do with me. It was after…"

He shakes his head, not finishing the sentence; *it was after the funeral.* He can still smell the oils of turmeric and sandalwood before they burned away, still see the ashes drifting across the river's surface like they were unwilling to sink into the sacred waters. Such a paltry scattering of ashes; there hadn't been much left to burn.

"Aside from my hand-to-hand instructor and the IDF guys teaching me the rifle, I didn't hear from anyone for a while." Nearly a year spent training. Easier to call it training than what it was in truth: exile.

Cayenne goes a little pale, though that might be from a wisp of cloud drifting in front of the early afternoon sun. "You…were seventeen, *cher*?"

"For a few months, I was. The sniper guys got me halvah for my birthday. Loved it. So hard to find the real stuff here." He smiles, changing the subject. "But yeah, I can see how it might be tricky to adapt your old fighting style. Especially if you have more muscle mass now."

Tentatively, Cayenne smiles back. They let him keep his distance, not trying to attack yet. Their expression is hard to parse; maybe apprehension, maybe gratitude, perhaps something like pride. It's hard to tell. Ravi isn't sure *why*; Cayenne has never hidden that the form they wear isn't the one they've always had. Makes sense, for a time traveler to change their face every so often.

"You know," Ravi says with a lopsided smile, "Krav Maga is about winning no matter what, so it's at least sixty percent groin shots. I'll admit I've been going easy on you. Don't want to damage the merchandise." He winks, hoping to reassure them.

Cayenne's voice pitches low and dangerous, and the hairs on the back of Ravi's neck prickle. "Oh, you've been going *easy* on me, pet?" Grinning savagely, Cayenne dashes forward into an attack.

Ravi moves to dodge, but suddenly Cayenne just *isn't there*. He blinks and they're behind him. Brutally, their foot snaps out to kick his knee out from under him.

There's a split second where Ravi knows falling is inevitable, so instead of a futile fight against gravity, he grabs Cayenne's wrist and uses the momentum of the tumble to roll them over his shoulder. It should toss them flat to the ground.

Instead, Cayenne flows with his throw, rolling head over heels and landing light on their feet, as if they were expecting it all along. Gathering his balance, Ravi stays low, crab-stepping back, keeping his distance and watching Cayenne with focused wariness.

This is new.

Cayenne spreads their hands in open invitation

with a sharp, vulpine smile on their face.

He's fast, too, trained to rely on speed as much as strength, and Ravi dives forward, feints right, aiming a flat-hand chop to the juncture of neck and shoulder. Before it even hits, he feels that satisfying certainty a blow is going to land true.

But Cayenne again is simply *not there*, Ravi's aim now inches off, and they nonchalantly push his hand off course. His palm goes sailing past their head, putting him way too close into their range. He's open, vulnerable.

Instead of taking the kill-shot, Cayenne grabs the back of Ravi's neck and reels him in for a hungry kiss. When they pull back, their expression isn't flirty in the least. Their speech is matter-of-fact. "Misdirection is the key. Surprise me, distract me. I may be able to slow time, but I still only have two eyes. Blindside me and I will take a punch like anyone else." And Cayenne hooks one foot behind Ravi's ankle and shoves him back hard, and he falls to the grass with a jarring grunt. "Even smaller and weaker, I will always have an advantage unless you take it away from me."

As Ravi regains his breath, Cayenne gives him a teasing little pout, then gallantly extends a hand to help him back up. Ravi bites back a wild grin and snatches a chunk of earth to fling it into their eyes. He kips up to his feet, supine to standing in an eyeblink.

"*Merde!*" Cayenne skips back and laughs, shaking grass out of their vision. "Yes, exactly like that."

And the two of them trade blows, a furious whirl-wind of power and ruthless grace, adapting to surprises and sidestepping tricks. Cayenne's ability to slow time makes them relentless, vicious, and *glorious*. It's one of the best fights Ravi's had in years.

Afterward, covered in sweat, dirty and grass-stained, both sport new bruises. If the whole day wasn't getting rewritten, Ravi has what would certainly be a black eye by sunrise tomorrow.

Cayenne apologizes, cupping his face in their hands. "Let me kiss it better, *mon tigre.*"

Ravi amiably shoos away their fussing. "Don't apologize for a good match. It'll be gone on the next rewind."

Cayenne's mouth twists. They attempt a careless tone that falls flat. "You know, it's *almost* a shame. It grants you a sort of, how you say, *roguish* charm." They inspect his face with an undue amount of care, brushing a thumb over Ravi's upper lip. A strange look shadows their eyes, and they swallow hard.

"You can make it up to me in the shower," Ravi murmurs, dragging their hand from his face to the swell between his legs. Cayenne's eyes flash down, the wide grin spreading over their face banishing any concern.

"Oh, *ho*, did you *enjoy* that fight, my sweet?" They squeeze, sending Ravi to his tiptoes with a hiss of pleasure. "Should I kick your ass more often?"

He rolls his eyes. "Just get inside."

*

CAYENNE'S MOUTH IS hot and welcoming, their hair plastered dark against their scalp under the stream of water, steam rolling up around them. Ravi can barely stay upright against the shower tiles. The sight of

Cayenne on their knees swallowing him down makes his chest feel tight, his breath short.

They're taking their time, drawing it out. Ravi's head knocks back against the tiles when he catches sight of Cayenne stroking themself as they suck him. Fuck, that's intensely hot. He sets his hands on the back of their head, not to guide or direct, but just enjoying the point of contact.

"You can fuck me, if you want," he ventures. "To the victor go the spoils, you've said before." The truth is that *Ravi* wants it, had thought about that one time at the Seychelles a *lot*, but Cayenne always seems content with the reverse, despite assurances of their varied tastes. Most guys assumed Ravi has a narrower field of interest than he does, and in any case, he never makes the offer lightly; but here, in this shard of frozen time, he trusts Cayenne. He trusts them with his secrets, with his body. With his heart.

Cayenne manages a laugh around his cock, the sensation zinging electricity right up through his spine. "Such a *generous* offer," they rasp, dragging the flat of their tongue from balls to tip. "After I make you come." They take him to the back of their throat, the fit unbearably tight.

Ravi bites back a tangle of Tamil curses as one slick, clever finger sneaks back between his thighs. With a thrill, he kicks his legs wider in silent invitation. It's… They have unerring aim. Sparks shoot through him. Panting, he braces one hand against the wall to stay on his feet.

"Fuck, Cay, that's—" He struggles to drag in enough air, the constant spray of the water already over-sensitizing his skin.

Cayenne moans, the hunger in it alone enough to pull Ravi straight to the edge. Their finger strokes just *so*, and Ravi tumbles over with a grating cry that scours his throat raw. Grinning, Cayenne pulls off with a chuckle, and Ravi craves nothing more than to have them right back where they were.

"Can you, um. Could we…go again?" Cayenne hasn't rolled out their time travel trick once, not even the small bedroom rewinds, the whole time they've been at the lake house. Ravi by habit never asks for more than is initially offered, but he's desperate enough to risk overstepping.

Cayenne winces. "As much as it pains me to deny you anything, *mon coeur*, extra rewinds *might* make it harder for your mind to recover between the big shifts. I think we get more time the less I fiddle with it. More possible days." They press an apologetic kiss to the crest of his hipbone, then another below his navel, and finally one at the top of his thigh above a faded scar, licking water from his skin in little cat-laps as they go.

"Oh. That's okay."

Brow furrowing, Cayenne sits back and gnaws on their already swollen lower lip. "But it might be harmless, just a *teeny*-tiny skip like this."

"Okay," he says, a touch hopeful.

"But I'm not sure, it's just a theory." They lean back with a calculating tap to their chin, ignoring their own arousal.

"Okay."

"But maybe…"

Ravi chuckles dryly. "Make up your mind, Cay."

Their eyes darken. "Hold on," they purr, and that paired with a tiny tug in Ravi's gut are the only warnings as Cayenne folds time back just far enough for it to happen all over again, and when Ravi comes into the hot clasp of their mouth, it's with a ringing shout of gratitude.

"*Kadavule*. I'm never going to get used to that," he manages in a series of gasps, hand curling fond around the back of their head, barely able to stay on his feet.

Cayenne licks their lips. "I'm not done with you yet."

*

AFTERWARD, RAVI STRETCHED out on his stomach in bed, what began fast and frantic has become slow and sweet, Cayenne pressing their lithe body so close against his it's as if they wear the same skin. The sheets tangle around Ravi's hands, his earlier impatience to get Cayenne inside him having pulled each corner off the mattress until the bedding fluffed around them like a nest of clouds.

"*C'est si bon,* you are *so…* You like this, my darling?" Cayenne's voice is ragged silk in his ear.

Languid and relaxed, Ravi murmurs back, "Mm-hm," and takes their hand. Their fingers tighten on his, knuckles white.

Cayenne comes with his name on their lips, a whispered prayer. They press shivering kisses across the breadth of his shoulders, asking hoarsely, "Again, *mon coeur?*"

"Yes."

And the hourglass turns over, sand rolling back, again and again.

Chapter Twelve

AFTER THEY SLEEP, Cayenne spins them back to dawn for the seventh time. Ravi keeps his eyes closed to wait out the dizziness. Only a little bit today; no worse than yesterday. When he opens them, Cayenne is watching him carefully.

"Good morning." He smiles, leaning in for a kiss. Instead, Cayenne avoids his lips, taking his face between their hands and inspecting him with a narrow glare. "Hey," he protests, but Cayenne hushes him with a hiss. After an intense handful of seconds, they relax, smile, and drop a quick peck to his forehead.

"*Je suis désolé*, my sweet. Just checking. Any dizziness? Nausea?"

Ravi levers himself upright and rolls his eyes. "I'm *fine*."

"*Indeed* you are." Cayenne drops a kiss to his collarbone. "And what desires can we fulfill for you today, my hot mug of chai?"

"I might actually be in the rare mood for chai," Ravi allows, "but you know what I've been thinking about?" He stretches languorously, ignoring the lurch of his stomach as he does so. He swings his legs off the bed, stands up, then knows nothing.

*

"*JE TE JURE*, Ravi, *je te tuerai si tu ne te réveilles pas!*" The distant sound of Cayenne's voice. Cool hands cradle his jaw. He opens his eyes, wincing at the brightness.

Muzzily, he asks, "*Kya hua?*"

They're sprawled on the floor next to the bed. Ravi is cold, even despite the way Cayenne bodily drapes across him. He's shivering, skin clammy.

Cayenne sobs with relief, tears making their eyes shimmer like cut gems. "You…you *idiot.*" Their lips collide with his in a graceless crush. They pull back just enough to meet Ravi's gaze, their lovely face tight with anguish. "Why didn't you *tell me?*"

Ravi swallows against a swell of nausea. The sunlight is too bright, a slight corona around Cayenne's pale skin.

"Because it's our last day together," he rasps, eyes hot and dry. "Isn't it?"

Cayenne sags against him. "Yes," they whisper.

*

TOMORROW'S DAWN FINALLY rises, the hourglass run dry.

I do hate goodbyes, Cayenne had said thickly, eyes tinged red. *So let's not, darling. I'll be seeing you.*

Ravi wakes alone.

He hadn't gotten much sleep. In the mirror, he regards his bitten lip and the passion-marks on his neck, visible even on his complexion. He buttons his collar high over them as he gets dressed. He's always been so careful not to be marked before. Careful never to show he might belong to somebody.

Ravi buttons the shirt, the waistcoat, slides up the knot of the tie, affixes the cufflinks. He cleans his gun on autopilot and holsters it under his jacket. With each familiar step it gets easier, the well-oiled routine keeping him grounded. Even then, it's only the peace that comes from standing in the eye of a hurricane; a center of calm but for a single step to either side, where he would easily become lost.

He takes his time to put the lake house in order, gathers his keys, and leaves.

*

TWO WEEKS INTO August and nothing happens. Each day is threaded through with dread, the anticipation stitched into Ravi's every waking moment. His sleep is plagued. Most nights he rises at uneven hours to go downstairs to the apartment's communal gym. There he methodically wraps his hands, pulling the fabric taut around his knuckles and over his wrists, and practices hooks and haymakers on the punching bag until weariness finally overtakes him.

No more than a day had passed for his teammates during his whole stay at the lake house. At least one of them still checks in every day, even though Ravi stays distant, responding coolly to texts and not answering any calls. They're all too perceptive, and he's far too raw to keep his guard up.

When Harry sends a group text, adrenaline spikes through Ravi, heart in his throat. But the message is fairly benign; nothing about an airport, no great emergency.

-Harry-

Heyyyy a weird thing happened at my apartment this morning. Stop by for refreshments and a small mystery. Though no refreshments actually. But yeah.

Everyone check in when you can, it's not pressing. I think.

Ravi relaxes. After suiting up he checks the mirror. Yeah, that's not going to fly. Two weeks of neglecting hair and beard maintenance are extremely noticeable.

Since Harry doesn't think it's pressing, Ravi stops by a barbershop, and afterward, he feels better, more like himself, his usual unflappable demeanor easier to maintain.

A second text comes in from Harry on his way to his car, this one direct to him.

-Harry-

Nothing peppery about this as far as I can tell, btw.

Just FYI. Didn't want you to worry this was the spicy situation we've been expecting.

-Ravi-

Appreciate it.

-Harry-

You know a lot about weapons, right?

-Ravi-

Yes.

-Harry-

Cool. Think I need your expertise.

You can make it, right?

-Ravi-

Wasn't doing anything better.

Be there in 15.

*

HARRY HAS ONE of those blocky old apartments built in the sixties, mostly concrete brutalism with a few flourishes added on in later decades that only highlight the stark design rather than soften it. Harry has repeatedly claimed she likes it there. Considering the team has a cache of diamonds at their disposal, it must be true or she would be living in a penthouse suite instead. She's a woman of simple tastes, she likes to say. The neighbors aren't nosy, and the view from the roof is well worth the creaky floorboards.

Ravi climbs up to Harry's floor. Outside her door he can hear a few low voices. No doubt the others were able to arrive sooner than he was. He knocks and Harry calls for him to come on in.

As suspected, the others are already here. Nate looks like he came straight from the campus in one of his tweed suits with the tie loose and jacket unbuttoned. The professor looks over and offers Ravi a friendly wave. Val, in her ever-present athleisure, doesn't look around to greet him, her frame blocking most of Ravi's view of Harry. The PI is perched cross-legged on her coffee table while Constance peers over her shoulder with a frown.

"What's the situation?" Ravi asks coolly.

Constance glances up. "Mine niece received a mysterious package at her doorstep after having an odd dream about the very self-same thing."

"A prophetic dream," Nate says with excitement. "There are tons of legends about them. I can maybe—"

"Ravi," Val says in her stone-slab voice, looking

straight at him. The hairs prickle on the back of his neck. The angel steps to the side.

Harry's in an oversized T-shirt and pajama pants, dark hair up in a sleep-tousled bun, and her under-eye smudges make her look as exhausted as Ravi feels. In her hand she holds a weapon, an enclosed hilted handle that sprouts four long, flexible whip-like blades. Harry waggles it a little, and the blades make a familiar ringing sound as steel strikes steel.

Glacial cold washes up Ravi's body as if he were plunged underwater, lungs freezing over into solid ice.

"How do you have that?" he rasps, voice hollow as the bottom of a dry well.

Harry brightens. "You *do* know what it is? I thought, yeah. This is an Indian weapon, right?"

"It's…it's an urumi."

"I've been thinking of it as a noodle sword." She flips it over. The blades sinuously follow the movement, reflecting light in long flashing stripes on the ceiling.

"It was my mother's," Ravi says, eyes locked on the urumi.

Val takes a step closer to Harry, mirrored sunglasses still fixed on Ravi, as if wary of him. He ignores her. He ignores Nate's surprised murmur, ignores Constance's puzzled frown. He ignores everything but Harry, pale and uncertain, his mother's urumi in her hand.

"What? But…this…" Harry blinks down at the urumi. "This was your mom's? Are you su—"

"Harry. Why do you have my mother's sword?" Ravi speaks evenly, steadily, not raising his voice. It's a wonder he can talk at all through the block of ice his body is rapidly becoming.

She throws herself to her feet. "Fuck if I know! I had a dream a package was left at my door. When I woke up, the package was really there, okay? Super freaky. Then this was inside, and…" Harry pauses and chews on her lip. "I got maybe, visions? When I first touched it."

Ravi can taste his pulse as it beats thick and arctic. "You got visions when you touched it."

"Yeah."

"Are they memories," he says, not bothering to make it a question. He already knows the answer.

Looking back down at the sword, Harry's brows knit, the tendons in her throat tensing as she swallows hard. "Yeah, but not *my* memories. They're—"

"They're the memories of all the previous Chosen. You're the *Chosen. You're* the Chosen." It doesn't make any more sense the second time Ravi says it. Suddenly he can move again, and he presses the heels of his hands hard enough for light to bloom in the darkness behind his eyelids.

"Sorry to interrupt, here, but *what the ever-loving fuck* is going on?" Nate sidles into view, arms crossed. He stands equidistant between Ravi and Harry, as if splitting the difference on who to support.

Constance props her hands on her hips. "Aye! Chosen by what? What has this to do with your mother, Ravi?"

Val stands at Harry's shoulder and takes off her sunglasses. Twin white-blue fires burn where a human would have eyes, flaring bright before banking low.

"Durga, goddess of demon-slaying. She chooses a champion to imbue with her favor once a generation. Her Chosen has heightened abilities to make them more effective at their task."

"Which is…slaying demons?" Harry sounds dubious.

"All sorts of supernatural threats, though demons in particular, yes. The blade imparts wisdom from the previous Chosen who have passed in the execution of their duties."

"Execution, huh," Harry says hollowly.

"The line of the Chosen goes back to the third century. There have only been three others like you, Harry, who were not born expecting to take on the burden."

Ravi turns his piercing stare onto Val. "How do you know any of this? You're not even from the right *pantheon*. You're not a deva, or an apsara, or—"

Val very slightly tilts her head to one side. "I do not understand the relevance."

"I'm missing something," Nate interjects with an upraised index finger. "The line?"

"Yes," Val says. "Ravi's line. The Abhiramnew line."

"Okay, I just—" Harry holds up a hand, turning away to face the window. Urumi held loose at her side, she massages her forehead. "So, this is some magical destiny bullshit, is what I'm hearing."

"Yes," Ravi and Val both answer simultaneously, then share a look.

"Fucking hell, guys, I haven't even had my coffee yet, this is…"

"Now *that* I can help with," Nate breathes with relief, moving to the kitchenette.

Harry takes a deep breath and looks at Ravi. "Okay, so… Your mom. This was hers?" She holds it up, and Ravi is torn between wanting to snatch the urumi away from her and wanting to back away from it, to never see the thing again.

"Tanvi. Her name was Tanvi. She was the last Chosen, yes."

"And…" Harry draws in a shaky breath. "She's not now."

"She died."

"Ravi," Nate begins, "I'm so sorry."

Ravi immediately puts up a warding hand, fingers spread. He cannot handle any sympathy right now. He can barely handle standing still. "She died eight years ago. You might not have seen it, yet. In the memories. It sometimes takes a few days for them all to fill in."

"Lucky me," Harry says dryly. "I've got that to look forward to." Her keen eyes drill into him. "After your mom died, who's been this goddess-Chosen demon-killing champion for the last eight years?"

Ravi's hands clench uselessly by his sides, then release. "It was supposed to be me."

"I… Fuck, I thought that might be it. Shit. Fuck. *Fuck*, Ravi, this—I didn't—"

"I know." He gets it. She didn't ask for this. "No one knew why it wasn't. The Trust has been scrambling for almost a decade trying to figure it out. All the predictions—the intel networks, the seers, everything—pointed to me being the next in line. I…trained for it."

Trained for it, sacrificed for it, ever striving to be

worthy, dedicated himself to it, *bled* for it; all those years of devotion and prayers answered with *nothing*.

"This is somehow tied to your Trust, then?" Constance eyes the urumi.

"Yeah." He rakes a hand through his hair. Questions are good. He can answer questions. Right now, he's grateful for any direction.

"The Trust started as a small cohort helping the Chosen fight evil. Over time it got…bigger." The urumi holds such gravity that Ravi can't break his gaze free. "We thought that was destroyed eight years ago, in the explosion that killed Tanvi and my uncle Nirav. The urumi has been destroyed before, and then it just reformed a little differently. It hasn't even always been an urumi, but that's ancient history. *That's* the same one," he says with a jerk of his chin at the sword, with utter certainty. "So many agents spent so many years searching for it before we gave up. And it just shows up on your doorstep."

Nate presses a mug of coffee into Ravi's hands. "Look, can we sit and talk?" He passes cups to Harry and Constance. Nobody moves to sit yet. Ravi automatically takes a sip, absently noting it has been served black with a dash of cinnamon.

Harry's shoulders slump. "Uncle too, huh?"

"They were twins," he says, by way of explanation. His teeth catch his bottom lip. It's a struggle to meet Harry's eyes. "The last person who wasn't an Abhiramnew to touch that sword was William Harbridge. His family was already in The Trust, one of the old families. It wasn't a surprise; the seers knew he'd be next. The urumi came to him by the usual ceremony in 1912." Ravi nearly burns his tongue on the coffee. He grimaces and sets the mug down. "And the last before him, Zhen Zi-Qi, was thousands of miles away when he was Chosen. Sixteenth century. The urumi was carried to him by an eagle."

"Fuck, I could have gotten an eagle?" Harry drawls. "I just got a dumb package at my door." She waves to her kitchen counter. The package is a plain, nondescript cardboard box with clear packing tape. Nothing notable about it aside from the name *Harry McAllister* typed, printed out, and taped on the cut-open top. "Believe me, I'm going to be doing a *thorough* investigation. I still know people at the crime lab who can analyze that thing down to the fucking atoms. I'm gonna be calling in some favors."

Constance prods at the box. "And I already peered through the veil of time to see who left it on the stoop. Naught but a city courier with this one package of many, not a chronomage."

Ravi flinches.

"My apologies, Ravi." Constance winces. "I thought that might comfort you. We hath all been expecting that particular Sword of Damocles to fall soon, but methinks this doth not look like Cayenne's... How would one put it? *Style?*"

Nate scoffs. "A plain brown package? They'd sooner die."

"Then we know not whose machinations hath drawn my niece into this obligation."

Ravi shakes his head. "You can't force a Choosing. People have tried. Sending the urumi to Harry doesn't guarantee anything. It's not like whoever is the first to touch it gets to be a goddess's living avatar. It's—"

Durga does not Choose wrong, his aunt had once told him, with perfect, terrible serenity. Harry's apartment suddenly smells like ashes. Ravi lets his gaze fall to his shoes, all at once exhausted down to the bone.

"Do you…do you want to touch it?"

His head whips up.

Harry holds out the urumi. "It's kind of yours, right? You should take it."

"I—"

"Here, Rav, please." Harry offers it up with a hopeful smile. "Take it. This is all clearly a big mistake. I can't be some kind of divine champion demon hunter: I'm a complete fuckup. I wouldn't know the first thing about how to use this properly. It's supposed to be yours, right, you trained for it and all? Take it!"

"I *can't*. It's not transferable." Ravi takes a step back, grinding his molars. "Durga has Chosen *you*, Harry. Not me." The hinge of his jaw is so tight pain lances into his temples. "It's you. Nothing can change that."

Val nods. "Ravi is correct. Though the delivery of the sword is a mystery, the choice cannot be influenced. You are Chosen, Harry."

Harry's face twists into sudden fury. "Yeah, right. So, who the *fuck* sent this to my door?"

Ravi breathes out slowly, forcing tension to release the iron grip on his muscles, and his hands to stay un-fisted. "I'm sorry, Harry."

Appalled, Harry looks at him as if he'd sprouted a second head. "Dude, you apologizing for this kinda makes me want to jump off the roof. Knock it off, okay?" She looks down at the urumi. For the first time since he's known Harry, she looks lost. Scared. "Look, can you just...try?" Pleading, she holds it out again, arm fully extended.

Ravi takes another step back, suddenly triggered into fight-or-flight, hyperaware of his surroundings; where everyone stands, the messy apartment around him, where the exits lie. He shuts his eyes and runs through sniper breath exercises. Once, twice.

On the third, he opens his eyes. He steps forward

and takes the blade.

Funny how it fits differently now. His hand was half the size then, when she would let him hold it. It didn't happen often, but he remembers those rare occasions with bittersweet fondness.

It's been a very long time since he's worked with one, but the body doesn't forget. Ravi adapts to the urumi's shifting, flexible weight, and he easily slides into the correct stance as he extends his arm to the empty side of the room. With a flick of his wrist, the blades rise up, steel whips cracking against the air. The others startle a little at the unexpected sound.

Ravi pulls his arm back and turns the urumi over, inspecting it for a long while before he realizes he's…waiting. Bated breath, senses poised. But in his hands, same as when he was a boy, it is only a sword.

He coils it up with a practiced flip and hands it back to Harry. "I'm sorry, Harry. I can't take this from you. It's not mine." He stares at Harry, with her bed head and pajama pants. Empty takeout containers under her sofa. The white guitar leaning haphazardly against her TV.

Her face, bloodless with dread.

"I have to go."

He's not sure where he's going to go or what he's going to do, but these are his friends, and he doesn't trust himself around them right now. They're safer if he leaves.

Harry clears her throat. "Okay. Yeah. Get some air. We'll be here."

"Yeah." And Ravi turns and walks out of the door.

*

A LITTLE OVER an hour later, he goes back. Everyone has seated themselves on mismatched stools around the kitchenette counter, fresh boxes of aromatic takeout piled to one side.

"It's Thai," Harry tells him as he walks in, as if he'd never left. He shakes his head and pulls up a chair.

"'Tis still but morning, but I could use a wee tipple." Constance sets small glasses in front of everyone, save Val, and pours out a jot of brandy in each. With a soft smile she pours Ravi a little extra. "Did thy walk clear thy head? I often find 'tis such for me."

Ravi can't remember where he walked. Stress response, he recognizes numbly, his thoughts a step removed. A welcome change, right now.

"Yeah," he says, taking a sip of the brandy.

Nate leans close and holds up an imaginary pad of paper with imaginary pencil readied, brows raised in expectation. It's just ridiculous enough that Ravi manages his first smile in weeks, though it feels weak. He rolls the liquor on his tongue, finally tasting it. It's not bad. He nods. Nate grins wide and marks an imaginary tick in the imaginary yes column.

Ravi sets the glass down. Pressing his palms flat on the table, he finally looks at Harry. "I'm sure you have questions. I will help however I can."

A sigh of relief wooshes out of her. "I'm glad. I need you on this." She smiles wanly.

"You have me."

"Val filled us in on some broad strokes stuff. History lessons. So, I guess I'm just shaky on... What comes next?"

"This should have been predicted, at least a bit. But considering the only agent of The Trust you have seen is me—" He narrows his gaze. "No one else has approached you, right?"

"Definitely not."

"Okay. Then right now, the only people who know you've been Chosen are in this room, and whoever sent that package to your door. Though it's not outside the realm of possibility it's..." Ravi's throat sticks. "You know. Divine will alone."

"Hm, that's *one* theory," Harry says with a hefty dose of skepticism. "Another theory is someone is trying to fuck with me. Or you. Or The Trust, or Durga, or all of us together. Or..." For a moment she goes distant, thoughtful. "Being Chosen is super dangerous, right?"

"Yes."

Nate sets a hand on Harry's shoulder, and she leans into it the smallest bit. "Someone might have it out for me," she says, "or they might want to protect you. I don't suppose maybe..." She runs a finger under the stretched-out collar of her shirt, grimacing apologetically. "Your dad?"

Ravi shrugs; that's a scab long since healed over. "No idea. Not in the picture. Mom managed to get around that bylaw by having me, but not marrying." That scandal had caused a few unsavory grudges leftover from Tanvi's time, even after Ravi's birth. "It was, by all accounts, a huge deal at the time."

Harry blinks at him. "Bylaw?"

Ravi worries his lip. She should know everything up front, he decides. If she's going to survive this, she should have whatever support he can give her.

"The Trust hires both career agents like me," he begins, "and freelancers like you. For the average asset, all you ever know is what we let you see: secretive monster-hunting organization with deep pockets, endless resources, and connections in the highest places."

Ravi sips the brandy. The burn helps bring him back to himself a little. "Agents work in teams. The team leads answer to the director of their branch. Branches cooperate globally, and as far as 99 percent of The Trust knows, that's where the chain of command stops."

Ravi pauses. Revealing secrets like this could get him in worlds of trouble, but he squares his shoulders and continues. "But there's a higher authority. The consortium makes all the big decisions for The Trust. It's exclusively made up of the old families, most of them founders of what The Trust is today. If you're from one of those families, you only get a seat at that table when you marry. And you only get a vote when you 'contribute to the legacy.'" He hooks his fingers into air quotes.

Nate arches a brow. "Are we talking financial contributions, or…"

Ravi shakes his head.

Nate snorts. "How delightfully heteronormative. No one thought that rule was going to run into issues?"

"It only came into being during the beginnings of British rule. So, it's been about two hundred and sixty years?"

"Fucking colonialism, man."

Harry shakes her hair out of its bun, finger-combing it out as she nods. "Hey, the family stuff and/or Trust stuff you were talking about. Your whole closet situation makes more sense now. Not just the Indian thing. I get it."

"Yeah," Ravi sighs, pinching the bridge of his nose. He feels like a turtle pulled out of its shell. He's had enough revealing conversations lately to last a lifetime.

Harry picks up the urumi, giving it an annoyed glare. "If we're the only people who know about this, I'd like to keep it that way for as long as we can. Until we can figure out who's behind this."

"Harry, it doesn't matter who sent it. It's immaterial. Whether by courier, by ceremony, or by eagle, the sword finds its way to the Chosen. It's done. You and the sword can't be separated now." He sits up straighter as a thought occurs to him. "And you can't just chuck it in a drawer, either. Keep it on you at *all times*. It's dangerous to be separated from it. Like Val said, it'll give you tactical wisdom. You're going to be more effective in fights." He leans back, idly tracing his beard with thumb and forefinger. Tactics are more familiar ground, a welcome anchor. "Team dynamics are going to have to shift, for battle. Might want to consider that."

Val nods in approval. "Yes. Harry must train to master her new abilities. In the meanwhile, she will be well protected." Ravi grunts in agreement.

Harry holds up a hand. "Let's…let's just back the fuck up a little." She shakes the urumi. "How am I supposed to keep this thing on me at all times? I can't carry a metal spaghetti sword around town."

Between one blink and the next, the urumi turns into a small scallop-edged coin.

"*Fuck!*" Harry drops it to the counter as if it had transformed into a giant spider, the coin falling into a clattering spin.

"Now *that's* cool," Nate says, inspecting the coin from a safe distance as it stills.

"Ooh, a weapon that doth disguise itself! Very cunning indeed."

"Yeah, it can do that. When my mom wanted to conceal it, it was a bracelet."

Harry squints at the coin. "I'm not much of a jewelry girl, anyway. What is this, with the lions?"

Ravi picks it up and flips it over, noting its unusual

heft. "The Lion Capital of Ashoka. It's a ten paise coin. One paise is a hundredth of a rupee."

"I'm surprised you even know what anything under a thousand bucks *looks* like, dude."

Despite himself, a sharp amused breath escapes through Ravi's nose. He sets the coin back down. "You might develop other powers, by the way. Strength, invulnerability, that sort of thing."

"Harry," Nate says with open awe, "you're a superhero. This is the coolest fucking thing."

Harry slams her fist on the counter. "*So cool* I get to die a horrible death fighting for a cause I never fucking signed up for. You know what these fucking memories are, the ones touching this asshole sword-coin gave me? They're not tea parties and sleepovers."

As the others fall silent, Ravi softly says, "Deaths."

Her eyes look haunted. "Yeah. A lot of them."

"Jesus *Christ*, Harry." Nate reels back. Constance's normally cheerful face is downright stormy and she drums her ink-stained fingers restlessly against the counter. Only Val remains unchanged, as perfectly placid as a statue.

Harry screws her mouth up to one side. "A *lot* of them, Ravi. And a lot of them *young*." She clearly doesn't want to ask the next question, but no one could ever accuse Harry of cowardice. "Don't suppose any Chosen have died of old age?"

Ravi sucks in a breath and shuts his eyes. Centering. Resolved. He opens his eyes and means what he says next with every fiber of his being.

"You're going to be the first."

Silence falls over the table.

"You're going to be a wild card for them, Harry. The Trust has had eight years to run the show however they want, without the guidance of the Chosen. It's going to shake up the balance of power when you decide you want to go public with this." Aunt Padme is going to go *apoplectic* when she finds out. Ravi feels almost hysterical at the thought.

Wrenching his mind back to the task at hand, he tries to impart his sincerity into every syllable. "But *you're* the Chosen, Harry. The heart of The Trust. It's been years since the Chosen has truly been the center of the consortium, but you'll still have significant sway. The right to make big decisions, and the freedom to implement them."

Nate sucks air through his teeth, as if unable to help himself. At Ravi's inquiring look, he winces. "Sorry, didn't mean to interrupt. Just thinking… You must have been counting on that, huh?"

"On what?"

"The freedom."

Ravi avoids Nate's insightful eyes. He adjusts the set of his cuffs before continuing, staying on task. He's *good* at staying on task. His inner turmoil is irrelevant and unhelpful. He needs to be helpful. Useful.

"The *purpose* of The Trust is to protect innocents and to help the Chosen save the world. To guard against supernatural threats and prevent apocalyptic destruction. That's the charge that was given to us over seventeen hundred years ago."

That's what Ravi is loyal to, what *all* of The Trust should be loyal to. Not the money, not the power, not a mire of family politics. But Ravi isn't a child anymore, and he knows it won't be that easy. It's going to take work.

Intently, Harry watches him speak. The tense line of her shoulders smooths out just a hair. After a long moment, she nods.

He returns his own nod, firm and self-assured. "What do you need?"

"I… What?"

"What do you need from *me*? I'll back your play, Harry." Ravi swallows, then stiffens his spine and plows through what he has to say. "My mother…" Voice catching, he clears his throat and tries again. "At the time, I didn't understand some of the things I over-heard. But she hated how The Trust had gone from sup-porting the Chosen into wielding them as a tool. It was supposed to be about guidance, about faith; that's why it was first called *Shraddha*. Trust. Faith. A sacred duty, to help Durga's Chosen however they could. She was always fighting what The Trust has become instead. I…I was just a kid. I didn't get it.

"She wasn't… She was…complicated. I didn't know her very well," he says through a dull, familiar ache behind his heart. "But she was an excellent champion. And Durga—" The name sticks in his throat until he clears it. "Durga doesn't choose wrong." Rising to his feet, Ravi places both palms together and gives Harry a small bow. She leans away from him, her eyes wide with alarm.

"I, Ravi Abhiramnew, scion of the Chosen family, bearer of the sacred charge passed down in an unbroken chain, pledge my service and devotion to you, Angharad McAllister, for whatever purposes you deem fit, and will ever strive to be worthy of your trust."

Constance merely nods her approval while Nate presses his steepled hands tight to his mouth, as if desperately trying to keep from laughing, or shouting, or holding back some unnamed emotion. Val watches with unreadable blue-fire eyes.

Harry's mouth flaps for a while. "Ravi, yeah, that's cool and sweet and all, but you *never* need to say my full name again. That would be great."

His posture loosens, determination tapped dry. "Fuck," he exhales, sweeping his hair off his forehead. Speaking of names… "Uh… They're going to want us to marry. Every time the Chosen has been found outside the Abhiramnew family, they've married back in."

"*Married*?" Nate shouts, hands dropping.

Constance gives a satisfied cluck of her tongue. "Ah, finally! The first thing that makes some sense about all this. An alliance of families. A union with my niece would be advantageous for you both, no doubt, if thou wilt hold some power over your nest of witch-hunters. And any issue from your loins will of a certain make very fine, strong babes."

Harry closes her eyes, head sinking into her hands. "Constance, I love you to death, you are seriously and without exaggeration one of my favorite people in the world, but *please* shut up."

She takes her "coin" in hand and scowls at it before shoving it in her jacket pocket. "Okay, folks, this is a *lot*, I think we can all agree. And all *this*"—she waves a hand vaguely toward Ravi—"might be a conversation for later, one-on-one. Right now, we keep this on the down-low. *That's* what I need from you, Rav."

"Of course. Anything I can do for you, I will."

His phone buzzes in his jacket pocket. He jumps a little, then rolls his eyes at himself and pulls it out. Caller ID redacted. His heart seizes. How had his aunt found out so quickly? Had the seer network caught up after all?

He looks up through his brows at Harry. She straightens up, and nods.

He accepts the call. "Ma'am—"

Padme's voice is uncharacteristically high, by a mere quarter octave. Likely no one but Ravi would ever notice the difference. "There is a situation at the airport. Bring McAllister's team to take point. We've managed to keep the incident off the news for now, but that won't last long." She pauses, to Ravi's great relief. Gives him precious seconds to cobble himself together into a reasonable approximation of a man, instead of a jangling mess of nerves and adrenaline.

"Ravi," she rasps, "The Harbridges are dead. All of

them. We are under attack."

The cool calmness that descends upon Ravi comes like a blessing, his body settling into readiness. His emotions all feel distant and remote, which is extremely welcome. His tutors would be pleased.

"We're on our way." She hangs up without another word. Putting his phone away, Ravi tells his team, "It's the airport."

"Jesus." Nate gapes at Ravi. "You are having the *worst* fucking day, my guy."

Chapter Thirteen

EVEN ANGELS HAVE limitations. The team learned the hard way that Val can only teleport two people at a time, else there's a good chance her passengers will be scattered and lost. Even that is a strain; it's tiring to carry mortal weight. Despite the urgency, the risk of angel-borne travel is too great, so they're down to more conventional methods of transportation.

Ravi's Escalade easily fits everyone plus their equipment. As a matter of course, Val with the longest legs gets to ride shotgun. Harry and Nate take middle seats, and in the way-back Constance uses the entire surface of the backseat to finish cobbling together a spell.

Upending the entirety of her leather satchel into a jumble of oddities, Constance claims she is fairly certain the finished spell will help keep Cayenne pinned down. The back of the car fills with mutterings and occasional sparks. A moth flutters up from a jar Constance hastily shuts again, cursing under her breath.

"How's it going back there, Constance?" Harry asks, waving away the moth.

"Beshrew this curséd posset, I hast nary—Ah, apologies, Harry." Constance pours something viscous and glowing from a folded paper cup into a small glass vial. "I am nearly certain I have something. I have been ruminating on the magic circle the time wizard crafted for our battle back in Chicago. If I can harness their chronal energy to power a similar spell, mayhaps…" She trails off into distracted muttering.

"That's promising. Keep at it, doll, you're our secret weapon."

"Hey," Nate muses as he zips up his sports bag,

regarding his heavily taped hockey stick with a furrowed brow. "Speaking of weapons. Should I get a sword? I could be a sword guy."

Ravi shoves aside any thoughts of the urumi for later. "I can get you a gun," he offers, for the third time since he's known Nate. Nearly anything would be an upgrade from a hockey stick. The professor is going to get himself seriously injured on one of these missions without some better protection, keeping at range, or both.

"Thanks but no thanks. The things make me nervous."

Harry grabs the front seat and pulls herself forward. "Speaking of, agent guy, you got extra clips somewhere?"

"Yeah," he says without thinking, "there's an ammo case under your seat."

"Jesus," mutters Nate.

Ravi frowns at Harry in the rearview mirror as she checks her gun. "Harry…"

"Yeah, yeah, I'm not planning on using my piece.

Can we even get into a post 9/11 airport armed?"

"The rendezvous is on the tarmac at the private plane zone. There aren't security checks for private planes."

Nate shakes his head. "Well, that paints a terrifying picture of wealth and privilege."

"I've gotta have some sort of weapon," Harry says. "I can't use this noodle sword." She gingerly holds the coin between thumb and forefinger. "I'll cut off my own hand."

"It isn't a noodle sword," Ravi snaps. "It's the Chosen's urumi, an ancient weapon forged by a goddess and delivered directly into the hands of my ancestors, who have wielded it for centuries."

There's a beat of silence.

"Okay, yes," says Harry reasonably, "that's just kind of a mouthful, so."

Ravi slumps and rubs his forehead. "Sorry. Yeah. It's… You can call it whatever you want, Harry. I'm…"

He has no idea how to finish that sentence. He's feeling everything and nothing all at once, both buzzing with energy and utterly exhausted. He's trying not to speculate about what they'll find when they arrive. Where they'll find Cayenne. Ravi knows how to stay on task, how to focus on the job at hand. He locks down the part of his mind still reeling from the revelation about Harry being Chosen. That's done. Nothing to be done about it.

All he can do right now is drive.

Constance leans forward and slugs Nate on the shoulder. "Send that up to Ravi for me, my good fellow."

"Ow," jokes Nate, but obligingly gives Ravi's shoulder two soft, supportive slaps.

Constance calls up, "Harry is attempting to lighten the mood of a difficult situation for us all, Ravi. We are as one on this."

"I…yeah," he says wretchedly. "I'm not trying to be an asshole."

"We know," Harry says. "Seriously, don't worry about it. We're used to your communication style by now. We don't think you're being an asshole. This is…"

She blows out her cheeks and holds up her hands around her head, simulating an explosion. "This is a fucking *day*. You need to be snippy, you go right ahead, my dude."

Ravi takes a deep breath. "Thanks." His knuckles bloom white on the steering wheel as he takes the airport exit. "I know it's going to be hard. But I have to ask." Though he's asking the whole team, he looks straight at Val. "Don't hurt them."

Val meets his gaze evenly. "As I have said, I shall act as the chronomancer's actions demand."

The wheel creaks under Ravi's grip. "Please," he croaks.

Harry sighs and strains against her seatbelt to briskly rub Ravi's shoulder. "Yeah, we'll do our best, Rav." She sits back and clears her throat. She crosses her legs, boot bouncing restlessly. "Okay. Whatever Cayenne does, we gotta be ready for it. We gotta be quick and adaptable. Sure, they took down a fuckload of powerful vamps, but they had who-knows-how-long to plan for that. We have to get this wrapped up in one go, before they go back in time and make sure we can't interfere. Nobody freak them out about future stuff; we have no idea how they'll react. As tempting as it will be to try and keep the Red Hot Chili Jerk from doing the kind of bullshit we know they are *going* to do, we have no idea what sort of repercussions that will have." With a meaningful lift of her brows, she lolls her head toward Nate, who frowns and folds his arms over his broad chest. "Let's just focus on keeping any damage they cause to a minimum. Our strategy is de-escalation."

Ravi nods once in approval.

Constance hums thoughtfully, rubbing her hands with an unsavory smelling ointment. "We cannot mayhaps tell them, 'Doth ye not dare to try thine rascally wiles on our noble comrade in yon future'?"

"*No,*" Ravi stresses. "I'm just going to be an asshole in a suit to them."

"Pointing Ravi out to Cayenne might put him more in danger," Nate adds, looking out of the window while chewing at his thumbnail. "Or be the very thing that causes them to be interested in the first place." Ravi can see his face twist sourly in the rearview mirror. "I've had toxic exes before, but *Jesus*."

Constance slaps Nate's shoulder again, and he startles. "Send it up," she instructs. He does as she asks, patting Ravi's arm once more as Constance says, "We shall do our valiant best, and all shall follow thy lead, Ravi."

Harry meets Ravi's eyes through the mirror and gives him a steady nod. He's about to say something—a thanks, perhaps—when they see the smoke.

*

A TRUST AGENT Ravi vaguely recognizes waits at the gate. He waves them through as soon as Ravi rolls his window down far enough to be recognized.

"Agent Abhiramnew. The Director is waiting for you by the crash site." The man points needlessly. Kind of hard to miss the smoking, fiery wrecks of two mangled jets spread across the tarmac, cordons set up all around. An attempt to shield the worst of the disaster from view has been partially achieved by parking trucks and luggage carts in a blockade around the area.

Probably some magic at work helping to conceal it, perhaps an artifact of some sort. Not Ravi's department.

"Fuuuuck," Harry says, peering out of the window.

A grim silence descends over the car.

A pair of agents move the cordon to allow them through. Ravi pulls up next to an ivory Rolls-Royce Cullinan and throws the car into park. He rests his forehead on the wheel for a few steadying breaths, gathering himself before he says, "Okay. You're going to meet my handler. My direct superior."

"Cool," says Harry as they all unbuckle their belts and ready their supplies. "Been running jobs for you Trusties a while. 'Bout time we get some face time with the brass."

Ravi licks his lips. "One more thing. It'll probably be obvious, but… She's my aunt." He slides out of the car before he can hear any reactions.

He hurries to button his jacket and smooth his lapels. He combs through his hair, attempting to be as presentable as possible. The rest of the team pile out of the Escalade as Ravi's aunt strides out of the back of her

Rolls-Royce.

Padme Abhiramnew is a striking bronze woman of indeterminable age with high cheekbones and a jawline like cut glass. Her onyx-black hair is tied back in a tight chignon. A full-length, high-collared dupioni silk jacket drapes over a classic pantsuit, the color shifting seamlessly from blood orange into black. Padme walks in heels like she could easily sprint in them, and her necklace of intricate filigrees of Sri Lankan gold takes up nearly the whole of her collar.

Ravi paces ahead to meet her. As the team's official liaison, it's his duty to make introductions.

"Ravi," she grates, eyes flinty. That's one feature they don't share; like the rest of her siblings, Padme's eyes are a lighter brown than Ravi's, more rust than topaz. "This is McAllister's team?"

"Ma'am." He nods sharply and motions to Harry. "May I introduce Harry McAllister?"

His aunt offers her hand to Harry, who clasps it for a business-like shake. "Padme Abhiramnew. Field Director. I appreciate your prompt arrival. We have a serious situation we wish to keep from going public for as long as possible. Your team has proven capable in the past. My nephew's reports have been favorable."

Ravi barely keeps his eyebrows from climbing up into his hairline. His aunt wouldn't outright claim him as family in front of outsiders unless she had an ulterior reason for doing so. Then Padme presses her lips firmly together and takes in all six-feet-plus of Val.

Ah. Right. Ravi belatedly wishes he had thought to inform Val of the lies he'd told his aunt about their relationship. A lot has happened since then. It feels like years ago now.

"It's a real pleasure to finally meet you," Harry begins, gushing in the likable fashion she often adopts on missions to charm the team into someplace they're not allowed to be. It usually works. "Wow, that outfit, you look seriously amazing. Anyway, this is my team. That's Val, she's an angel. This is Dr. Nathaniel Corbin, and this here is my sorta great-aunt Constance Shaw. And of course, *you* know Ravi." At this, Harry claps a hand over Ravi's shoulder in a shockingly proprietary gesture. He stands frozen as Padme's eyes narrow a hair. "Yeah, my team. Any idea what caused the crash yet?"

Taking in the group with one sweep of her piercing gaze, Padme reports in a gunpowder voice, "At 09:45, two private jets collided midair during a faulty takeoff. There was no warning beforehand and no maydays given. We have agents investigating the wreckage, but there were no survivors. At this time, we have no other information."

"But you must think the cause is supernatural, or you wouldn't have called us."

Padme shoots Ravi a veiled look that sends more steel into his spine. "One of those planes carried the entirety of one of The Trust's founding families, our London branch." Her chin lifts. "The number of supernatural forces that would seek to target us are beyond measure. This loss will be met with severe retribution."

"Plus, a real bummer for whoever was on the other jet too, right?" Nate interjects mildly.

Padme gives him the same look she'd give a dog who suddenly started talking, dark eyes glinting frost.

"All loss of life is, *of course*, a great tragedy, Professor Corbin. And who or whatever is responsible will be held accountable. Agent," she adds sharply, and Ravi snaps to further attention. "A word in private." She stalks back to her car, not waiting for his assent. Ravi spares an apologetic glance back before joining her.

Once they are out of earshot, she touches her necklace before she speaks; a subtle tell she's feeling out of sorts. Ravi automatically positions himself so both of their expressions will be shielded from view, crossing his arms over his chest.

"All the Harbridges?" he asks in a low murmur. That bloodline has long been staunch allies, tied to the Abhiramnews by bonds of battle and occasionally matrimony. Some of them were even likable. And some were children, which Ravi is desperately trying not to think about.

"All of them. Even young Archibald. They were here for an emergency meeting." Padme purses her lips and takes a half step closer. Her voice drops into a conspiratorial hush as she switches from English into a pidgin mix of tongues, a translanguaging cipher. "This cannot have come at a worse time. There have been a string of accidents and embarrassments across the old families for months now, and we are increasingly stretched thin to correct these errors."

"Accidents?"

"Indeed. The Eatons, who happen to be our most politically connected family here, have been compromised with various unfounded drug scandals. The Bhagavatis, our most magically inclined, have suffered a series of break-ins in at their Mumbai hold. All of their totems of power have been stolen or destroyed." Her lips curl into a snarl. "And now the Harbridges. They had significant sway over The Trust's purse strings. Without them, the families are going to be scrabbling at each other's throats for financial control. And the networks are less than useless. There hasn't been this much confusion among the seers since the Chosen fell."

Ravi can't lock down his tiny flinch. She notes his lapse with a disapproving downturn of her lip, then draws even closer until their shoulders are nearly touching. She's close enough he can catch the familiar scent of her jasmine perfume. "Our own branch suffered a data breach six months ago. It seemed unrelated until recently."

"A…data breach?"

"Yes. The Atlanta archives saw a minor break-in. Some of our records were compromised; nothing highly classified, but investigations have turned up nothing."

"Why didn't you tell me about this?"

"What good would that do? You're a field agent, Ravi." She sniffs, looking away. Her lips twist in brief conflict before she turns back to him, all solemnity and stoicism. "This is the kind of responsibility you will get to wield when you are wed. It's not very appealing, I know." She sighs, exhaustion hardly even showing in her exquisite posture. "Knowledge can be a great burden."

The words are out before he can think better of them, before he can remember his place. "I'd help you share it."

She scoffs. "Why do you think I've been pushing so

hard to find you a bride? There are factions—" The rest is bitten off sharply.

Ravi keeps his thoughts carefully compartmentalized. Between keeping Harry's new secret and his own old ones, he's on the knife's edge of deception, and this revelation stirs up such a searing, sudden spike of *anger* that it threatens to topple him off entirely.

"Factions within The Trust?" he asks slowly, steadily. At least, if his organization was being targeted from within, it meant Cayenne might not be involved.

Cold comfort.

"That is for me to worry about," Padme says, stern, shifting back to English. "Your mission is to find out who or what is responsible for this." She points Asian-style, with her chin, at the wreckage.

Ravi squares up and gives his aunt a firm nod. "*Ji.* Yes, ma'am."

Briefly, she brushes her fingertips to his shoulder, a faint touch that nevertheless imparts some strength, before they both rejoin the team.

The four are in a huddle, and by their serious faces

and Harry's expressive hand movements Ravi would wager they're talking strategy. Harry looks up as they approach. "Okay, here's the plan. Since your agent types got the wreckage covered, my team's going to check inside the airport."

"Is that so?"

Ravi leans a fraction away from his aunt as her voice achieves all the warmth and flexibility of stone.

"Yup," Harry breezes. "Ravi, you guys got any badges or anything that can get us in armed?"

Padme speaks before he can answer, her grating voice reaching new depths. "Very well, McAllister. It is your team; you *may* allocate them as you see fit. After a crash, any identification we can provide you with will only get you so far. There's Homeland Security to contend with." She sniffs with disdain. "No one will stop you investigating, but anything more suspicious will draw unwelcome attention."

"Discretion is my middle name," Harry says cheerfully.

"Your middle name is Alexandria." Padme smiles,

smooth and benign, and Harry's eyes widen. Padme gives Ravi a severe nod and waves toward the Rolls Royce. "Agent. The necessary materials are in the trunk."

He comes back with badges and hands them out before clipping his own on his breast pocket. Once situated, Padme reviews the team, her lips drawn into a firm line. She levels a significant glance at Ravi, both a gesture of support and a warning. "Report in if you find anything. I may seek you out, should new developments arise."

As they head toward the airport's private entrance, Harry spins around to Ravi, walking backward as they go, grinning in genuine pleasure. "Your aunt is *amazing*. Terrifying, obviously, but what a fucking presence!"

Ravi huffs a small laugh. "Yeah. In another era, she would have been a general."

Harry's grin fades into speculation, appraising Ravi head to toe. "Yeah," she says, turning back around. "Interesting."

They cross the hot tarmac for a few silent moments.

Eventually Nate asks, "Anyone else think she's smoking hot?"

Horrified, Ravi recoils from him.

"What? Sorry, striking. Handsome. Whatever you're supposed to call older women."

Constance hums agreement. "Clearly the Abhiramnews have been bred for qualities beyond simply carrying warrior blood."

"Good to know you're not a fluke, man," Nate says, clapping Ravi on the back. Ravi snorts and rolls his eyes, warmth creeping up his neck.

"Got any straight cousins?" Harry gives Ravi a salacious wink along with a nudge of her elbow.

"The chronomage has crashed two planes, killing many," Val says with all the nuance and finality of a tombstone.

Everyone falls silent.

When they reach the doors, they flash their badges and are quickly allowed through. Ravi finally dredges up some words as they enter. "They wouldn't. There's another explanation." His words are hollow, a thin vine of hope with no roots.

Archibald Harbridge was barely ten.

"Okay," Harry agrees kindly, and a swell of fondness for her climbs into Ravi's throat. "Could easily be a mistake. All we gotta do is find the Pepper and get them to reverse it, right? Even if they didn't cause this, they can fix it. We know they're here, we just gotta figure out where. And I have a hunch."

*

"WELL, FUCK. LOOKS like there are a few more highflyers lounges than I thought there'd be." Harry inspects the airport map with an irritated frown.

Nate peers over her shoulder. "Which one is the fanciest?"

"It doesn't exactly have a fanciness ranking on the map, Doc."

"Admirals Club," Ravi says absently, scanning the crowd for trouble.

Harry rolls her eyes. "Of course you'd know." She taps the spot on the map. "Okay, we start here. Unless anyone thinks it more likely Pepper is gonna slum it somewhere else?"

Ravi's face twists, frustrated with himself. "It's as good a guess as any." Why couldn't Cayenne have given him explicit directions instead of vague apologies? Why hadn't Ravi asked better questions? Too busy screwing and playing basketball. Some agent he was.

Rolling a palmful of yellowed snake vertebrae, Constance pipes up, "I've thrown the bones many times, and the divinations show they are indeed here still at this hallowed hub of flight." She spares a wide-eyed look up at the high-vaulted ceiling before fixing her attention back in front of her. "I am nearly certain I have devised a spell that shall work. I have not tested it, but it should suffice. One hopes."

"Well, it's worth a shot," Nate sighs, flipping through a battered little Moleskine notebook before returning it to his back pocket. "I've found virtually nothing credible in folklore. The only records about chronomancers hint they're incredibly rare, and any information about them goes for big, big money on the magical black market."

Ravi can't quite keep the distasteful curl from his lips. The occult market is a constant menace for The Trust. Trying to stay ahead of the trade of dangerous artifacts is a never-ending battle.

"I still have my maul," Val says helpfully, once again obscuring the celestial fire of her eyes with dark glasses.

Harry slides her penetrating gaze up to Ravi. "And should all else fail, we can tell Director Padme the whole unvarnished truth, and get the full might of The Trust in on this time wizard hunt, right?"

Ravi hesitates, teeth nearly cutting through his lip.

"Okay, so that's the second-to-last resort, before hammer time. Any idea what they're gonna look like? Since this is gonna be pre-Lucy?"

Ravi blinks at her. He hadn't told the team about that yet—but of course, she would have remembered that detail from Chicago. Not much slips past Harry.

"Not…exactly. I think…smaller," he says hoarsely, vividly flashing to their breathless, exhilarating spar, barefoot in the grass. "Not as...strong." Their thighs wrapped tight around his waist while drumbeats pulsed in the darkened club, eyes glittering golden.

Harry curses under her breath, walks up to Ravi, and digs into his breast pocket. She pulls out his mirrored sunglasses and shoves them into his hands. "Wear these, for chrissake."

He puts them on, relaxing a little behind their welcome shield. *Keep your shit together, kid.* He can do this. Just because he's recently found ways to let his wall down doesn't mean it's gone. Ravi builds it back up, brick by brick, while the group merges through the crowd.

On the way, Nate nudges Harry and points at a TV. Someone managed to get phone footage of the crash, and the local news has finally picked it up, despite Trust interference. Passersby slow down to watch, murmuring to each other, hands to mouths. The crowd's mood grows fraught with tension.

"No problem," Harry mutters to the team. "It's all going to be reversed." She shoots Ravi a companionable crooked smile. "We're eternal optimists, right?"

Despite himself, he barks a laugh. "That we are."

The Admirals Club concierge insists upon seeing their membership cards until the combination of their badges, Ravi's perfectly tailored attire, and Harry's smooth-talking convinces them otherwise. They make their way through the hall, the entryway winding back to the nearly empty lounge.

Alone at the bar with a flamboyantly tropical cocktail, Cayenne raises their half-empty glass up to the TV broadcast with a celebratory grin.

They look different, which Ravi expected. They look, as ever, *good*, which he did not.

Out of long habit he catalogs Cayenne's appearance, assessing threat. Ginger hair a completely unmanageable mop, more muddy orange than the smooth copper-red Ravi's fingers have learned so well. A sharp-featured face smattered with freckles, set off by russet brown eyes. Age difficult to discern, but somewhere close to Ravi's, maybe a few years older. Clothing nondescript but well-made in a flattering cut, with no identifying features. They have a waterproof bandage taped over the back of their left hand, cling film peeking from under the tape. Their clock tattoo must be fresh and unhealed; Cayenne once told Ravi the mark helped them shift more precisely and invisibly. A possible advantage to exploit, there.

They're alley-cat thin and wiry, unarmed but self-assured, confident, hidden claws ready to strike. Ravi's assessment remains the same as it had been back in Chicago; this one will fight dirty.

A few unchanged features. The same full lower lip, the same carefree smile. They carry themself the exact same way, as if they were sprawling across the lap of the world while looking up through half-lidded lashes.

Why had Cayenne bothered changing their form when they were always like this anyway? Beautiful enough to make the air in Ravi's lungs heavy, each breath an effort to draw?

Ravi keeps to the back of the group, blocking the door more because he's frozen in place than because of a conscious effort. By unspoken consensus, the rest of the team take position between him and Cayenne, Nate and Constance creating something of a human shield while Harry walks straight up to Cayenne with a friendly smile on her face.

With her long legs, Val easily overtakes her and looms over Cayenne as they watch the news of the crash with apparent delight. Though quiet on her feet, Val gives off a considerable presence, and Cayenne spins around on their barstool.

"*La vache!*" They look Val up and down with a slightly stunned expression. "Where did *you* come from, *maman*?" Same accent, same cadence. They grin with an expressive tilt of their head, such a familiar gesture that Ravi's heart aches.

Harry draws up beside Val and bumps her shoulder companionably into Val. Val doesn't move a single inch. "*Maman* here's a gift from heaven, wouldya believe it?"

"I absolutely *would*," they say, still with that flirtatious grin. "Would you ladies care to join me for a little celebration? I can call the bartender back." They raise their glass in salute.

"Maybe we would." Harry smiles and bats her lashes. "Whatcha celebrating? Did you kill a bunch of people today?"

Cayenne's grin freezes in place. They look past her to the rest of the team, gaze catching on the badges and the blocked exit. Ravi watches the set of their shoulders, the way they lean casually on the barstool while their feet are set to bolt.

"What a thing to ask, *chérie*."

Harry bobs her head to one side as if conceding a fair point. "Only weird if you didn't do it, Cayenne."

Every line of their body tenses and the mask of flirtation drops entirely.

"Huh. I suppose that isn't your name, is it?"

"It'll do well enough." They set down their drink and lob Harry a fox-quick smile. "Sure you don't want that drink? You can bring all your lurking little friends there." They aim their finger at Constance as she inches her way forward, then cock it back as if shooting a gun, their eyes skating back past her to size up Nate and Ravi.

"Sure, yeah." Harry smiles back, stepping in front of Constance as if by accident. "That sounds fun. It would also be *super* fun if you go back in time and stop those planes from crashing. Don't you think that'd be fun?"

Val somehow manages to loom even taller without moving a muscle.

Cayenne's smile fades. "And just who exactly are you, *ma chérie*?"

Constance sidles up beside Val. As she takes that last step to join them, Cayenne's attention snaps to her, reeling back as if she's a ravening beast instead of a mild-looking brunette in an eclectic mix of fashions.

"And *what* the fuck are *you*?" They gasp, rubbing their arms as if their skin is crawling. Cayenne's eyes dart. They're going to jump through time any second — Ravi can see it on their face. He moves closer, heart in his throat. Nate curses and sticks to his heels.

"Oh, me?" Constance says brightly. "Just a silly girl, really." She sweeps both hands up into the air and her pupils go pure white.

A series of things happen in sudden succession. Cayenne slips off the barstool and they move back a half step before their attention is caught by movement in the doorway. Their face twists from alarm to a furious, feral rage unlike anything Ravi has seen on them before. He glances over his shoulder to see his Aunt Padme enter the room.

"*Trust*," Cayenne snarls. They brace themself, a subtle tell Ravi recognizes from their many rewinds, but their hand doesn't go to their fresh tattoo—instead, they *flicker*. Their outline blurs in the air. Constance clenches her hands into fists and slams them together. Cayenne halts in place, expression contorting in confusion.

A sudden lurch tugs Ravi's gut. He can't move, stuck as if encased in glass; then, with the sickening feeling of being pushed off a cliff, Constance pulls her fists apart like ripping a blanket in half.

Then she sways and turns green. "*Bollocks*," she groans, staggering into Val, who doubles over with her hands on her knees. Harry, Nate, and Padme all slump to the ground, pale and disoriented. The grip of nausea is familiar, and Ravi sucks in a breath and swallows hard against it.

Shuddering, Cayenne falls over while swearing a filthy string of French, face so pale their freckles stand out like a reverse night sky. Instinctively, Ravi steps forward to go to them, but his head swims violently, dizziness threatening to drop him. Almost as bad as that last day at the lake house, but manageable. He straightens, shaking it off.

"Jesus *fucking* Christ." Nate groans from the ground. After a few labored breaths, he throws his hand in the air, and Ravi helps haul him back to his feet. "How in hell are you standing right now, man? *Ugh.*"

Once Nate can shakily manage to stand, Ravi crosses to Padme and helps her up. She leans against him for a handful of seconds before forcibly pushing away to stand on her own, her eyes slitted.

"Apologies, friends," Constance says in a tremulous voice as Val helps Harry. "Methinks I carried all of us backward in time? *God's blood,* that art unpleasant."

Cayenne snarls and gathers their feet under them.

Then they suck in a pained breath, and their eyes roll back as they curl up on themself like a beetle, the very picture of silent agony. Ravi lurches toward them, but the pain seems to only last for a second. Panting, Cayenne pushes to their feet, leaning heavily against the bar. They shuffle away from Constance. "*Où as-tu appris que? Bien joué, espèce d'idiot!* Where did *you* learn time travel? You could have killed us all!"

While everyone else is still reeling, Ravi looks up at the television screen. The timestamp places them hours ago, well before the crash. He turns to Padme. She's breathing raggedly, a hand pressed to her stomach. "It's before the crash. There's time to stop it from happening."

She eyes up Cayenne and opens her mouth.

"There's no time," he urges.

She glares at him in reproach but nods sharply.

"Oh, this is *perfect*," Cayenne crows. In the next blink they flow forward in a quick, snakelike strike. Val steps into Cayenne's way, but with a shifting blur Cayenne is no longer there, appearing well past her as she grasps onto empty air.

Ravi shoves Nate out of the way to safety and places himself between Cayenne and Padme. He remembers clearly the lessons they taught him back at the lake house—*distract me, mislead me*—but they move so fast, and his head still spins with Constance's spell.

He moves into a defensive pose, ready to block them. Cayenne sinks low and slows time, their slight form flickering at the edges, and they duck under his arm. The blade of Cayenne's open hand chops Ravi across the neck and they're easily past him, leaving him coughing.

Ravi pivots around. Cayenne has Padme by the throat, pushing her flat up against the wall with her arms trapped behind her back. She struggles in vain. Ravi tries to call out but has to work to drag in even a single breath, his windpipe bruised. Good hit.

"Whoa, hey." Nate raises his hands placatingly, face still wan and sweaty. "Let's not do anything crazy, eh?"

Cayenne scoffs, teeth bared. "*Oui,* we wouldn't

want to do anything crazy, now would we, Padme?" Their fingers tighten on her neck.

Cayenne knows his aunt by name. *How do they know her name?*

Imperious even now, she looks down her nose at them with a sneer. Cayenne draws in a deep breath, tensed to strike.

"*Bi-Aji, sa-wadili-ísa nanichi líhi bókoton,*" Ravi forces out the words they taught him over spiced hot chocolate in a warm cabin surrounded by falling snow. Another time, another life.

Cayenne's head whips to the side, brown eyes wide with surprise, grip loosening just enough for Padme to suck in a rattling breath. For the space of a single second Cayenne looks shaken, before their face twists in disdain.

"First, your accent is atrocious. Second, you fucked up the pronoun, you moron. And third; beautiful? Hardly. This *vieille salope ridée?*" With a venomous laugh they lean in closer to Ravi's aunt. "Very, very clever, Padme. Guess your seers are good for something after all." They tilt their head back sideways to aim a dagger smile at Ravi. "Are you one of her flunkies? Why don't you tell me where you were born? I'll make sure it never happens." They flutter their lashes. Then their free hand snaps down and deflects Padme's knee; she'd attempted to take advantage of their distraction, but barely moved at all before Cayenne blurred slightly and caught it. They coo in mock admiration and press harder against her throat. "Look at *you*! Those old bones still have some fancy moves, hmm?"

"Cayenne," Harry warns, slowly walking forward with both hands raised. "Just listen for a second."

Cayenne glares at her and spits, "If *anyone* makes a *move*, I will throw this bitch into the past before this airport was built. You know what was here, right where we stand?" They lean in close to Padme, pitching their voice into a loud stage whisper. "A racetrack. How'd you like to see those vintage automobiles up close and *very* personal, darling? It'll be quick. Better than you deserve, really."

"Easy," Ravi chokes out desperately. Is this it? Is

this what Cayenne was so sure Ravi would hate them for? Killing his aunt?

"Shut the fuck up, you fucking errand boy." Cayenne barely spares him a glance, giving Padme a shake.

"There's no reason anyone has to get hurt," Harry says calmly. "We've already jumped back in the past, so nobody is dead yet, right? We don't have any problem with you. There's no need to do anything rash. No one needs to get hurt here."

Val's hands clench into fists. Ravi knows she's not used to restraining herself from battle and is desperately grateful she's trying. "Why did you do it?" The angel's voice is a low, thundercloud rumble. "What reason to kill the Harbridges?"

Heaving a sigh, Cayenne rolls their eyes. "For fuck's sake, I *didn't*, big girl! The *only* reason I am here in this *dreary* little city in the swampy asshole of this country is because *this* cold-hearted bitch *told* me I'd be here." They sneer at Padme. "*You* accused me of killing all of your precious London family this very day. So, I thought, well? Why not? Sounds fun. So I came here to do just that, but someone beat me to it. The crash happened before I even got here."

A wash of relief spreads over Ravi like one of Constance's soothing balms. He knew there had to be some explanation. Cayenne couldn't have done it. He wishes he could stop time himself, to take a moment to sink into a chair and shake for a while.

"Already dead?" Harry asks, brows knit tight.

Nate still has both hands up in a soothing gesture. "Okay, that's good. That's *great*. You didn't crash two planes full of people. So why even come here? If you hate her so much, why do what she says?"

Cayenne gives Nate a sweet smile. "So many questions! And they say blonds are dumb. I came because it would have been my *pleasure*. The less of these Trust spooks around, the better." Padme's throat goes white under their grip, and Cayenne hisses, "Less of them to torture me."

Ravi's heart stops.

"We got to know each other pretty well, after all those months in your little dungeon, *n'est-ce pas,*

Padme?"

"I've never seen you before in my life," Padme grates.

"I'm a time traveler, sweetheart, *do* keep up."

Val steps closer. "No, Cayenne," and she unfurls her wings, white feathers spreading wide and reflecting the light.

"*Un ange?*" Cayenne whispers incredulously, shrinking away.

Constance steps closer, which Cayenne seems to take as the first credible threat, true alarm on their features. In a flash of sinuous movements, they spin Padme into a shield in front of them. They lock an arm around her throat, both her wrists caught in one hand at the small of her back. Ravi has never seen his aunt look so coldly furious; as a child, she had much of the same combat training Ravi had until her younger sister had been Chosen instead. Being helpless is an unfamiliar indignity.

"Don't *you* touch me, witch," Cayenne hisses, glaring warily at Constance. "I'm telling the truth. I had *nothing* to do with the planes. Though I can't say I wasn't pleasantly surprised."

"A lot of other people died," Nate barks, hands falling into fists.

Cayenne shrugs airily. "Lots of people die all the time, hot stuff. Like this bitch here is going to." They give Padme another little shake. Her bladed eyes lock onto Ravi's. *Take the shot,* they say. He shakes his head the smallest fraction. He couldn't even if he wanted to. He'd purposefully left his gun in the car.

Noting the exchange, Cayenne's arm tightens. "Oh, ho, what are the two of you plotting, hmm? So, this little pest *is* one of yours, Padme?" They turn a speculative look on Ravi. Val's wingspan stretches, feathers arching behind her back, and Cayenne's attention shifts back to her.

Ravi lifts his chin. "If you wanted to kill her you would have done it already."

Cayenne laughs at him. "You simple thing! I could have *already* killed her five times and just gone back so I could enjoy it a *sixth*." They bare their teeth in a ferocious grin.

Ravi stares at Cayenne, at their hatred, their rage. This side of them he'd never seen. What could he possibly say? *Sorry my family tortured you? Sorry the noble organization I've dedicated my life to has done the unthinkable to the person I love?* No. There were no words in any language that could express what he wanted to say.

"Why don't we all just take this down a notch?" Harry proposes. "Let's relax and have that drink, huh?"

Again, Cayenne laughs. "*This* one, I like. But no, *chère*, I think I *will* take care of that plane after all. If it pisses you Trust assholes off this much, it's worth doing."

"We're *not* Trust," Nate says emphatically at the same time as Harry says, "Come on, Red, just let her go, and we can all forget about this whole thing. You go your way, we go ours."

Cayenne pretends to consider this. "Hmm, tempting offer. Counteroffer—I just kill this withered cunt and be done with it." They press their cheek alongside Padme's in a grotesque parody of intimacy. "It'll be *très intéressant* to see what *that* does to the timestream, won't it, darling?"

Constance speaks in a rush. "Hark, I think I've chanced upon what I did wrong hence! Let me just…" As she raises her hands, Cayenne's eyes widen in alarm, and they push Padme roughly into Ravi and back away from Constance, nearly to the entrance of the club.

"*Putain*, you'll kill us all, you—"

Constance's hand blurs as it moves, leaving the arc of a ghostly afterimage as she holds her hand in front of her face. She puffs over her hand as if blowing a kiss to Cayenne.

Cayenne blinks, shakes their head like a wet dog, and staggers.

"Ah," Constance says with satisfaction. "I doth believe that hath done it."

Cayenne glares daggers at Constance, but the fury is a veneer over growing panic Ravi has seen before, after the nix's bite. That terrified, pinned butterfly look.

"Interesting *trick*, Glinda, but it won't last lo—"

Teleporting in front of Cayenne in a flurry of white

wings, Val kicks them hard in the chest. Cayenne goes flying into the wall and tumbles to the floor. The plaster doesn't crack, so it must have been a mere angelic love-tap.

"I did not use my hammer," she says.

Padme stiff-arms away from Ravi. "Quickly," she rasps, even more hoarse than usual. "Before—"

With a sharp Gallic curse, Cayenne bolts, clutching their shoulder. Before anyone can move, they dash around the hall.

"A rabbity one, 'pon my oath!" Constance shakes her hand and flexes her fingers like she's working out pins and needles.

"Fuck." Ravi drags both hands through his hair and moves to give chase.

His aunt stops him with a firm hand to his chest. "Foolish to go dashing off without a plan, agent. Here." She hands him her phone, open to a locator app. Her throat is bruised, every word clearly a struggle, but she ignores it. "Tracker in the front pocket."

"*Nice,*" Harry says in admiration.

"I shall take care of the planes," Padme continues. She touches her throat, scowls, and pulls her hand away. "You retrieve the chronomancer." Her eyes lock onto Ravi's. "Alive, agent."

He wants to grab her, shake her by the shoulders. Ask her what she knows about the torture. Is it only in an avoidable future, or in the present too? Or fuck, the *past*; is this what The Trust is? Is this the legacy Ravi was always supposed to inherit? What else is under the surface he's never been allowed to see?

But instead he swallows it all down, another leaden weight in his belly, and nods.

"Let's move," he says, and the team heads out with him.

*

"HOW LONG HAVE we got on that spell, Constance?" Harry asks. They struggle to weave through the thick throng of travelers until Valiance pushes out in front. The crowd parts around her, flowing easily to either side.

The hedge-witch taps her chin, following along in the angel's wake. "No more than fifteen minutes, I'd wager. If that."

Ravi checks the tracker app. "They're heading to the lower levels, by departures."

"More of a crowd to get lost in," Nate speculates, "or they're going to hop on a plane."

Val grunts. "If there is any chance the chronomage is still set on crashing those planes, we must stop them."

"Ix-nay on the ashing-cray, Val," Nate mutters with a nervous glance over his shoulder. "We're in an airport."

Harry groans in frustration. "Fingers crossed they aren't trying to board a plane. That would be super inconvenient."

"No," Ravi says distantly, then stops. "They wouldn't get on a plane unless they…" He breaks off from the group and strides to the nearest directory map. He holds the phone up, comparing positions.

Harry joins him. "You got something?"

Ravi chews his lip. "I have an idea."

"Great, 'cause I'm really coming up empty on those. Let's hear it."

"Harry, Nate. Can you two get to the control room for the airport tram?"

"The… You mean the Plane Train?" Harry's eyebrows go up. "I guess so?"

"Good. Cayenne…" Ravi can't meet anyone's eyes. He feels like the lowest, slimiest thing for breaking this promise, but his own personal honor doesn't matter if there are lives on the line. Keeping a promise, even one he made to Cayenne, isn't worth anyone's death. "They can't time travel at high speeds."

Harry blinks a few times. "Huh."

Nate says, "The tram isn't exactly a bullet train, my guy."

"Then make it faster."

Harry and Nate exchange a look.

"Okay," Harry says, cracking her knuckles. "We'll give it a shot. Val?" The angel turns to Harry, awaiting instructions. "Stay with Ravi. Help him however he needs."

An actual discernible expression crosses Val's face; reluctance. "I would prefer to stay by your side, Harry. But I shall see it done." She steps beside Ravi, and he can't deny he feels more at ease with her there, the same calm he would feel having a trusted weapon in his hands.

"I am useless with machinery," Constance offers. "Mayhaps I can help get the common folk out of harm's way?"

"Yeah. If we can clear a car, get Cayenne on it, and keep the tram moving, then I can…" Ravi swallows. "I can distract them until Val can get a hold of them. And…and we can decide what to do from there."

"A sound enough plan," Constance agrees. "There be no wriggling out from an angel's firm grasp. If mine spell—"

"No more time magic," Harry cuts in, looking downright queasy.

Constance scrunches up her nose. "Aye, that is likely wise. Many kinks still to work out."

Harry ties her hair into a messy topknot. "We have

a plan. Let's move."

"Wait," protests Nate, "we're just going to leave Ravi alone with that—"

"I know how to fight them," Ravi rasps. "In the Admirals Club, they had no trouble getting past *Val*. Nobody else..." He looks away, licking dry lips. He must do this himself. There's no other way to ensure Cayenne will stay safe. It has to be him. "I can do this."

Harry doesn't hesitate to say, "We believe you. Good luck. C'mon, Doc, time's a-wasting. Let's go hijack a train."

Nate throws his hands up. "Sure, I always wanted to go to federal prison in the Deep South." Together they veer off away from the concourse.

"We can use your magical powers."

"*My* magical powers? Which ones are those?"

"Being a good-looking, cis white guy. You're unarrestable."

As they disappear into the crowd, Ravi turns to Val and Constance. "I appreciate you—"

"Piffle!" Constance waves a dismissive hand.

"Time enough for fellow feeling later. The hunt is on!" And she starts marching away toward the tram. Amused despite himself, Ravi joins her, Val staunchly at his side.

Chapter Fourteen

DHYANA HAS ALWAYS come easily to Ravi, the practice of fixing his mind on one singular point, whether that point be a physical target or a more abstract goal. An essential tool in every form of combat he's learned, especially marksmanship, and usually Ravi can slip into a heightened state of dhyana without his concentration wavering.

Usually.

Half-hidden by the concourse pillars, in the very back of the empty tram car, Ravi leans against the furthest pole from the sliding doors. The doors are about to shut, and Cayenne will get their powers back any second. After a moment's hesitation, Ravi tosses up a quick prayer or two to any deities who might be listening. He hasn't exactly been the most devout for the past eight years, but it can't hurt.

The instant Cayenne skips backward into his view through the tram windows, Ravi's breath snags. Cayenne sidles back, avoiding Constance's advance from the left. Val flanks from the right, biceps popping as she crosses her arms and blocks the exit. Cornered, Cayenne skids to a halt. They glance over their shoulder, grin, and jump onto the tram the instant before the doors begin to close.

"*Bien tenté, connards,*" they laugh, giving the ladies a triumphant middle finger through the glass doors. The tram starts up and pulls away from the station. They turn, chuckling until they see Ravi.

Ravi would have sworn he was ready for anything, but when Cayenne merely heaves a put-upon sigh with a theatrical slump and a roll of their eyes, he admittedly hadn't prepared for that.

"*Merde*! Don't you assholes have better things to do?" Cayenne groans, kicking back to mirror Ravi's relaxed pose, leaning against a far pole. Orange hair tumbles into their eyes and they unsuccessfully try to puff up a breath to shift it, disarmingly unsuave. Harmless, amiable. They toss Ravi a fetching smile, with only a hint of mockery. "Why don't we talk a bit, hmm? You seem a chatty sort."

"Yeah," he tries, voice gravel. "We could talk about you not crashing those planes."

Cayenne's smile curls into a slight sneer. "Straight to business. Aren't *you* a hero in your secret agent sunglasses. You do know we're indoors, *oui?* Well, no one can accuse you Trust stooges of having an overabundance of intellect." They glance to the window. Ravi licks his lips, internal clock ticking down the two minutes between stops. By now Val will have already teleported Constance to the next location to guard the door, in case Harry and Nate haven't yet gotten control of the tram.

"I get why you want revenge." Insufficient words. Not even close to what Ravi wants to say to Cayenne, to *his* Cayenne, not this eerily familiar stranger who would have killed a woman if Ravi hadn't stopped them; if his Cayenne hadn't decided to teach him the right words to say. "That's why you've been targeting Trust families."

A derisive laugh. "Keep up, you empty suit. I didn't do *anything* to their precious *families*. Seems like an awful lot of work." Cayenne tilts their head to the side, tapping their bottom lip. "Not a bad idea, though." Shrugging, they hook an elbow around the pole as they peer out the car. "Well, as *riveting* as this conversation has been, hero, this is my stop. *Au revoir!*" They push off toward the doors in anticipation. As the tram continues without slowing down, Cayenne stops and slides a narrow glare at Ravi from the edge of their eyes.

Ravi masks his relief. The others must have managed to get control of the tram. It passes right by the terminal without stopping.

"Cleverer than you look," Cayenne snorts.

The tram jerks. Cayenne throws their hands out to

catch their balance as the speed increases. Their gaze locks onto Ravi. Every hair on the back of his neck stands up. "Is it just me, darling," Cayenne says brightly, "or does it feel like we're speeding up?"

One moment Cayenne stands with one hand to their canted hip, smiling blithely, and the next instant they flow forward in a staccato blur, one hand already fisted in Ravi's hair. They slam his face into the nearest pole. It's a quick, brutal strike, and it nearly knocks him out cold.

Pain blooms sharp at Ravi's upper lip as his sunglasses fly off his face. Instinctively, he twists his thumb up over the pressure point of Cayenne's wrist. Their grip breaks. He ducks under their arms and jabs an elbow hard into their solar plexus, buying himself some space. Feet planted, he brings his arms up to shield his face, heart rabbiting. A wet trickle makes its way down into his beard, the taste of copper thick on his tongue.

Cayenne skips back, teeth flashing through a wide grin. "Oh, look at that! Seems as if that little inhibitor spell is wearing off." They shake their head in pretend sorrow. "Uh-oh, and here's little old you, locked up in here with *me*."

This isn't his Cayenne, Ravi has to remember, forcibly blinking off unconsciousness. He's a stranger to them. This is not a sparring session. This is a dangerous chronomage capable of anything. Ravi could never hurt Cayenne, but *this isn't Cayenne*.

If he keeps telling himself that, maybe he'll believe it.

Next time Cayenne advances, Ravi is ready. They fly at him with fast, precise strikes. Ravi concentrates on blocking the worst of the blows, staying on the defensive for now. Hopefully Cayenne will underestimate him, leave an opening he can use. *Nobody guards against a dull blade*, his instructors often said.

Cayenne fights a little differently than he's used to, likely from the new tattoo. They move in a faint blur of motion, like an afterimage on film. No doubt they could still send their consciousness back to an earlier state, which is the chief danger. If Cayenne can concentrate enough to rewind their mind to before the team arrives

Cayenne growls and launches into a ruthless series of unrelenting strikes at vulnerable spots: a kick at his groin, a rake at his eyes, a brutal knuckle strike to his temple. Deflecting each blow, Ravi notes from the depths of his battle-calm that those last two hits are potentially lethal.

Cayenne levels more curses at him. Every time they do, they leave their flank slightly open. Typical. More concerned with getting the last word in than in properly protecting themself.

Cayenne is fast, but Ravi is too; trained to end monsters with quick, ruthless efficiency. He ducks under their guard. Spinning up behind Cayenne's back, he slips an arm around their throat. Forearm on one side of their neck and Ravi's bicep on the other, he applies pressure to the carotid arteries. A few seconds more should render Cayenne safely unconscious.

Cayenne scrabbles against him, jabbing up for his eyes. Ravi keeps his head out of reach between their shoulder blades and squeezes.

The tram jolts as the speed increases yet again,

knocking Ravi's grip loose for a split second. Cayenne squirms sideways. They yank out of Ravi's chokehold and mule-kick him back into the wall.

"*Merde*," they cough, twisting away from him. They're having a harder time slowing time now, their shape skipping like a broken record instead of a smooth blur. Cayenne steps in for a kick, and Ravi shifts his block low. Cayenne blurs up instead, and fuck, it's a feint, and he fell for it. Ravi braces for another merciless blow. He doesn't expect a simple, hard, backhanded slap: not any sort of martial technique, just raw fury and hatred. Ravi's ears ring. The sting takes him by surprise, enough for Cayenne to spin around onto his back and lock both arms around his throat.

Instead of struggling, Ravi uses their momentum to slam Cayenne back, trapping them against the reinforced glass. The air releases in a pained whoosh, their arms loosening. Ravi grabs their elbows and flips them over his head, their heels brushing the ceiling before he slams them down onto the floor.

Like a far-off mirage, their edges go fuzzy. Ravi

curses, grabbing the pole to jump up, barely keeping his feet off the floor as Cayenne unblurs, exploding into a sweeping kick that would have knocked Ravi's legs out from under him.

"How the *fuck* are you doing that? Did that bitch used to have a better quality of thug back now?" Cayenne hops up onto their feet and slams forward while Ravi is still off-balance.

Ravi's head narrowly misses the wall as Cayenne tries to bear him down to the floor. Cayenne is smaller than him, slighter, but in any melee fight, strength always comes in second to speed. He blocks another hit to his face and takes their wrists in a disarming twist.

Time skips like a poorly edited film and suddenly Cayenne is straddling Ravi's chest. Their knees dig into his shoulders, trapping his arms at his sides. It's a bad position to be in, one of the worst. Ravi let himself get overconfident, thinking one friendly spar could have prepared him to match skills with a damn time traveler.

Cayenne grins over him, a different face wearing the same beautiful smile. The last time they'd been in this position, Cayenne had smiled like that. The memory lances through Ravi with more force than when he'd been slammed into the metal pole—guiding Cayenne's toned thighs as they slid down onto his cock; the indent of his thumb on the plush pinkness of their mouth as they sucked his fingers while riding him; taking him in greedily everywhere their body possibly could, as if they would never get enough of him.

Cayenne winks and says, "Decent moves, asshole, but I'm getting dreadfully *bored*," then they lean the blade of their forearm against Ravi's throat and press down.

He sucks in one last breath before his oxygen is cut, wriggling uselessly. Cayenne has him completely pinned. He let himself get fucking *trapped*. Cayenne smiles pleasantly as they press harder on his windpipe, so close he can feel their breath ghost across his mouth. Ravi twists and squirms but finds no leverage. No way to mislead them, nothing to distract them, he's choking and *helpless*...

Ravi surges up and kisses them.

Cayenne jerks back, eyes wide with shock.

The train speeds up, and the whole tram shakes with the force of it, rails creaking alarmingly. Ravi takes advantage of Cayenne's surprise to buck them off balance, fisting his hand in their shirt and throwing them off, sucking in big lungfuls of air.

Cayenne glances around with panic as they stagger to their feet, a familiar trapped expression before their gaze locks onto Ravi, a thin line creasing their brow. Using the wall for balance, Ravi pushes himself up, rubbing his throat.

There's movement behind Cayenne, a brief rush of wind. They're too busy staring at Ravi to notice. A smear of his blood reddens their lip. For once, Cayenne seems to have nothing to say.

Ravi looks past them and nods at Val.

The angel strikes. Her arms close around Cayenne, easily holding them up off the ground as if they weigh less than one of her wing feathers. Kicking wildly, Cayenne struggles, but Val's grip is tight and immutable. After some fruitless effort, they give up. Sagging in her arms, Cayenne sucks in breath after breath while their eyes dart around, a cornered animal.

"Stop," Valiance orders. "There is no point in fighting anymore."

Cayenne curses creatively in French.

Ravi coughs, massaging his windpipe. "Thanks, Val," he chokes out.

"You said to come when the train was at its top speed."

"I did. Thanks anyway."

"What shall be done now?"

Cayenne struggles anew, pleading, "You can't take me back to that fucking cell, *s'il vous plait, non—*"

Ravi's heart seizes again behind his breastbone. Nothing he can do about that now. Or yet. Or will do. *Fucking* time travel. "The lake house?"

Val shakes her head. "I do not think it wise to keep a chronomancer in a densely populated suburb."

Ravi touches his tender lip, tasting copper. "*I don't know, Val, I...*"

"You could let me go," Cayenne wheedles, ceasing

their struggle.

Ravi quirks a brow at them.

"Look," they say seriously, "your friend was right. No one has died, no one has even been hurt." They give Ravi a dismissive once-over. "No one of importance, anyway, so what is that delightful American expression? No harm no foul, *oui?*"

Val and Ravi trade inscrutable glances.

"*Mademoiselle Angélique,* as beautiful as you are surely compassionate, there's no reason to do anything rash, *oui?*" Cayenne's pleading expression falls, and they bite their lip, silvery voice a barren husk. "I was just…so *angry.* Seeing that woman's face. After everything…everything she did to me. To make me obedient." They droop in Val's grasp. "You can't know what it was like."

This isn't my Cayenne, Ravi has to tell himself to keep his feet in place, to keep from taking Cayenne out of Val's arms and into his own.

"But you're right. I haven't done anything *wrong.* As much as it pains me to admit, thank you for stopping me, truly." Cayenne peers up at Val, eyes wide and sincere. "I don't want to hurt anyone."

Val glares, then sighs. "Ravi?"

Cayenne scoffs under their breath. "Isn't that amusing. Ravi the *ravageur*. Very fitting."

Ravageur, a destructive, ruining pest. On that dock in the Seychelles while under the influence of the nix venom, Cayenne had spat that at him, and he had, at times, wondered about it. Maybe they'd been hallucinating back to this fight on the tram, or some version of it that had now been overwritten. No telling what else has changed since Cayenne has been stopped from crashing the planes or killing Padme.

A little thrill of elation begins to take hold, the first edges of optimistic hope Ravi had cautiously shelved this whole time. He'd changed Cayenne's past. Without this hidden regret of past mistakes, there was no longer any reason to think he and Cayenne couldn't have a future together. It's *beyond* what Ravi had hoped for.

He gives Val a weighted look.

There's a downward curve to her mouth, but she

nods. "Very well. I will teleport you to a park in the city of Chicago. That will put you well out of harm's way. Do not try coming back here to reverse anything we have undone."

Cayenne shakes their head emphatically. "Definitely not, no way. I would be a fool to try and trick an angel, and I'm many, many, *many* things, but never a fool." They slant a suspicious glare at Ravi, tongue swiping at the smudge of blood his kiss had left on their lip, before telling Val, oozing sincerity, "Take me *wherever* you like, I swear I'll be well out of your hair. I won't even stay in this *year*. You won't be seeing me again, *je vous promets*."

"Too late for that promise, but see that you keep the other. I shall see you shortly, Ravi." Ivory wings flare wide, and both she and Cayenne disappear.

Alone, Ravi sucks in a shaky breath, absently tunneling his fingers through his hair. He leans back against the wall, swaying with the rocking of the tram. He sits there for maybe a minute before he startles, suddenly remembering where he is. Hijacked tram going at unsafe speeds. Right.

He calls Harry and gives her the all-clear. The Plane Train immediately slows with an unhealthy squeal and comes to a halt at the next stop. Ravi buttons up his jacket, fixes his cuffs, and walks off the tram.

*

"HEY, HOW'D IT go—*whoa*. Are you *okay*?" Harry is the first to lay eyes on Ravi as the group reconvenes in a secluded area near the doors leading to the private jets.

"I'm fine," Ravi says, brushing aside her concern. "Are you? Nice work with the tram. Any trouble getting access to the controls?"

Harry waggles her hand side-to-side, but any further explanation is interrupted by Nate bounding up with Constance alongside him, both beaming smiles.

"Okay, so that went pretty good, right? No crashes, no deaths, no rampant destruction of the fabric of time. Yeah, pretty damn good, I'd say." Nate slaps Ravi on the shoulder and double-takes. "Except for your face! *Jesus.* Did Cayenne do that to you?"

Ravi touches his lip again. Annoyingly, the cut is still bleeding. No wonder people in the hallways had given him such a wide berth. "It's just a split lip," he says with some bafflement. The team have seen him get worse from a dozen monster hunts. Hell, he's had worse from catching the wrong end of a staff while training as a kid. There are more important things to focus on right now.

Constance snorts and grabs Ravi's chin in a firm, unyielding grip. Good thing he keeps his beard shorn so close or doubtless she would have yanked it without hesitation. "Just a split lip *and* cuts all around thy brows, *and* mayhaps a cracked eye socket, thou great brawny fool." She gives his face an insistent tug until he awkwardly bends to put his eyes level with hers.

"Ow, Constance, what the—"

"Stay still. *Honestly.*" One-handed, Constance fishes a small jar out of her satchel and flicks off the top. "'Tis merely an unguent. Hold thyself." Despite her stern tone her touch is gentle as she swabs ointment over Ravi's forehead and at his temple.

His head does ache a lot, now he thinks of it. That pole hit him pretty hard. Lucky he hadn't been knocked out. A slight tingle permeates into his skin wherever the medicine is spread.

"What's in this?" he asks warily.

"Cockerel blood and mashed frogs' eyes." Constance winks at his alarm. "Only comfrey and honey, you numpty, with some healing magic to speed matters. There," she says with satisfaction, finishing with one last thick smear over his split lip. "Attempt to not lick the remedy off for a few minutes, if you can resist." She lets him go with a pat to his cheek.

"I… Thanks, Constance." Ravi isn't sure what the correct response is to mothering. Also, he has no idea what a "numpty" is.

Constance waves his thanks away. Val teleports into being next to Harry. Her wings are again hidden wherever angel wings go when not brandished.

Grinning, Harry rocks up on her toes and stuffs her hands in her jacket pockets. "There's *maman* now! How was the trip?"

"Acceptable. The chronomage has been safely deposited in Illinois. I am satisfied with their assurance they will not attempt to return to this airport."

"If you're satisfied, then I am too." Harry sighs with relief. "So, the fight went okay?"

Ravi shrugs one shoulder. "Only because you two got the tram under control so quickly. Seemed like smooth work."

Harry fake-coughs into her fist. "*Ahem*, yeah, so I got into a *little* tussle with the guy operating the tram."

"Harry is invulnerable!" Nate butts in excitedly. "She's got maybe bulletproof skin or something?"

Harry groans and covers her eyes.

Ravi's entire body tenses. "Someone *shot* you?"

"*No*," she says with a glare at Nate. "But normally I would have been cut pretty good on that metal panel." She holds up her pristine hands.

"I did say you might get special Chosen powers in addition to the visions. You got the invulnerability. That's great news." Ravi smiles. "Makes my job keeping you alive easier."

"Cool," Harry breathes, examining her hands.

"She's crazy tough," Nate adds. "We did some experimenting."

Harry looks horrified. "Okay well, I'd love if you made it sound less like middle school frottage, Doc, *fuck*."

"I'm dying to know." Nate easily changes the subject, turning to Ravi. "What was that you said to Cayenne when they were about to…well, back there with your aunt?"

Ravi shakes his head ruefully. "Not sure. I wasn't able to find any translation online, but I only learned it by ear."

Val cants her head aside, her high ponytail falling in an ashen waterfall over one shoulder. "One moment." White flame briefly flickers past the frames of her dark glasses. "*Bi-Aji, sa-wadili-ísa nanichi líhi bókoton* is an imperative that in English may be translated as 'You must protect this beautiful boy.' The language is Lokono, also known as Arawak. It is rare, but still spoken by a handful of native peoples in South America. By the dialect, the location of origin may be French Guiana or Suriname."

Everyone stares at Val.

"And you can just speak this rare South American language?"

"Knowledge of human languages may be granted to me if it is deemed of significant importance."

"What?" Nate slaps a hand to his forehead. "'Granted'—you're literally able to download from the *cloud*? That is unbelievably cool! Val, why have you never mentioned this before?"

"Nobody has ever asked."

"Just…wow. I've got a lot of historical texts I'd love you to try and translate."

Taking advantage of the distraction, Harry slings an arm around Ravi's shoulders and walks him a few steps away from the group. She lowers her voice. "Be real with me, Rav. You're okay?"

"I'm…" He forces a short, paper-thin laugh. "Yes. No. It's been…"

"It's been a day."

"Yeah. Are *you*?"

"Yes. No." She offers a smirk she swiftly drops. "I know we're due a celebration for fixing whatever bad shit Cayenne was gonna do—you gotta be *stoked*—but there was some heavy stuff revealed back there. Did you…" She gnaws her lip, then asks frankly, "Did you know The Trust employs torture?"

Ravi jolts as if stricken by an electric shock. "*No.*"

Harry sighs. "Okay. I didn't think so. This is…" She ruffles her messy bun into an even more tangled mess. "This is the world-saving organization that guides the Chosen? This is who my monster-hunting team has been working for? This is— It's your *family* fucking *business*, Ravi, *fuck*, I'm so sorry."

He doesn't allow their eye contact to waver, his jaw tense. "It might be only in the future. In which case… Harry. *I'm going to change it.*"

Her gaze sharpens, and it feels as if she can see through him, examining how far down his sincerity goes. Seemingly satisfied with whatever she finds, Harry nods. "What if it isn't just in the future?"

"Then I'm going to tear out any corruption by the roots," Ravi says, a simple declaration he means with every atom of his being. "My aunt let slip there's inter-factional disputes within The Trust. I don't care how long it takes me. I'm going to fix it."

"I suppose that would be easier with the weight of the Chosen behind you."

"Harry, you… I never got to have a choice; being Chosen or not, being involved in The Trust. You do. If you want to keep this secret, I'll help you."

She looks away. "Let me think about it."

"Whatever you decide, I'll back your play."

"I know, dude." Harry shakes off a fragile smile and slips back into her customary casual slouch. She jams her hands in her pockets and wryly laughs, "Now we just have to deal with your terrifying aunt."

Chapter Fifteen

THERE'S A TRICK to staying straight-faced through any truly scathing scolding. Ravi learned the technique years ago; he listens with one ear, in case he'll be called upon to repeat any details of the rebuke, but otherwise he lets his mind race ahead. How soon can he get in touch with Cayenne? Where best to start Harry training with the urumi? How to even begin unraveling the rotten threads woven into The Trust?

"—cannot fathom how you allowed something so important, so unbelievably dangerous, to slip through your grasp. Do you have any idea how much havoc a chronomancer is capable of—"

"Hey, lady." Nate's voice cuts through Ravi's spiraling thoughts, bringing him back to solid ground. "Wherever you bought your opinions, I hope you kept the receipt."

Aghast, Ravi slowly turns his stare onto Nate. The professor's irked expression doesn't quaver in the slightest as Padme draws herself up. Ravi would swear he feels the frosty breeze pouring off her like dry ice.

"Your team had an objective to fulfill, and—"

"And we did it. The objective was to uncrash those planes, and mission accomplished. Your London branch is alive because of us."

He interrupted her. Nate actually *interrupted* his Aunt Padme. Always running heedlessly into danger, this guy, and without even the hockey stick. Ravi braces to throw himself between them the same way he'd block a ravening monster attack.

With only one more ounce of pressure, Padme's caustic voice could physically cut skin. "And in doing so, you allowed an unthinkably dangerous individual loose. A couple of planes may be the least of our worries."

"A dangerous individual who *knows* you," says somebody. Oh shit, it was him, Ravi realizes. *He'd* spoken those words.

Fast on his heels Constance adds, "Your future actions and infractions against the time wizard will spark this whole event, Lady Abhiramnew." Constance shapes her speech with a soothing, deferent tone; a verbal curtsey absent of thees and thous. "Surely any further hostilities will be avoided if you merely resolve to not engage with the time wizard."

Padme sniffs disdainfully. "You are referring to the ridiculous accusation I keep people in some sort of torture chamber? You believe a thing that came out of that chronomage's mouth? Use your brains. We don't torture powerful mages we wish to recruit. The whole notion is ridiculous, clearly a ploy to gain sympathy. I've known many accomplished liars in my life, and he is certainly one of them." It's punishingly hard not to correct the pronoun, but there's no way for Ravi to explain how he knows that personal detail.

Constance's manner is carefully respectful. "Trying to control those who possess magical abilities rarely ends well, my lady."

"Your clan was infamous for killing demons, Miss Shaw, but our histories show you often hunted dangerous mages as well, did you not?"

"Aye," Constance says, a little of her harmless demeanor receding, a subtle shadow of something hard and unyielding underneath. "Indeed we did. Better us than the witch-hunters."

"Yet you were the one to devise a spell to hobble a chronomancer, Miss Shaw, not us 'witch-hunters.'" Padme's sharp gaze turns speculative.

"Look," Harry interrupts with hands spread wide. "I appreciate it's been a stressful day. But like Nate said, we've done the job. Wild success. Yay, team."

Padme turns a viper's eye on Ravi. "I suppose you have nothing useful to add, agent? Perhaps rather than make me wait for your surely insufficient report, you could simply tell me what it was you said to convince the hostile party not to murder me. A trigger phrase? Code words? How did you come to learn them?"

Ravi curses himself as the worst kind of idiot. Saying that right in front of his aunt? She *taught* him a fair amount of spycraft, how could he have been so *careless*—

Val lifts her head from her still, silent vigil over Harry's shoulder. "I know many human languages," she says.

Ravi clamps down on his surprise before it can show.

"On occasion, I receive useful information from my superiors before dangerous missions," Val continues. It's the closest to deception Ravi has ever heard her get; every word the complete truth but arranged in such a way that Padme will inevitably draw the wrong conclusion from two unrelated statements.

Padme purses her lips. "Any other useful information you feel inclined to share, Valiance? Perhaps McAllister doesn't mind running her team so lackadaisically, but in my experience withholding vital intel often has disastrous results."

"It is insubordinate for you to speak of Harry that way."

Ravi tenses. Harry's eyes flash wide with alarm. "Uhhhh hey, Val—"

Val ignores her, speaking as calmly to Padme as if she was discussing the weather. "You owe Harry your fealty."

Eyes narrowed, Padme takes a quick appraisal over the team's nervous expressions and postures. "Ravi," she says slowly, voice dragging like wet silk, "what is your angel talking about?"

Ravi swallows and looks to Harry, mind racing for any plausible explanation besides the truth.

Harry meets his eyes, sets her shoulders, and nods.

He's incredibly proud of her.

"Harry has been Chosen," Ravi says, faintly astonished his voice doesn't waver. "The sword came to her this morning."

Padme sniffs. "What nonsense are you spinning

now?"

After a deep inhale, Harry mutters under her breath, "Fuck me, okay, here we go." She pulls the scalloped coin out of her pocket and holds it in the flat of her palm. She glances at Ravi, gulps, and the coin turns into the urumi.

Padme steps back with a sharp, shocked gasp.

"It's hers," Ravi says softly. "It's the same."

Padme stares. "I know it better than you," she says faintly, without rancor, before she stretches out her fingers, only to jerk them back as if singed. Jaw tight, she asks Harry, "May I?"

"Sure." Harry shrugs. Padme takes the urumi, implacable expression melting into equal parts uncertainty and reverence. Ravi looks away, giving her a moment of privacy. He knows how she feels.

Padme doesn't linger overlong before she passes the urumi back. Once it's in her hand, Harry staggers a little. Murmuring concern, Constance steps in to clasp her elbow.

"I'm fine," mutters Harry, "just more memories."

Padme turns away, taking a few seconds to collect herself, and when she next speaks much of her frost has been shaken off. "We thought it lost. We thought maybe…" Her eyes dart between Ravi and Harry. "We thought perhaps there wouldn't be another Chosen, despite the signs. But here you are." She turns her gaze upward with a slight shake of her head. "I expect Ravi has filled you in on the details?"

Harry tucks the urumi, a humble coin once more, away. "Think so, yeah. I'm supposed to prevent an apocalypse, right?"

"That is broadly true, yes. Not every Chosen thwarts a world-ending event, but should such an event come to pass, the Chosen is the only one who can stop it. This is…" Her focus shifts to Ravi. He must be mistaken, but for just a split second he could swear he reads sympathy there.

Whatever odd mood leaves Padme as soon as it arrives, and she draws herself up with dignity. "This is excellent news. It finally answers a question long unanswered. High-ranking members of The Trust have long known the next Chosen would be revealed in this city. That is why key members have relocated here. There were some contradicting visions, but they all agreed on that point: the Chosen would be found here."

"Contradicting visions?" Constance asks.

Padme sniffs and rolls her eyes. "Some said there would be some kind of great storm, a hurricane or a monsoon, that would wreak devastation upon us. The sort of poetic nonsense the clairvoyant are fond of. An equal number insisted the storm would miss us altogether and was no threat. I have been arriving at the conclusion that our seers were becoming increasingly untrustworthy, but…" Briefly she lays a hand on her bruised throat, frowning. "With a chronomage in the mix, perhaps it is no wonder after all. This changes a great many factors."

Monsoon. Ravi briefly becomes a statue, an unfeeling thing of stone, before he wrangles the roiling chaos of his thoughts into a manageable shape. He's vaguely aware of Padme and Harry speaking to each other, other teammates occasionally adding to the conversation, but

Ravi is present in body only.

Only two people in the world would hear *monsoon* and know it translates to *Cayenne*. But Padme had said the seer's opinions were split, an equal amount claiming there was no threat. And hadn't the team averted any great disasters Cayenne might have caused today?

Ravi's dread gives way to relief. Cayenne hadn't killed anybody, and they got away unhurt and uncaptured. There's time enough for Ravi to undo any harm they may face in the future. They hadn't even caused some sort of paradox where Ravi and the rest forget they ever met Cayenne, or whatever time travel bullshit they had been so worried about. Things turned out fine, navigated through to the best-case scenario.

If Ravi didn't have a responsibility to Harry, he would have already left to call Cayenne. Meet them somewhere and tell them he's forgiven them. That he's never going to let them go.

He snaps back to the present as Harry claps him on the shoulder. "Yeah, he said something to that effect already. I can sign up for some training, sure."

from bouncing with anticipation. It feels like it's been forever since that last rewound day at the lake house; long, endless weeks without seeing Cayenne, without their touch or their voice or their smile, without hearing them whisper in his ear, hesitant but heartfelt, *I love you.*

Ravi has never said those words to anyone before. Which language should he use? Will they be more delighted with the Hindi —*main tumse pyaar karta hoon* — or would it mean more in their own tongue? If he took their face in his hands and whispered *je t'aime, j'adore* in between kisses? His heart swells, and he has to wrench himself back down from his reverie to catch the tail of the conversation.

"More intel is always useful, of course," Harry says. "Sounds great to me, whatever you can offer. The thing I'm still hazy on is… What's my *job*? You keep talking about guiding me on my path, and how The Trust and the Chosen are, like, integral parts of each other, but what am I supposed to *do*? Day to day." She illustrates the passage of time with an expressive twirl of her hand.

Padme leans closer. "You are the tip of the sword,"

she tells Harry, her throaty voice carrying a clarion ring. "You are a light in the darkness. A guardian between this world and the supernatural forces that threaten to destroy it. You are the living avatar of the will of Durga. You are humanity's shield against evil."

"No pressure," Ravi adds with a crooked little smirk. Harry's visible nervousness breaks into a grateful grin.

"So I don't have to quit my private eye gig, is what you're saying."

Padme's lip twitches downward. "Your finances will be taken care of, if that is a concern."

"It's not." Harry shrugs. Looks like she still wants to keep the diamond money a secret. Ravi says nothing.

"Very well. You may, of course, live your life as you choose, insofar as it does not interfere with your responsibilities."

Harry snaps her fingers. "There it is. My responsibilities. What are those, exactly?"

"There is much to discuss, but that can be saved for another time. For now, know we will send you briefs on likely occurrences we believe your team's talents are suited to. We don't expect you to leap into an apocalyptic scenario without some field training." Padme favors her with a slight smile.

"Yeah, I'm down for that. It's basically what we've been doing anyway; investigating and solving supernatural threats. That's our comfort zone, for sure. As for training, Val has already voluntold me I'll be working with her every day to get more, you know, swole. But the weapon stuff? I'm already a pretty good shot, but I know fuck-all about swords and shit. I suppose you can give me the rundown, Ravi?"

"Sure, some stuff. But for the urumi, I can only teach you basics." Before today, he hasn't touched an urumi in nearly a decade.

Padme adds, "The urumi itself will assist you in battle, but to become truly proficient we will have you meet with one of our masters. It is not an easy weapon to wield."

"No shit." Harry glares at the coin.

"The urumi is like the power of the Chosen itself. A

fearsome weapon to your enemies, but also a danger to you, if you do not understand how to wield it." She's being metaphorical; the urumi cannot hurt the Chosen who wields it. But not knowing how to use its centuries of wisdom can be more fatal than the whip-like blades.

For once, her veneer of nonchalance fades, and Harry goes thoughtful. She picks up the coin and flinches, blood draining from her face. She shakes her head and sticks it in her pocket, then stands up. "Excuse me a moment," she says thickly and makes her exit, bedroom door shutting behind her.

Padme uncrosses her legs, adjusting the fall of the fine fabric. "The memories," she guesses.

"Yeah."

She sighs a note of regret. "It's a much easier transition with the proper ceremony." She scrutinizes the apartment. Harry had done a hasty decluttering when they arrived, kicking laundry under the couch and sweeping a counter full of half-empty glasses into the sink. Her video game controller and headset still rest on the coffee table. Padme looks at them as if they were

"If you finish that sentence, Director, it is the highest treason," Ravi says mildly. He keeps his heart rate from pounding, his face impassive. This is a test. Everything with her is. Nothing is ever straightforward. She's testing him…only he's not sure which way she wants him to fall.

"She is unsuitable," Padme hisses through her teeth.

"She is Chosen."

He can almost hear her teeth grinding.

The door swings open. Harry plunks back down in the armchair, her eyes faintly bloodshot. A few water droplets cling to her hairline where she must have splashed her face in the sink. She avoids looking directly at Ravi. "Sorry, right, I'm back. What did I miss?"

"Nothing of import," Padme says smoothly. "Well, if you have no further information about how the urumi came to you…"

"I'll let you know as soon as the lab finds anything. I'm dying to know that myself."

Padme pats Ravi's knee, and he can't help but

startle. She's never done that before in his life. "Then let us discuss the wedding," she says brightly.

Harry coughs. Ravi shuts his eyes.

"Surely my nephew told you this would come up. My apologies if this comes as a shock."

Harry strikes her breastbone with a closed fist, as if dislodging a stuck frog. "Uh, yeah, he mentioned the, uh, the possibility." She squeezes her eyes shut, and when she opens them, she meets Padme's gaze unflinching. "Look, we can save the bulk of that convo for later. But I'm not outright saying no."

Ravi blinks at her incredulously. Why would she... What was...

"Excellent," Padme says, satisfaction snipping her syllables clean. "A union with my nephew would bring you many advantages as Chosen, Harry."

"I'm not insensible to the politics involved. Look, I've never seen wedding bells in my future, and you can't work very long as a private eye before the whole notion of romance itself collapses as an ideal, so, yeah. It's not out of the question. Ravi's obviously gorgeous, loyal, a genuinely good person, and almost frighteningly competent at everything he does. As far as marrying for convenience goes, I could do way worse."

Ears hot, Ravi attempts to not sink straight through the couch. He had no idea Harry held him in that kind of regard.

"Also, your nephew is sitting right here and can speak for himself. Whaddya think, Rav? Something we can talk more about later?"

Ravi's mouth opens on an automatic prevarication, but then he gives the question some serious thought. Harry wouldn't care if he saw anybody on the side, and he certainly wouldn't stop her from pursuing her own interests. Cayenne already told him they wouldn't mind this kind of arrangement, and as for the legacy… It's the twenty-first century, as Cayenne had pointed out. Lots of options. There weren't fertility clinics in the time of the British Raj.

To think he'd been so terrified of this possibility. The best Ravi had ever hoped for was a wife who wouldn't despise him. It never occurred to him that she might be his friend.

"I'm…not opposed."

Harry grins. "Ooh, ease off, hot stuff! You're gonna make a girl swoon with that kind of talk."

He barks a laugh. Padme watches them both with her brows raised.

"I think that's enough for today," Ravi tells his aunt.

She gives him an arch glare before sighing and inclining her head a respectful degree to Harry. "Very well." She ascends to her feet with a grace that belies her age, and Ravi instinctively stands up with her. At least she won't be able to condemn his manners. "There will have to be a formal ceremony to introduce you to the families. I will get those wheels in motion presently and will keep you apprised with everything you will need to know."

Harry smiles at Padme, her easy charm masking steel underneath. "Oh, you can send that stuff through Ravi. Probably easier, right, since I see him all the time?"

Padme's frozen smile cracks a little at the edges.

"As you wish, Chosen." She dips into another perfectly correct bow. When she straightens, she nods once at Ravi, turns on her heel, and leaves.

When the door shuts behind her, Harry falls back on the couch with a whoosh of breath. "Yeah, she's not gonna be happy giving up even a teeny bit of control, huh?"

Ravi sits back down and nods solemnly. "That's why I've been building up an immunity to all known poisons. We should get you started on a regimen."

Harry gapes in horror before she sees through him. "Oh, fuck you, I bought that," she laughs. He smiles. Harry's grin slips and she looks away.

She's...nervous? Something a little like grief, maybe? "Harry...I'm not going to make you do anything you don't want to do. I promise you, no one can make you. We don't have to talk about it right now, but the marriage thing—"

"Oh, dude, for sure." Harry waves him off. "I know. That's... Yeah, we do not have to do this tonight, I agree one hundred percent. This hell day just *never ends*—" She sucks air in through her teeth and tugs at her hair roots.

Concerned, he lowers his head to meet her eyes. Their color normally shifts depending on clothes and lighting, kind of an ambiguous blueish-hazel, but now they look too dark. Shadowed. "What's up?"

"*Ugh.*" She groans so loudly that Ravi jumps back a little. Harry digs at the inside corners of her eyes with thumb and forefinger. "Can you… Fuck, I'm sorry, but can you tell me what you know about how Tanvi and Nirav died?"

"Ah," he says, a little distant. "You got that memory."

"Hey! I'm gonna get us some booze." Harry practically jumps off the couch to grab a couple of buckwheat beers from the fridge. "I know you're not a beer guy, but the only other stuff I have is vermouth, so."

"I'll take the beer."

She hands it over and folds up on the opposite end of the couch, knees hiked up to her chin.

Instead of taking a sip of the beer, Ravi holds the

cool neck of the bottle up to his sore lip, trying to decide where to begin.

"There was a demon cult, base was hidden in an old factory beneath the city of Guangzhou. They abducted people and used some kind of magical artifact on them. An ancient wooden idol that could warp victims' bodies into…" He takes his first swig while considering how best to word it. "Into the image of the cultist's demon god. They thought if they sacrificed enough people who wore the face of their god, they could raise the demon to corporeal form."

"Jesus," Harry says, recoiling. Her beer is already half gone. "Can that work?"

"It almost did. Mom and Uncle Nirav first snuck in disguised as cultists and got most of the abductees out. Not all. But most."

Ravi takes a breath and draws one leg up onto the couch under him. Harry watches solemnly over her knees. "Then they got caught, we think. The only eye-witness accounts were from a few starved survivors who had no idea what was going on, so we don't have a full picture of what happened. And the seers had trouble looking back, which…happens sometimes." Ravi pauses for a second, remembering his aunt earlier mentioning conflicting visions. "There was a battle, and then a massive explosion. Took out the whole cult, and…" He gestures wordlessly with his beer bottle. "And everyone left in the factory."

Harry's lips catch tight between her teeth. "What about the idol? What happened to it?"

"Lost in the explosion, like…" Ravi laughs mirthlessly. "Like we thought the urumi was."

"What do you know about it?"

"About the artifact?"

"Yeah. Could it only change people into demon-y shapes, or could it be used…differently?"

"I'm not sure." Ravi leans back to assess her. "Are you going to tell me what's up? Was…was that memory stronger than the rest, because it's the most recent?" He wishes he was better at offering comfort. He can probably manage a pat on the back, but that's not likely to help much in her situation.

Harry fidgets, kicking her feet out and crossing them under her. She drains her beer and tosses the empty bottle onto the carpet. "Look, Ravi… bandage off, right? I'd bet you're a rip the bandage off kind of guy."

"I am."

"Okay. Okay. *Shit*." She scrubs a hand over her face. "Okay. So, in the memory, I saw the whole thing go down. I saw the cultists, this busted old factory, your family in disguise. I saw them freeing people, and I saw them getting found out. And yeah, this big climactic battle, dodging bullets and shit. Fuck's sake, but your mom could throw down. Nirav was like…like her shadow or something, they—"

"Like reflections in a mirror," Ravi murmurs, remembering.

"Yes! Really impressive. But then, the battle turned, and things were looking pretty dire, and Tanvi went for the urumi. I could see it through her eyes. I saw what she saw." Harry holds her hands in front of her, staring at them intently. "She went for her wrist, where the urumi should have been. But it wasn't there."

That can't be… "She always had her urumi."

Breathing uneven, Harry looks away from Ravi, her nails scraping raised lines over her collarbone. "Some of the cultists were dead nearby. They had semi-automatics on them, which is… There's a second where your mom remembers no guns, but then, suddenly, they've always been there, and…and so your uncle grabbed them and handed one to her. They start shooting, but there are way more cultists than they think there are, and without the urumi it's…" She swallows, staring into a memory only she can see. "They're surrounded, back-to-back. Almost out of ammo. There's…there's these big rusted, dripping tanks right behind them. And Tanvi and Nirav look at each other, and they…they shoot the tanks."

It's an old wound, but no less painful for it. Ravi closes his eyes for a moment and takes a long breath. They died together. At least there's that. Most Chosen didn't get that privilege.

When he opens his eyes, Harry's hands shake. "*Fuck*, okay, Cayenne was there, she saw them before they disappeared, just before everything goes white. Bandage on the back of the hand, same clothes from the airport. Holding the urumi in one hand and a creepy wooden idol in the other. The idol that can change people's appearance even without knowing a somamancer." She stops abruptly like she just hit the bottom of a sheer drop.

After an eternal silence, Ravi looks down at his beer bottle, inspecting the label. It was designed to mimic woodcut printing, probably inspired by Dürer. "She died with a gun in her hand," he says, softly running the pad of this thumb over the raised lettering in the glass. "She would have hated that. A coward's weapon, she used to say."

"That's… Do you… Ravi, you get what I'm saying, yeah?"

"I understand the implications, Harry." His lover had willfully caused the death of his two closest family members, stolen his birthright, and lied to him from the start. The moment Ravi had met Cayenne in Chicago, he had met the person responsible for the greatest catastrophe of his life.

And then they asked him out to dinner.

"Okay, because you're being *horrifically* calm about it."

"Would you feel better if I punched a wall?"

"Uh… Maybe?"

A ghost of a laugh slips free. "I'm not really a punch-the-wall kind of guy." Ravi takes a long pull of beer. "You're right about this being a hell day. And I've had some bad fucking days, Harry." He tilts his head. "I think I'm at emotional capacity, to be honest. I'm…sort of numb?" He flexes his hand and can barely feel it. He doesn't feel much of anything, aside from a slight ringing in his ears, like when the auditory exclusion of battle wears off after he's fired his rifle. Apart from that, Ravi feels nothing. He's a ghost.

Harry scoots close enough to take his hand, and the warm press of it registers through the emptiness. "Did you know my mom died of cancer?" she asks.

Ravi shakes his head.

"It was…bad for a long, long time. So, I get it. You

can only take so much. After a while you just kind of…shut down." She squeezes his hand and lets go.

"I'm good at processing things internally."

"Fuck," she says, a bitter laugh. "I don't doubt it. The more I learn about you, the more impressed I am with your—you know. Your squishy insides." The fluttery motion she makes with her hand somehow manages to illustrate the concept of empathy; an impressive feat of sign language.

Ravi snorts, leaning over with his elbows on his knees. "Hardly. Everything good I've ever done I did to prove all of them wrong. To prove Her wrong." He points upward, then drops his head into his hands. "But I guess that's not why I wasn't Chosen after all, huh?"

It was just Cayenne.

Ravi's mind skitters away from the thought. Easier to focus on someone else right now. He lifts his head and swallows. "Harry. I'm sorry if I…if I brought this on you."

"What?"

"Contracting with you. Offering the freelance gig.

If that…got you tangled up in my family's bullshit. Put you in the line of fire."

Harry eyes him, then smiles crookedly. "Rav, as much as I wish I could lay the blame at someone's feet, I stumbled across an angel when I wasn't even a believer in weird supernatural shit. Then my sorcerous ancestor jumped forward eight hundred years to join the party. And *then* you and The Trust. And if I'm being brutally honest, there was some fucked-up spooky shit even before that I've been sort of…ignoring. So, yeah, weird shit has been happening to me for a *while*. Maybe, fuck, I don't know." She stretches her feet out over the coffee table and musses her hair. "It's not your fault, is what I'm trying to say. If I were the kind of naive simpleton who believes in things like fate and destiny, or that witches and angels and goddesses were real, then maybe I'd also believe someone like *you* was sent to me too. You know. If I was that kind of superstitious idiot."

Ravi ducks his head, biting his lip. "So, what's Dr. Corbin been sent for?" He attempts a smirk he's fairly certain comes across as natural. Though he's been distracted with his own shit lately, over the last few weeks it seems like Harry and the professor have been getting chummier.

"You kidding? Once, before a fight, he told me my bootlaces were untied. Probably saved my life. Heart of the team, that guy."

"He's a good guy," Ravi agrees.

The two of them sit in silence for a long moment.

"I...I think you're my best friend," Harry says while looking at her socks.

"Fuck, McAllister, you trying to compete with me for saddest personal revelation?"

"Fuck you, man," Harry laughs, snatching up a piece of laundry from the floor and lobbing it at him. He bats it away with a barebones smile. A good distraction, the camaraderie, the banter. It helps. He can keep this act up; it's just a different kind of wall. He's good at those.

"You really care about The Trust, huh?"

The question takes Ravi off guard. "Of course I do."

Harry rolls her eyes. "*Of course*, he says. I wouldn't,

if I were you. You haven't told me much about…your life in it, but I am both observant and imaginative." She gets up and grabs them both another beer before flopping back down next to him. "But as far as I'm concerned, as a living goddess avatar, as ridiculous as that is, you *are* The Trust. I'm sure lots of folks on your end aren't going to be thrilled who their long-lost Chosen turned out to be, but you and me together?" Tenacity edges into her mercenary grin. "We're gonna help a lot of people."

How did a cynical, hard-drinking, lifelong skeptic and self-professed fuckup like Harry evolve so naturally into the leader of their little band of monster hunters?

She leans over and gives Ravi a one-armed side-hug. "I know you're in my corner. I'm in yours too."

It's no wonder, really. "Thanks, Harry," he manages thickly.

Clearing her throat, Harry stands and briskly rubs her palms on her jeans. "It's been a rough day. I'm not going to pretend like I'm not rattled after everything. Any chance you'd be willing to stay over? I'd feel better."

And she's got to know he's not in great shape to be alone right now either. She's something else. "Yeah, no problem. I'll take the couch." Having someone to protect will help him a lot, ground him, give him something to focus on besides…

"*Pfff*, you'll take the fucking bed, dude. After the day you had? Fucking hell. You've had an *unimaginably* bad day. I love sleeping on that couch, by the way. Seriously, do not argue."

Pushing himself to his feet, Ravi shrugs and checks the window. "You're the boss. How many entrances does your place have? Security system, alarms, anything like that?"

"Taking this 'you have my service' thing pretty seriously, huh?"

"Yup."

She rolls her eyes. "Nothing besides locks on the door and windows. Entrances are the front door and the fire escape outside the bedroom window."

"Fire escape?"

"Yeah, it goes from roof to ground. Nice view up there."

"Security risk."

"It has a lock, geez. Look, the apartment's shit, but I definitely spent a bit of diamond money on a choice bed. Fresh bedding, pinky swear."

Ravi feels like he weighs a thousand pounds, like he wants to bury himself in covers and never emerge, but knows he won't be able to sleep tonight. "Sounds good."

"One last thing before you turn in." Harry nibbles her lip. "Do…do you want me to keep the truth about Cayenne a secret from the others?"

Staring out of the window, he considers the question for a long time. Stars begin to peek through the darkening sky. "I don't know." His voice cracks. Ravi runs a weary hand over his face. "I am so tired of lying, Harry. Of keeping secrets."

"Yeah." She gives his arm a squeeze. "I'll do whatever you want me to do here, dude. If you want me to keep this secret with you, I will."

Every secret Ravi has kept from these people has made his life harder, smaller; penned him further into a box of his own making. Every truth has opened it up, bit by bit; freed him from hobbles he'd been too accustomed to wearing to even realize other options existed.

"You should tell them. It's best if everyone knows what they're capable of. If we run into them again." *If.* He almost laughs, a bit of black humor.

Harry joins him in a pensive stare out of the window. "I just don't get why Cayenne was so adamant they hadn't caused the plane crashes to begin with. Once we rewound time, they weren't able to cause the crash. Nothing else did, so ergo ipso facto, it *must* have been them."

It didn't seem possible this day had anything more it could take from Ravi. He'd been torn apart and stitched back together into a hollow, walking shell. But with perfect clarity, Ravi recalls the moment Constance skipped time backward a few hours, the moment Cayenne had twisted with pain, their face racked with it. A much harsher penalty than the nausea and dizziness that affected everyone else, getting torn back in time. Ravi assumed it had been a clashing of Constance's magic with Cayenne's.

We can't exist here at the same time, my old self and me, they had told him. *It's agony.*

The Cayenne they met at the airport hadn't caused those original plane crashes.

His Cayenne had.

Epilogue

ON THE ROOFTOP the night wind whips through Ravi's hair, still too warm and clinging even in his sleeveless undershirt. Cayenne, of course, is already there. Waiting.

They breathe fast, almost panting, both hands twisting in the hem of their shirt. The moon above is a neatly halved circle, its waning light painting Cayenne's fine features into delicate, otherworldly angles. They're so fucking beautiful it's like a bullet to the back.

"Why?" The word slices out of him, a razor, and

Cayenne flinches.

They close their eyes and drag in a long breath. When their eyes open, they are composed, nearly as calm and cool as they had been when Ravi first met them in Chicago.

"After months of captivity, they thought they had me properly cowed. That all of time was theirs to control, and that I was an obedient little tool in their arsenal. *Mais c'est moi,* so I tricked them." Cayenne's shoulders lift in an airy shrug. "I escaped, and I found a way to make my powers more precise." They hold up their tattooed hand with a playful waggle of their fingers. "All the better to get revenge. And then I went to the airport to get started."

"I gathered all that. Why did you do *this*?" Ravi slams a hand into his own chest, unsaid words carrying on the Georgia breeze as audibly as if spoken.

Cayenne laughs bitterly. "*Why.* Why do I do anything, darling? Because it was fun, wasn't it?" A sharp smirk, hips canted at the same careless angle.

"It was *sadistic,*" Ravi grates, barely able to hear

himself speak over the jackrabbit thump of his heart.

Cayenne's insouciant smirk crumples. They cover their face with both hands. "I know."

"I always thought it was something I had done. Or who I was. Why I wasn't good enough for Her. But there was no reason at all. I was just your collateral damage."

Red hair silvered in the moonlight, Cayenne drops their slender hands to their sides as they run their tongue over dry lips. "You should have gone away with me, when I asked at the cabin."

We can skip the next few months. Ravi squeezes his eyes shut. "Yeah. That would have been a lot easier for you."

They slump. "For you, I thought."

"Did you?"

"Ravi, *please.*" Cayenne takes a step forward. They freeze when Ravi slides his foot back into a ready stance. Teeth catch at their lip, and they ease back. "It's a couple of years from now, when they capture me. You can't change that, but even if you could, then we wouldn't ever know each other. And I just...I can't give up this version of you, Ravi! I don't care about what happened to me, you are *worth* it. Months of captivity, years or decades—you'd still be worth every second, *mon amour*."

Ravi wipes his mouth with the back of his hand, distantly noting the catch of his knuckles on the scab over his lip. *You're worth a little inconvenience, sweetheart.* Fuck, he wishes fervently they hadn't ever said that. But it's his own fault; he gave them the knife himself, pulled back his armor, and showed them exactly where to strike so it would count. *I'm very easy to break.*

"When I was fourteen," Ravi begins, "there was a party. There were lots of parties. Gowns and jodhpuri suits. Trust families loved to trot the kids out and make them dance with each other, hoping for an alliance down the line." He crosses his arms over his chest, gaze fixed in the barren space between them. "We were in Italy visiting the family there. And Isabella—she's basically the heir—she kept asking for dances. I'd already learned how to be as unapproachable as possible by then, but she was…tenacious. Wouldn't take no for an answer. So we danced.

"Later, when our chaperones were tipsy and distracted, she tricked me into going somewhere alone with her. She…got handsy. Fortunately, my mom was walking by and found us before anyone else did." He looks out over the edge of the building, at the distant glow of Downtown. "She told me that if another of the Cattanos had found us alone, whether I wanted to be there or not, Isabella could have claimed anything she liked. Forced an engagement." Tanvi had been forthright, matter-of-fact. His mother never spoke to Ravi like he was a child, even when he had been one.

"She told me that was going to happen all my life. There would always be someone trying to play me. It's funny. All that training, all those years of being so fucking careful, looking over my shoulder everywhere I went, and…it turns out it was easy. All you had to do was say you wanted me."

Cayenne's green eyes flash. "This would be Isabella Cattano?"

Ravi looks at them sharply. "*No.* Don't." But then it hits him. "Fuck, you already did," he hisses, yanking at his hair. Blood rushes in his ears. "The skiing accident Jessika mentioned."

Cayenne clucks their tongue and sets a finger aside their mouth, pretending to consider carefully. "A skiing accident? Yes, that sounds just the thing to teach little Bella to keep her hands to herself. What an *excellent* idea, *mon tigre*."

"Don't you fucking *dare*," Ravi snarls. "Don't you hurt anyone for…for *me*. I don't want that."

"But you say I've already done it, sweetheart." They give him a lazy smile, lifting their hands in a helpless shrug. "If I don't do it now, the paradox could unmake reality. I won't *kill* her, relax."

Guilt snatches at him, drags him down. His mistake, and others would pay for it. "If you're so concerned with paradox, why fuck with the Chosen line? Why did you give the urumi to Harry?"

"Now on *that* subject, pet, I am as puzzled as you are. A few hours ago, I was weeks ahead in the future, and seeing dear Angharad with that damned thing gave me *quite* the shock."

"You expect me to believe that you didn't do it?"

"Wasn't me, darling. I took the urumi and locked it up in a safe in the middle of Moscow, decades in the future. Fucking thing cut up my arms to ribbons. I intended it to be lost for all time. How it came to your fearless leader and why *she* of all people was Chosen, I have no idea. Perhaps it is divine will, after all." They spread their arms out and tilt their stance back, as if supplicating to the heavens.

No scratches on their arms at the airport. Another revelation hits Ravi, another punch to the gut. "You hadn't done it yet. Killed them."

Cayenne flinches, mockery slipping. "Yes."

"We… I let you go and you…"

Cayenne drags in a ragged breath. "Yes. Right after. The Trust had all sorts of plans, after they believed they had me leashed. Wrongs to correct. A lot of talk about saving more lives at Guangzhou, and in doing so showed me exactly where to hurt them most. Practically drew me a map." Pausing, they twist their hands together as if not sure what to do with them. "I had hoped maybe, this time, I'd hear you say those words to me, to protect you, my beautiful boy, and I'd *fucking* listen. But I didn't. I'm…" They squeeze their eyes shut tight for a brief second, then words flood out of them. "I didn't *know* you, Ravi, I thought you were just some Trust lackey. I didn't know who the Chosen was, or what she was to you, I had *no idea* they were your family, I—" They bite off their words with a hastily swallowed gasp. "It…wouldn't have mattered, though. I wanted them all to pay."

Every word, another shovel full of dirt falling on him, another log thrown on his crackling pyre. "You could have told me to stop your past self. You could have changed everything. You could have… The whole course of my *life*—"

Cayenne gives Ravi that same winsome, charming smile they had in Chicago, the one they wore while pressing their lips to the back of his hand. A sweet smile that promises more. "I could have, but then we wouldn't have met, my love. You'd be someone else. The Chosen, probably."

"If I *were* the Chosen, I could do whatever the fuck I want with my life and no one could tell me different. But *you* made that impossible."

For a moment, Cayenne looks unsure, forehead creasing, but then they shake their head. "It would only be a different cage for you. Besides, how could I give this version of you up, darling? Everything that has happened, every hardship or struggle, it's made you *you*. You, like this? You're *perfect*, Ravi. We fit together." They take a step forward, both hands over their heart. "How could I risk losing that?"

Ravi reels back. "Fuck," he breathes, unable to find words to express.

"I know I'm not worthy of it, but I love you, Ravi. A monster, *oui*, but *your* monster. Please."

Ravi looks down at his shaking hands. "This version of me. Alone. Weak. Fragile. At the cabin, that's what you said you liked about me when we met. What drew you in." His voice is so soft it's more breath than speech. "Broken, you said."

"We're *both* broken, *mon coeur*. I'm sorry for what

I… But *I'm* here, Ravi. We're both here *together*. Nothing has to change between us."

"*Are* you sorry? You could have stopped any time, if you were sorry. Stopped all this from happening. Not lied to me the whole time. Even that confession at the cabin was half lies."

Cayenne buries their face in their hands. It takes them a full minute to speak again, to plead, "Can't we do what we did at the lake? Forget the past, darling? We can forge a new future together."

Every cherished memory now tastes bitter, the tang of poison thick on Ravi's tongue. Every day spent with Cayenne had been the best day of Ravi's life, and every perfect moment had been a lie.

Real's better than perfect, isn't it?

He'd been such an idiot.

"That future have anything to do with what you did to the Eatons? And the Bhagavati family? The 'little project' you've been working on?"

Cayenne swears under their breath.

"*You* crashed those planes."

"I tried to," they sigh. "But once my past self was there in the new time-jump, I couldn't be there. I had to skip away to a different time." The tip of their tongue presses to their front teeth, and they shake their head in disgust. "You'd think I would have learned. But I thought I could manage it this time, get it tethered to the timeline, but—it doesn't matter. It's like I get to read the last page of a book, but even knowing the end, I keep fucking up anyway."

Abruptly their posture loosens, an exhausted actor dropping a pose as soon as the curtain falls. Cayenne glances around and tips their chin toward the broad cement ledge bordering the roof. "Can we sit?" At Ravi's stony silence, they roll their eyes. "Oh, are we going to draw pistols?" They sarcastically shape their hands into guns, quick-drawing like a gunslinger at high noon. "Come on, it's been a long day, *mon chéri*. Promise I won't push you off." Cayenne walks over, pulls themself up onto the edge, and turns out to the street, legs dangling.

After a moment Ravi joins them.

Folks wander a few stories down, weaving through pools of light and shadow under yellow streetlights. On their phones, walking their dogs, talking with each other, holding hands. Normal life. Right now, it's like watching an alien planet.

"Sorry about the lip," Cayenne mentions softly.

Ravi keeps his gaze steady on the street below.

They sigh, rubbing at their forearms though they couldn't possibly be cold. "*J'ai une question.* Something I've always wondered. Why did you tell The Trust to keep off Lucy?"

Surprised, Ravi finally looks at them. It's a mistake. They've dropped their cheek sideways into their palm and their emerald eyes scan him intently. "What?"

Their tongue flashes pink over their lips. "You didn't turn her in, but you didn't leave her out of your reports either. That would have been much, much easier, to lie about her creating those little blood monsters. But you didn't. You told the truth, and then you…you *fought* for her. To keep her with her family."

"Why are you asking me this?"

"Honestly?" Cayenne smiles, the kind of blade so sharp it slips between your ribs before you even know you've been cut. "It's why I wanted to meet you. Really meet you, not that nasty little murder attempt in the airport."

"*That's* why you wanted to meet me? Just because of that?"

"*Just*," Cayenne laughs.

Ravi shakes his head. "You don't even know her. You've never met." Just another one of so many lies they're nearly beyond counting.

"True. But I *was* her, once, in a way. Without the 'loving family' part. But nobody fought for me." Cayenne leans back on their palms, face turned up to the washed-out stars. Their throat bobs, swallowing hard. "It was in your reports. I knew your name from the airport, I knew you were stationed in Atlanta. I knew you were unexpectedly good at anticipating my moves, *mon tigre*, though at first, I thought some lucky seer stumbled on my weakness.

"It was *quite* the internal debate, for our jet to the

Seychelles, if I would tell you about my inability to jump time during high speeds or not. But really, all things considered, that encounter on the tram could hardly have gone *better* for me. I got away free and clear, The Trust had no *idea* what I would do next, and I had a little mystery on my hands to unravel."

They slant over a sidelong, teasing smile. Ravi flinches. "Who *was* that empty suit who had so cleverly distracted me? Was it merely sound tactics? A surprisingly tricky ploy? Or was there something more? *En plus*, telling you gave me the opportunity to see what you'd do. If you'd slap some cuffs on me and have a team of gun-toting agents waiting for me when we landed."

Smile fading, Cayenne heaves a sigh. "So, I found my way into the archives. That's when I figured out who you were, when I realized the asshole agent who foolishly let me go was the son of the woman I had killed right afterwards. That this same agent helped a little girl who had an ability like mine. So, you see, everything's kind of your fault, *cher*. I felt…I had a debt to pay."

Debts. Making amends. Ravi closes his eyes, feeling stupid for taking this long to put it together. "My reports… You read all my reports. You never knew any of us. The team. All that about working with us in the future was more lies. You just got your information from the archives."

"*Oui*. After I broke into the records, I went back and watched you all perform a couple of missions, to fill in some gaps. Your reports weren't exactly *comprehensive*, darling. I did some reconnaissance, I believe you would call it, real proper spycraft. Haven't done that in a *while*." They smile wryly. "It looked like it would be fun though. Being in your merry little band of misfits. I thought, maybe if I changed things enough, I could be. Believe me, I tried *many* times to make that future stick. To make the story I told you at the cabin…*real*. Not just another lie." A long sigh escapes them, and they twist their hand out over the empty air. "But I could never manage it. Only in my dreams, I suppose."

"I didn't put everyone's favorite picnic food in my reports."

"Hmm? Oh, *oui*! A *very* irritating endeavor. I had to approach each of you individually, figure out how to get you to tell me what your favorite food was, and then rewind. Easier to do with that girl and her beach hat; you folk are a *very* suspicious bunch. Took me ages, you can't imagine. And then nobody even ate it, *honestly*. A good lesson for me, no doubt, in where to focus my energies." Cayenne chuckles, a warm, fond sound that tears at Ravi like knives.

He runs shaking fingers through his hair. They come away damp with sweat. "I suppose you don't know James either."

"*Ugh*, no, him I *do* know. I sought him out, after…well, after my second jailbreak of three. You can't *imagine* how disappointed I was to finally meet another time traveler, and he turns out to be the human equivalent of dry toast. And the constant *moralizing*," Cayenne groans with an exaggerated roll of their eyes, accent sloping into a nasal imitation of American diction. "*Your actions have consequences, Cayenne.*" They huff a laugh which quickly grows sour. "Guess he was right all along."

Ravi's face sinks into his hands. "I'm going to fix things," he rasps through his fingers. "I'm going to make The Trust what it should be."

"You can't, dearest," Cayenne says wearily, "because you didn't. In my past—your future—you are every bit as much a pawn as you are now."

"I'm going to stop it. If you aren't taken, if you stay safe, then none of this happens."

With a furious, feral snarl, Cayenne turns on him. "You noble, self-sacrificing *idiot*. I can't *believe* you." A sharp, anguished laugh as they press in on their sternum as if staunching a wound. "After all this, you still talk about keeping me safe. It already *did* happen, my sweet. You can't change that. But I can. I'm going to free you."

Their voice drops low and fierce, their hands balling into pulsing fists, opening and closing over and over. "My father ran a prison, long ago, and though I never set foot in it, I was his favorite prisoner. When I escaped—oh, my love, you can't imagine how *sweet* that freedom tasted." Eyes closed, caught in some pleasant memory, Cayenne leans out over the edge. Ravi tenses until they roll their shoulders back with a wistful sigh. "But then I found another like me…or I *thought* he was, anyway, for a time. And for him, I was a *weapon*." Earnest, they turn to face him, one leg pulled up under them. "Like *you*, Ravi, another thing we share, another reason we fit so well together. We were both honed by others into something meant to kill."

They are silent for a while, watching the people down on the street walk by. "But of course, it was just another kind of jail. A gilded cage. He deserved to have his favorite weapon turned on him. Freedom is worth *any* cost, my love. And I'm going to free you too."

"No. I can do it myself, Cayenne. I can fix things. Make The Trust what it should be. Not the way you'd do it, but the right way. One step at a time."

"You can't, pet. If it was possible, you would have already done it."

"You don't know that."

"I know I can't change my past."

"But *I* might be able to change my future."

"Why would you even *bother*? You're talking about…about getting nicer *bread* and *water* for your own *jail* cell, Ravi. I thought I knew everything there was to know about being a prisoner, but *you, mon Dieu!*" Cayenne laces their fingers behind their head and hangs on tightly, as if their thoughts were about to fly away. "You're the *only* good thing about your entire terrible Trust, and they don't give a *shit* about you. You did everything they ever asked but when you didn't fit into their plans, they fucking *left* you. You've lived your *whole life* just a…a fucking tool to be used and thrown away. Even your own mother didn't want you."

Was this what love was supposed to be like? You give someone everything they need to tear you apart, and just blindly hope they never use it? Ravi's hands twitch against the cool concrete. He wishes he could be a ghost again for a little while, wanting that comforting numbness.

"But I do, Ravi, *I* want you. And one day soon we are both going to be truly free. Even if we have to grow a new life together from rubble, your monsoon will tear this entire world down for you. I'm going to save you."

"Save me? *Kharâbetam.*" The Persian slices out like broken glass, a word that by inflection can either be an endearment or an accusation: *You've ruined me.* "There have been two great tragedies in my life and you're both of them."

A long moment passes where the only sounds are what rise up from the street. Tears roll down Cayenne's perfect face. "I never meant for this to happen. For either of us to feel this way. I truly didn't think I was capable of it. I…I'm grateful, if you can believe it. Loving you has been the singular greatest privilege of my life."

"You're still doing it," Ravi says hollowly. "Still trying to play me."

Their teeth saw at their lower lip. "You think I'm lying? About loving you?"

That's the worst thing of all. "No. I don't."

Cayenne looks away and nods, wrapping their arms around themself despite the warmth of the night. "Aren't we a pair."

Ravi tries to take a deep, grounding drag of air. "I'm not going to let you tear down everything I believe in, Cayenne. It's…" He's never been good with words, and he struggles to stitch the right ones together; The Trust is his legacy, his duty, his responsibility; it's over a thousand years of standing vigilant against the forces of destruction, years of training and dedication and *vision* — Ravi can see it *so clearly*, its potential, what The Trust can become, even if no one else can…

"It's *mine*," he finally growls.

Cayenne wipes their nose with the back of their tattooed hand, pride and disappointment forged together into an expression of strange, begrudging admiration. "I know, *mon tigre*." They drop off the ledge onto the rooftop with feline grace, then turn back to drink in the sight of him. They step away, touch their tattoo, and smile.

"I'll be seeing you."

Acknowledgements

Shout-out to the irrepressible band of novelists of the Quills Critique Clique (I still think we should've named ourselves the Lit Cliquers) and to the wonderfully supportive folks at the Loft Literary Center. Special thanks to Ritika, who went above and beyond a mere sensitivity read and introduced me to the new love of my life: chole bhature.

About the Author

Fox Beckman is an author with a penchant for spicy stories about swords, sorcery, and smooching. Her books feature strong, nuanced characters who interrogate the status quo and subvert expectations.

A member of both the Loft Literary Center and the Author's Guild, Fox lives in the Twin Cities with too many hobbies and a very patient spouse.

Email

fox@foxbeckman.com

Twitter

@foxbeckman

Website

www.foxbeckman.com

Other NineStar books by this author

Trust Trilogy

Stolen From Tomorrow

Coming Soon from Fox Beckman

Built from Ashes

Trust Trilogy, Book Three

"I DO NOT like this," Val mutters for the third time, her voice low.

"Me neither," Ravi sighs, his eye not wavering from the scope. The rifle is a cool, sturdy presence under his hands. Something he can rely on. Rare as it is for him to roll out his sniper skillset on hunts, he's strangely nostalgic for his time in Israel. The simplicity of training and nothing else. Being so worn out each day he could slip into a deep, dreamless slumber.

Val rumbles a little under her breath like a building storm. Normally the angel is perfectly content to spend any time with Ravi in companionable silence—one of his favorite things about her—but he agrees the situation is less than ideal.

The pair perch on the second story of an abandoned big-box department store, a building slated for demolition in two months' time. Scouting hours ahead of the rendezvous, they'd found this vantage point hidden by a defunct escalator with a clean line of sight down to the meeting place. The perfect position to keep an eagle eye on the proceedings.

It's harder than Ravi expected it would be, staying on the sidelines while Harry and Nate are up close and personal with so many potential enemies. Even with Harry's Chosen invulnerability and her recent training regimen, she's still not ready for this kind of threat on her own. But as the most personable members of the team, she and Nate are the best options. One peek at Val's eyes and it's obvious she's not entirely human, and if this information broker is as savvy as Nate's vampire contact claims he is, the team can't afford to take chances.

Through the scope Ravi watches the broker, a gentleman of Filipino descent approaching middle age and fighting it tooth and claw. Clothes too flashy, recent hair plugs, rings on every finger. The man gesticulates through a joke, and Harry throws her head back to laugh with him. Nate joins in, grinning wide. He's leaned up against the broker's desk, dragged into the middle of the dead mall in a parody of legitimate office space. Several men surround the trio, big slabs of hired muscle in identical plain gray suits and sunglasses.

The broker's laughter fades as he eyes Harry with speculation. He falls silent, tapping a finger on the desk, one of his rings glimmering.

Something's off; the guy has twigged. Ravi lines up a shot, breaths slow and measured. Kneeling beside him, Val glances at him and tenses. Her massive maul materializes into her hands.

Nate throws a nervous glance up at their sniper nest and thumbs his nose.

That's the signal. In the space between seconds, Val disappears from Ravi's side, a faint rush of displaced air the only sign she had ever been there.

Two of the goons are lined up right next to each other.

Perfect.

Ravi exhales and squeezes the trigger.

Connect with NineStar Press

WWW.NINESTARPRESS.COM

WWW.FACEBOOK.COM/NINESTARPRESS

WWW.FACEBOOK.COM/GROUPS/NINESTARNICHE

WWW.TWITTER.COM/NINESTARPRESS

WWW.INSTAGRAM.COM/NINESTARPRESS

www.ingramcontent.com/pod-product-compliance
Lightning Source LLC
Chambersburg PA
CBHW071523120726
47907CB00012B/259